QUEEN OF DARKNESS

THE BLOOD MOON PROPHECY

BOOK TWO

SUSAN PERSON

PERSON
PUBLISHING

For those who experience profound grief as I did while writing this book

PRAISE FOR SUSAN PERSON

THE TRILOGY ENDS ON FEBRUARY 14, 2023

Pick up Book 1 to find out what sacrifices were made that led to the Darkness, and pre-order Book 3 to be the first to see how the trilogy ends!

QUEEN OF DARKNESS

> > ● ((

The universe decided to fuck me. Brie Danforth, vampire hunter, Queen of the Witches, and the universe proved she was a bigger bitch than me. A few months ago, I hunted vampires, and now, I'm engaged to one. The Elders believed our love brought about the start of not only a war but the apocalypse.

Much had changed since I found the love of my life, Nick. My aunt died and passed the proverbial crown to me. My father, Sorin, returned only to die on the battlefield and be brought back from Hell by my pink aura. My aura now tainted by the Darkness of Sorin's. Nick supported me all the way. He saved me from myself, so I could save the world. But the universe's cruelest twist came as a sacrifice I'm required to make. *Love for Light or drown in Darkness like my father.*

I stared out the window into the almost cloudless blue sky over the grassy knoll of the Great House. Winter's touch was gentler this year, but Spring brought a freshness with it along with repairs to the Great House from the battle with Stefan, Nick's vampire father, brought to our backdoor.

When Spring blew in this year, I stood full of hope in front of my future husband. Hope we could avoid the sacrifice The Blood Moon Prophecy necessitated. Hope our love would survive the immense pressure of our position. Looking into the sea of emerald-green eyes, I knew who I was, and what kind of queen I wanted to be. I promised both of our people change, and I hoped I could deliver.

I motioned for my guards to wait at the door and ambled over to my love. Nick's thick hair laid to the side in a fresh cut, shorter than when I saw him in the club five months ago. Enemies were what we were expected to be, but we'd rekindled something that started eight years earlier.

His arms spread welcoming me. I ran my fingers through the dark mass on his head.

"Are you sure about having the wedding on April 4 during the next Blood Moon?" Nick whispered in my ear as he pulled me to him. "It's not that far away."

I never tired of meeting him on the grassy knoll in the back of the mansion. Spring and a little magic had washed away the events of the battle. Our meeting spot restored to the original lushness it had once been.

"The ancestors chose the date. I want to honor their wishes given the gifts they have bestowed on me," I answered taking in his angular features.

"The veil between Light and dark wanes then. Remember the pull the Blood Moon had over you during the first one? I am worried about you." He kissed my cheek, and I closed my eyes leaning into him.

The Blood Moon's strength was consuming like Darkness. I wasn't ready to feel it again, but I didn't have a choice. It would come whether I was ready or not.

"I made my choice for Light," I said. "Besides the thin veil will make it easier for you to enter the chapel." The chapel ceremony created the only point of contention between us regarding our wedding. Nick sighed.

"I can't steal the honor of walking you down the aisle from your father, and I can't walk in the chapel without your help. How am I to make the beautiful future Mrs. Domenico happy?" He lifted my chin to force me to look him in the eyes. I opened my eyes allowing the connection to flow between us. Love filled me, and my pink aura enveloped us.

"Who says I will change my name? Maybe you should become Mr. Danforth?" I smiled at him, and he chuckled.

"Or Vladislav?" He said as a joke, but the smile left my face at the mention of my father's last name.

Sorin came back different after he sacrificed himself on the battlefield and my aura kept him from death. His eyes burned like embers from Hell's Fire, and he disappeared often. I figured it wouldn't be long before he did again. My worst fears grew as I could see Darkness creeping back into him. He left us so long ago to deal with the Darkness, and the responsibility for the hold it had on him today rested solely on me. "Hey, I was joking." Nick's voice filled with concern.

"It's not the last name bothering me, Nick. Of course, I will take yours. I'm worried about Sorin," I said like I had a revelation, but we both knew I had been worrying about him more and more in the weeks since he cast Nick's father away. Stefan hadn't tried to summon Nick or bargain for me once which left me with an uneasy feeling. The more time passed without a Stefan sighting convinced me he knew more about what was happening with Sorin than we did.

"I think you are right to be worried. He's battling internally a struggle you know well. I neither crave his blood nor am repelled by it. Before we were Blood Bound, I craved yours with intensity, but most witches' blood repulses me," Nick said.

It confirmed to me what Grandmother had said the night my mother and I called her to the chapel to view Sorin's body. I watched him die and lay lifeless on the battlefield his blood mixing with others who perished there. Yet, we saw his wounds heal in front of us. Grandmother told us of those who returned were not dead or alive and were not witch or vampire. He could barely look me in the eyes, barely slept, and rarely ate. He had become more reclusive, but he never turned me away when I sought his counsel. I wondered if he would stay long enough to attend the wedding. I wanted him to walk me down the aisle, but I wasn't sure if he could.

"My father is forever changed, and the blame belongs to me. If I'd done more when he tried to teach me to control my powers." Tears brimmed my eyes as I looked at Nick.

"We all change, Brie. You can't blame yourself," he said.

Except I could and I did.

"Look at the changes you have endured the last six months. To expect someone to not change is to try to stop progress or movement forward." He studied me. I saw concern in his eyes.

I nodded, not convinced and not able to agree verbally. I tucked the conversation away for now.

"Grandmother is waiting for us to go over wedding plans." I smiled at him.

)) ● ((

WEDDING PLANNING OFFERED an escape from the worries of being queen except when Grandmother reminded me of the royal wedding pageantry. The requirements of a royal witch wedding were exhausting. We had reviewed many of the details, but she was focused on the activities the day before the wedding this time.

"The night before the wedding there will be a large party where witches and dignitaries will be in attendance to offer their allegiance to you as their queen and blessings for your wedding." She paused giving me the stern look she did when Brandon and I were kids and not paying attention. "Then just before midnight, you two will be escorted to the chapel with only the elders. The elders will perform a binding ritual." She glanced at Nick. "Similar to the Blood Bound ritual among vampires."

Nick and I exchanged knowing looks. A tinge of guilt hit my gut.

"This could be tricky for you two given what happened when you performed the new lovers' spell."

I cleared my throat and looked at Nick again. His eyes widened a little. Nick shifted back a few steps from Grandmother like he was afraid of what she would do if I divulged our secret.

"I'm going to just tell her." I moved between them.

"We're Blood Bound, Grandmother. We have been since the night before the first battle."

I was sure she would chastise us for not only doing it but not revealing it sooner.

She raised an eyebrow and nodded once.

"You are basically married in the vampire world then." She thought for a moment, her expression unreadable. "There should be no issues with the binding ritual then. The blood mixed is much less than in the Blood Bound ritual."

Hopefully, we didn't have to divulge it to anyone else. I wasn't sure the witches, especially those of rank, would have accepted our decision as well as she did. There were already those who protested our right to marriage. They would be mortified a witch bound herself in a vampire ceremony.

Both witch and vampire were ready for the peace we brought, but few on either side believed we should be allowed to marry. The elders fought every step of the way until I threatened to leave. It was an empty threat, but they didn't know that. The notion I might pull a Sorin and disappear concerned them enough they gave in to my wishes. Once they publicly accepted our pending union, the rest fell silent on the matter save a few. Those few managed to gain support, and some of the very lives we saved on the battlefield now refused to support our choice. It pissed me off, but the queen had to swallow down the disdain for her choice. I thought of myself as the queen in the third person more and more as if being queen was a persona and Brie was personal.

"Do you think Sorin is going to leave again?" I asked Grandmother. Just the thought made me uncomfortable.

She sighed. "I honestly don't know."

"Me either," I responded. "But my gut says he won't stay." *Because of how dark his aura is.* I hated keeping it from her or the rest of my family, but it was his to tell. As one of the few witches who could read an aura, I didn't have a right to divulge something so personal.

There was a knock at the door. The wedding planner entered the room, and we dove into the details of our special day.

☽ ☾ ● ☾ ☽

NICK and I left Grandmother with the wedding planner and walked toward my quarters to steal a few minutes. I looked down at our swinging hands and smiled. I turned my gaze to him and found him smiling too. His happiness filled me with so much love. I wanted to stay in simple moments like this.

"We could elope and avoid all the parties and cere-monies," I said, giving him a sly smile. It was wishful think-ing. Duty demanded a production.

"We could." Nick agreed. "But we need to be transparent with our people right now, and they need a royal wedding in the public eye. We need them to trust us."

"My head knows this, but my heart craves a more simplistic approach," I said. Nick squeezed my hand.

I stopped, tugging Nick to move us out of sight as I watched Sorin enter the chapel. I looked up at Nick with pleading eyes. I wanted alone time with him, but Sorin seldom walked the halls these days. His trip to the chapel furnished a rare opportunity. Nick kissed my hand and motioned for me to follow my father. I mouthed a thank you to him and hurried through the doors. The sanctuary's age only visible in the architecture. The coven maintained the ornate beauty.

My heart almost stopped when I saw him standing in the exact spot where his body once laid. His Darkness shadowed around him, and my own dark aura pulled me toward him. The strength of his aura had grown each day since his return, and every once in a while, I could break through to feel his struggle. The waves of despair ate away at his hope. I stood behind him until he turned around to face me. Not even the tears he shed would extinguish the burning embers in his eyes. I wrapped my arms around him and tried to send some of my calming energy to him. He relaxed for the first time, and I sent a prayer up in thanks.

"Dad, I'm so sorry." Fresh tears welled in my eyes as the words left my mouth.

"Sssh. It's not your fault.," he said.

"But it is. I did this to you," I said, a sob shaking my body.

"No, you didn't intentionally do this. You didn't even know you could." He had said it before, but he still couldn't convince me.

"I'm going to keep searching for an answer."

"I know you will, Brie. It's part of the goodness in you." He smiled at me. It was strained and sad and matched my insides. "I'm going to go away for a while, but you have my number. I will only be a phone call away if you need me." I feared him leaving since the day he returned. He'd been back for a short time, and I didn't want to lose him. To ask him to stay would be a selfish act I refused to do. I now battled the same Darkness he had, and I considered going into seclusion myself for relief. My love for Nick and my destiny kept me moving forward.

"I understand." I nodded at him and fought back the tears. This time was different. He wasn't disappearing for a few hours or a day. It was a withdrawal like he'd done when Brandon and I were little. "When are you leaving?"

"This evening."

"Mom is going to take it hard," I said. She would be a mess, and Brandon and I would have to put her back together as best as we could.

He sighed and looked up at the altar.

"I have put her through so much over our lifetime. Take care of her for me." He pleaded with me.

"Of course," I said, even though I figured she would blame me. She'd be right to. I brought him back from the fires of Hell. "I'll miss you."

He wrapped an arm around my shoulders and rested his head against mine. "I'll miss you too, and never forget I love you, my daughter."

"I love you too, Dad," I said as he let go of me.

He knelt down in front of the altar, and the elements began to swirl and push his dark aura tight to his body. His ability to call the elements rivaled mine. Maybe exceeded my own strength.

I watched for a moment before turning away. I left him alone in the chapel to pray and prepare for his journey.

◗ ◗ ● ◖ ◖

By DINNERTIME, Sorin embarked on his new path. He had taken the time to say goodbye to all of us individually. The pain on my mother's face broke my heart. After all the years of discord, we were finally a family, and just as we were reunited, we were torn apart. We ate in silence barely uttering to each other. Nick eyed me as I picked at my food. I forced some down until I couldn't sit still any longer.

"Excuse me." I dropped my napkin onto the table as I stood. I walked until I was out of the room, and then I started to run. I ran as fast as I could until I tripped over my own feet in the hall, but I never hit the marble. Nick caught me in his arms, and we sank to the floor together. The anguish flowed from me as my tears fell. He held me tight against his chest, and let me cry until there were no more tears left.

"Better?" Nick handed me a handkerchief.

I studied the square fabric. *Who carries a handkerchief anymore?*

"Not really, but I guess I have to be since a queen can't be running away all the time," I said weakly.

"You're still allowed to feel. You don't have to stop being —" Nick paused.

"Human?" I raised an eyebrow at him at the elusive word. "I've never been human. Remember? Witch. All my life." I pointed to myself, and he gave me a weak smile that matched my pitiful attempt at humor.

He stood and pulled me up with him.

"I know. It's not really very different," he said, brushing the hair from my face. I cocked my head and waited for him to continue. "So, you have powers. You still feel. You still age even if it is much slower. You love. You have children, and you eventually die. You have the same life cycle of a human."

I hadn't given a whole lot of thought about children. I really never thought I would get married. My life seemed whole as a huntress. *Or so I thought.* I'd never considered a family of my own as a possibility.

"Children? Can vampires?" I asked, having never heard of it. Nick sighed like he was disappointed.

"No, we can only turn those we wish to make our family." He wrinkled his forehead. "We never really talked about it. Can you live with not having children?"

I thought for a moment. *Did I even want them? Having them had never been on the table as a vampire hunter.*

"I love kids, but I never planned children into my life. A huntress doesn't exactly fit in the married with a family life-style." I shrugged.

"But do you want children?" He pushed forward. Worry lines creased his forehead.

"If I can't have yours, then I don't want children," I answered honestly. He kissed my forehead and pulled me tight against him. His silence worried me.

"Come on. Let's go to our room and watch a movie. We can have a perfectly normal human kind of night." He took my hand and lead the way to our room. His attempt to distract me with something normal was welcome.

The strength of the full moon permeated the space around me as we watched the movie. The power pulsating around me. I tried to ignore it and focused on Nick. Our desire took over, and we never saw the end of it. When I removed Nick's shirt, I froze. A tattoo almost identical to mine marked his skin. I studied the Celtic-style sword marking his pectoral. It differed from my own, but there were three Blood Moons and one white one just as on my arm. Instead of intricate scrollwork, mine had, his had snakes, and I shivered at the sight of them. The reptilian forms shimmered like black diamonds. It was repulsive and beautiful at the same time.

I said nothing but grabbed his hand. I led him to the bathroom to show him.

His eyes widened seeing his reflection in the mirror. "It's true."

"What's true? Did you do this?" I asked, confused.

"No, but Stefan told me repeatedly I held a destiny of my own." He stared at the mark.

"What does it mean?" I ran my hand over it. Nick placed his hand on top of mine.

"After he turned me, Stefan said he had a special destiny for me, but I thought he meant in his design of the world. I had no interest in it so I didn't listen intently."

"We need to find Grandmother," I said, unable to ignore this was a sign. The universe positioned herself to fuck me harder.

TWO

Nick and I looked everywhere in the Great House for Grandmother. Her hiding place eluded us, but we found my brother, Brandon, in the library combing through books. I enlisted his help searching for any mention of Nick's mark. My twin and I sat at one of the tables and flipped pages.

Nick stared out the window handsome even lost in thought. I warmed inside thinking how I'd like him to press me against the window when we are alone. He turned toward me like he could sense my stare. The smile on his face disappeared. He doubled over. *What the hell?* His arms clasped over his chest, he sank to his knees.

I jumped from my chair to get to him. My stomach rolled. I gasped at the pain radiating through me. My ability to feel what another feels consumed me. Torment wrenched through me. It was Nick's agony. He collapsed on the floor, clutching his chest. Brandon caught me and lowered me to the floor. I tried to crawl but couldn't move fast enough.

"Get me to Nick," I whispered. Brandon wordlessly helped me as I half crawled to my fiancé. I knew whatever excruciating sensation I felt, Nick's torture was worse. Brandon moved slowly and grimaced. Our twin sense sent him a dose of the pain.

Blood oozed from Nick's eyes like crimson tears. His eyes rolled back in his head. He couldn't die. He wasn't alive. Immortality meant he could exist forever, but he wasn't invincible. I gently lifted his head, fighting against my own pain, and placed it in my lap sending up a prayer to spare his life. *Goddess, please.* Tears rolled down my cheeks landing on his face and mixing with his blood.

"Nick, can you hear me?" I said close to his ear. His wrinkled forehead matched his tightly closed eyes and pursed lips. His teeth ground, top against bottom, sending chills down my spine. A hand touched my shoulder, and my affliction eased. I let out a breath and looked up into my grandmother's worried eyes. "Grandmother, what is going on?"

"I don't know, but it feels like he is changing." Her eyes fell on his mark where his shirt gaped open.

"I'm going to try to send my aura around him," I said, shifting my focus to him. Grandmother squeezed my shoulder.

"Brie, remember your father. The consequences could be devastating if this is supposed to be his time." She sat down beside me and began to pray. I didn't believe it was his time, and I would fight like Hell to keep him here.

Refusing to let Nick writhe in agony, I placed my fingertips at his temples and concentrated on sending my aura out to protect him. The pain became mine and eased. His body visibly relaxed as the tension left, but his eyes remained closed. The vibration from Nick's phone startled me. My gut was telling me it was no coincidence.

"Brandon, can you reach into Nick's pocket for his phone?" I glanced at him. He raised an eyebrow at me as he reached for it. "Who called him?"

"It was Ella." Nick's ex and I had let go of our animosity. We might not be friends, but we didn't hate each other either. Nick loved me. I knew this, and she wasn't a threat. For her to call meant there was major vampire business. "It's ringing again. Malachi this time."

"Answer it." I nodded to him.

"Hello?" He stood and paused. "Malachi, it's Brandon. Nick's not well." He walked out of earshot, and I couldn't hear the rest of the conversation. My focus remained on Nick. I would have sworn days had passed in the time it took Brandon to return when in reality it was only moments.

"Did Malachi know what was going on with Nick?"

"No, he called with news from the vampire castle. Stefan is dead. They don't know exactly what happened." He paused. "You know this means—"

"Nick is the king now." I finished his sentence. Everything would change for us again. I stared into Nick's face afraid for what Stefan's death meant for him. I stroked his face with my fingertips in a soft caress. Fear "Nick, you need to wake up." I leaned over to kiss his forehead. His skin was colder than even a vampire's should be. I inhaled to control my panic, so close to breaking through.

"Maybe he should rest, Brie. He may not get any for a while," Grandmother said quietly.

"He's a vampire. They don't actually need rest." I bit my lip at the harshness in my voice. "I'm sorry, Grandmother."

"It's ok. You're worried." She gave me a small smile and squeezed my hand.

"Nick, please open your eyes." I coaxed in almost a whisper. His eyes darted around before his lids slid back revealing his emerald-green eyes in a sea of red. The shock of it caused me to gasp.

"Hey." He raised a hand to touch my face. A smile crossed his own. "You need to relax. I'm fine."

"You scared me." Fresh tears spilled in relief.

"For that, I am sorry." He sat up and brushed his lips over mine. The familiar sparks between us ran their course through my body.

"We need to talk."

Nick searched my eyes, but the normal connection was absent like he held back. A hollowness formed in my gut and spread through me.

"I know." He looked away.

"What do you mean?" I studied him waiting for his response. His posture closed off from me.

He turned back to me, and his normally bright emerald eyes darkened to almost black. It reminded me of Sorin's aura. My heart pounded in a heavy sluggish rhythm. I tried to swallow down my dread but couldn't.

"When a vampire king dies, the successor goes through a sire fracture. The bond is broken. It happens for all vampires that lose their sire, but the successor bond is more intense. Not all of them survive it, but they are free for the first time since becoming vampire." I expected him to have some semblance of happiness to be free, but his tone was emotionless.

"Similar to the bond between a Witch Queen and her successor." I remembered our battles with his father. Nick had prepared to kill Stefan himself then.

He winced, giving away a hint of pain in it. "It's not unlike what you have experienced with other witches passing or when Queen Cecily passed."

The torment death left in my soul provided the fuel to keep the Darkness at bay. *Was it the same for Nick?*

He wrapped his arms around me, and I melted into him. Although she was my aunt, I didn't know Cecily well other than as my queen, but Nick looked at Stefan as his father for a very long time. Regardless of the evil things Stefan did, the loss hurt Nick, and I didn't think he experienced just physical pain.

"Grandmother? Brandon? Would you mind giving us some time alone?" I asked, even though we should be talking to the council. The council could wait a few minutes. It's not like the world would end in the hour.

"Of course," Grandmother said. "My condolences, Nick."

"I'm sorry for your pain," Brandon said.

Grandmother took Brandon by the arm and left, closing the door behind them.

"Are you really okay?" I asked, knowing I wasn't that day on the battlefield with Sorin. I was so broken, and Nick put me back together that day.

"I will not miss Stefan," he said. "If that is what you are asking, Brie."

"But you wouldn't be a vampire if it wasn't for him," I said.

"No, I wouldn't have, which means I wouldn't have met you." His forehead wrinkled. "And that's the only good thing he can claim in my life."

He seemed more like himself. I pulled him close to me and rested my head on his chest.

"I need to go to the vampire castle and be with my people." He kissed the top of my head and wrapped his arms tighter around me. "They will need my leadership."

"Of course. I can come with you." He'd been there for me when Sorin died on the battlefield, and I would be there for him in the same way.

"You need to stay and lead your people." He pulled back looking me in the eyes. Our connection tugged at me, but I fought getting lost in the moment. "I will need to find out what happened and administer retribution. I don't want you to be a part of it."

If Sorin hadn't returned, I'd have made someone pay, so I understood. But his statement lacked emotion and made me wonder if he was obligated by some twisted vampire loyalty.

As I thought about what he said, the resounding reason circled in my head. My thoughts led me to one person. My father said he was leaving for a while, and he didn't know how long. The coincidence with his departure and Stefan's death convinced me the relationship between vampires and witches would only get worse. Panic swept through me like a tsunami. I had to find my father first.

"Everything is going to change for us again." I looked

down, not ready to meet his eyes and acknowledge my suspicions.

Nick crooked a finger under my chin, lifting it to study me.

"We change every day, but we will always be together. I love you, my impressive witch fiancée." He gave a small quirky smile and kissed me.

"I love you too," I whispered as he disappeared with his lightning speed.

The hollow vacancy grew in me as I looked at the empty space where he once stood. A twinge of Darkness beckoned me for pain and anger to feed it. I called my pink aura to push it away. I inhaled, filling my lungs with a cleansing breath, and let it out slowly after a moment.

Finding Sorin and getting him out of harm's way jumped to the top of my list of priorities. Stefan had a lot of enemies who wanted him dead, but Sorin had made it clear he regretted letting him go. He did it to show me control over the dark and compassion could drive it away. He'd shown remorse for allowing Stefan to live that night, and my gut told me Sorin corrected his mistake by ending Stefan. I sent a prayer up to find him before Nick and the vampires figured out Sorin held the answers they wanted. A warlock killing the vampire king would divide us further and destroy the tiny step forward we'd made. Leaving the comfort of the library, I searched for Grandmother and Brandon.

I found them in the office and shared my concerns.

"There is no way Sorin ended Stefan!" Brandon yelled at me. "He spared him the night he returned. He could have killed him then if he wanted him dead."

I stared at my brother. An outburst wasn't normal for him. He was the calm one.

"Brandon, he believed he made the wrong choice that night. I think he wanted to protect us," I reached out to touch his arm, but he backed away. Our twin sense made me fully aware of just how angry he was. The intense emotion strained my control over the dark aura mixed with my pink.

"No! He wouldn't do it, Brie. I don't believe it." He shook his head.

I looked at Grandmother. She tilted her head toward the door and squeezed my hand. It hurt a bit to be excluded, but Grandmother could reach my twin and me when no one else could so I left them alone. She would talk him down from his anger.

Much of my life meant fighting battles on my own, and the decision almost made itself for me to find Sorin on my own. The loneliness of doing it by myself was new. Sensing my father since his return was difficult, and scrying seemed my only option. It was considered lesser magic and often linked to the dark and calling on my dark aura to locate him wasn't an idea I relished. Each time I touched Darkness there was a risk that I might be lost to it, and I was afraid I would hurt someone I loved. But Sorin and I were linked by the Darkness, and it offered a sure result.

Locking the door to the library with a magical seal, I prepared the big table with my map and objects. Magic never made me nervous before Darkness became part of me. My hands shook. After sending up a prayer for the Light to lead me even though I would be accessing the dark, it was time to begin. The pull of the dark threatened me as I visualized

Sorin. The power of the dark took over, and my blood cooked in my veins. I both hated and relished how strong the power was. A protection spell guarded Sorin, but the dark broke through it. The dark drew the charm in my hand to the map, and I watched it drop right on the Vampire Castle. Chills spread over my body. *They found him.* Pain gripped me that Nick hadn't told me.

The dark aura still flowed through me, and images of Sorin filled my thoughts. I saw him bound in the same dungeon I had once been held in by Stefan. Darkness lapped up the hatred of that memory. With his battered and bruised body, my father stood strong in the same chains. Even with his left eye swollen shut in a purplish hue and dried blood around his lip and nose, he held up. The Darkness had him fully, and Darkness was skilled at removing pain. A small thing to be thankful for in this case. I could tell from the flame raging in his right eye. The flicker that had been there turned into a raging fire.

Once again, I accepted the responsibility for his meta-morphosis, and he needed me to save him. It took him over twenty years to find his way back to our family and losing him for another twenty wasn't something I would risk. I tele-ported to my room and geared up, determined to succeed. I figured leaving the library locked would buy me some time before anyone knew I was gone. Grandmother and Brandon would try to stop me. There was a chance I could get back before anyone noticed. I thought of the dungeon and tele-ported there.

Seeing him in person conflicted me. The warlock in front of me didn't resemble the man I had come to know as my father. The Darkness waving over me from him nauseated me. He glared at me, and the wicked way his lips curled up made me take a step back even as my own Darkness urged me forward.

"Light," I whispered softly. My tension eased as the pink aura surrounded me like a hug and pushed against the dark. Sorin's face relaxed as my pink aura entwined with his dark. The tentacles of Darkness burrowed deep in him, but my hope to reach him grew as I watched my pink aura breakthrough.

"Brie, you must go," Sorin said with the strength of his voice. His battered body didn't look as strong with my aura holding the dark at arm's length from him.

"Not happening," I said watching his Darkness fight against the barrier I'd created. If he stayed her, the vampires would surely kill him. "I'm going to get you out of here."

"It's too late for me. I'm lost to the dark, but you still have a chance." He winced as his dark aura fought to push me away. "They will kill you. The war between the witches and the vampires hasn't been stopped. It is only enraged by Stefan's death."

"Sorin." I paused and shook my head. "Dad, Nick is the King now. Everything is going to be all right." The words sounded hollow to me. I wanted to believe Nick wouldn't hurt my father, but he'd said he would have retribution. I reached for his shackles, but his aura pushed me away. "Let me get you out of here," I pleaded to him.

"Remember my warning to you about choosing better friends? You need to go now. The Darkness is breaking your hold." Hell's Fire burst up between us forcing me back further. Disappointment at my failure seared my heart worse than the flames could burn my skin. "I'm sorry."

Tears trailed over my cheeks as I teleported to the library. My head down, the hot liquid fell into my hand. *Should I go back?*

The pounding on the door pissed me off. It had to be Brandon. Grandmother wouldn't make a scene by hitting a door like that. Evidently, going off grid for even a half hour garnered more attention than I wanted. Being Queen of the Witches sucked and being the demise of your family and your race sucked worse. I swung the door open prepared to unleash my fury when I saw Brandon standing there. He hugged me tightly.

"I'm sorry I was so bent early," he said, pulling away. I yanked him inside by the arm and shut the door.

"If you weren't my brother, I would smack you."

He smiled. "It would hurt you too given how strong our twin sense has been lately. Speaking of... what just happened to you?" He raised an eyebrow at me as he eyed the scrying paraphernalia.

"I found Sorin," I said, dreading telling him the rest.

"Let's go get him." Brandon smiled. He took a step toward me. His boots echoing on the floor reminded me of the hollow sound of the dungeon.

I cleared my throat to push the knot forming there away. "He doesn't want us there." I looked up into Brandon's confused eyes feeling the hurt he felt.

"What do you mean? Where is he? And what is that smell?"

"I don't smell anything. I teleported to him, but he used Hell's Fire to keep me from releasing him."

"Releasing him? Where the hell is he?" His voice lowered an octave.

"Trapped in Darkness." I looked away while continuing to avoid the truth of his location I would, at some point, have to share. He would want to attempt a rescue of our father, and it would put them both in danger. "Listen to me, Brandon. He's not going to let us near him. You understand the power of Hell's Fire, right? Or maybe you don't since you can't wield it." The snarkiness of my voice surprised me. Brandon turned to walk away, and I touched his shoulder. "I'm sorry. I didn't mean it like that."

He shrugged my hand from his shoulder and walked out of the room.

"Damn it!" I said, running my hand through my hair after the door shut. *Was it stress? Was it Darkness that made me say it?* Darkness infected my mind with vile thoughts of inflicting pain in any way possible. I got a whiff of what Brandon was talking about. Hell's Fire singed part of my leather cuff. I gagged at how much it smelled like burnt flesh.

I contemplated ways to get to Sorin through Hell's Fire. I could wield it, thanks to the Darkness living in me, but I couldn't walk through it like Sorin. *Darkness.* The thought made me cringe, but Darkness presented the only option. Accessing it meant giving up a piece of me, and I chanced not ever getting that piece back. Inviting Darkness to me allowed it to consume like it had consumed Sorin twice. The last thing I wanted was to be the Dark Queen, and common sense told me I should enlist help. Neither my family nor the council would approve of me turning to the Darkness which left me as alone in the quest as I was this morning.

I waved a hand to seal the door again and pulled down the books on dark magic. They resided in the library as reference tools when fighting dark magic, but they aided me today in figuring out how to save my father. I studied the books feverishly, and Darkness didn't offer solutions ending in happiness. Darkness existed in power so most of the paths were about gaining strength and magic. As I read, I found the only references to walking through Hell's fire were for witches who live in Darkness. I thought of the repercussions if I allowed Darkness to consume me. I was sure I would be lost to it if I gave into it fully. The thoughts of hurting people I loved angered me, and the anger let Darkness drive worse thoughts of war. I tabled the option and went on to look for scenarios where Hell's fire was suppressed or quenched. The only thing I found involved two dark warlocks who battled with Hell's fire. The battle took place in the early time of the witches, and no record existed of another one. Both warlocks ended up dying in the battle. I slammed the book closed in frustration surprised when a small flame shot out.

The one viable option wasn't really an option at all. Rage built in me for my father, Nick, and this situation. I closed my eyes breathing in to calm the Darkness stirring within me. Warmth grew around me and beads of sweat formed on my forehead. I opened my eyes to see Hell's Fire forming a small ring around me. *Had I called it? No.* My senses told me to quench it, but I decided to test the boundary. I reach my hand out, and it intensified the closer I got to it. I placed my hand up against the flame wall, and the excruciating burn of the flame caused me to jerk my hand back. Studying the wall gave me an idea. I took a step forward, and it moved with me. If the ring of fire could protect me, I could pass through Sorin's wall unharmed. *I think. It's worth trying. The only option.*

The Darkness sang to me with the promise of power. I stopped to calm myself by thinking only of Light. My pink aura skimmed across my skin and enveloped me centering me in the present. It reminded me of when Grandmother held me as a child. The pureness of it equated to love. To choose Light was to choose love. It wasn't the sacrifice the witches believed.

I tried to call Nick, but he didn't answer. My phone vibrated, and I jumped a little.

I'm not going to make it back tonight

Really? Nick's text pissed me off. He held my father prisoner, but he couldn't be bothered with a phone call. My first extinct was to throw the phone, but the wiser part of me told me to hold that thought. I sent a text back as simplistic as his.

We need to talk now!

I usually wasn't demanding with him, but he owed me an explanation. No response came from him which infuriated me. I started shaking uncontrollably and slid to the floor.

Brandon and Grandmother sat on the floor beside me. *When did they get here?*

The vision was terrible, and it repeated multiple times. I could see on their faces I had projected the events to them. Dad's prediction resonated with me. He was right when he said the war was not over. Our war had only begun, and the future was horrific.

"The elders should know what is coming." Brandon, visibly shaken by my vision, was pale and trembled as hard as me.

"No, my gut says we keep it to ourselves for now." The elders would push for action, and it could trigger apocalyptic events. I looked to Grandmother. She nodded.

"They'll want to attack, and it would mean certain failure right now." She sounded more convincing than I did.

I checked my phone and got to my feet. "Nick hasn't returned my text, and I want to know what he has to say."

"He either has or will betray you and the alliance you formed, Brie. We all saw the vision. He will try to end all witches. Why would you want to talk to him? He's the enemy," Brandon said with a voice full of venom.

"He's my fiancé, Brandon, and we don't know what is going on. The visions are subjective and ever-changing. You know this," I defended Nick, but my heart was breaking at the thought of fighting against him. My role as Queen was compromised, and I knew it. If the fragile peace we had fostered broke and ware came, I'd be the one to blame and all the deaths would be on my hands.

"Grandmother, talk some sense into her," Brandon pleaded.

"She is the Queen first, and she has proven herself to be wise. She will make the right decisions for her people," Grandmother said with a small smile in my direction. "Let your light guide you, Brie." Even as she said it, my thoughts turned to the night we faced Stefan last. I had chosen Light, but the Darkness crept in when I wanted to end Stefan. Sorin stopped me that night which is why it made little sense for him to kill him now. The more I considered it, the more it didn't seem plausible for him. *But maybe someone wants us to think it was my father.*

"I need to meditate," I told them wanting to be alone more than meditate.

THREE

I locked myself in my room and sorted through the facts as I knew them and tried to come to terms with what the vision meant. I saw death on both sides, and it amounted to significantly more than in our other battles. Nick had yielded Hell's fire against the witches, and it frightened me how it could even be possible. While they often aligned with the dark and dark witches, vampires didn't have magic and, therefore, had no control over Hell's Fire. There were only two witches in existence that could wield Hell's Fire, and that was me and my father. Tears pooled in my eyes, and I swallowed hard to push them down.

My ancestors chose me because they believed in my ability to bring peace. If Nick betrayed me, he would pay. It would wreck me forever, but I would hold him accountable. Even as I thought it, I doubted my resolve to go through with it, and if I did, I'd die inside. Dad warned me multiple times about loving Nick and the cost for myself as well as our people. I inhaled deeply. *No, Nick wouldn't do this to us. I believe in us. I believe him.*

Involving myself in vampire business risked peace in the worst way possible, but my determination to rescue Sorin led me into a precarious situation. The unplanned familiar rush of air carried me to the Vampire Castle with ease as I thought of Nick. Unfortunately for me, the result landed me in the throne room and the middle of a major vampire meeting. I cut my eyes around the room and recognized a few faces but didn't know them. The look on Nick's face confirmed my mistake. The love in his eyes vanished and replaced the light with anguish as he turned from me.

How could he? The rejection gutted me.

"Take her to the dungeon," he proclaimed, as the King of Vampires. The shock of his reaction spiraled me through anger. Darkness took control and Hell's Fire radiated around me incinerating the two vampire guards. I gaped at the pile of ash and never saw the blunt object that connected with my head. *Again! Damn it!* Everything went black as I fell toward the floor.

I woke to a pounding in my head followed by nausea at the damp musty smell of the cell. *Fuck.* My hands were shackled, but I could still heal myself. Healing would require sleep which I couldn't afford right now. I tried to focus through the pain. I let out a small sigh when I recognized the figure shackled next to me. *Sorin. My father.*

"Dad, you're still alive! Thank the Goddess," I said surprised by the weakness of my voice. He looked up.

"I was worried about you. I'm glad you're awake. You are

weak, but you should have enough strength to teleport out of here. Do it now," he whispered, his voice strained.

He didn't want my help. Nick sent me to the dungeon. *Why?* I didn't have a big ego, but they chipped away at what I did have. My hurt ego didn't change what needed to be done.

"I'm not going anywhere without you this time." I kept my voice low. He wouldn't die at the hands of vampires. *Not today if I can help it.*

"You're in danger, Brie. They will kill you," He argued, his voice heavy with desperation.

"How long have I been out?" If they wanted me dead, they could have done it earlier in the throne room instead of putting me here.

"A couple of hours at least which means you don't have much time."

"Why don't you want me to rescue you, Dad?" I didn't understand why he was so against being rescued.

His face softened, and the dark aura lightened a little.

"You have a genuine pureness in you which is why you are a good queen, Brie. I am lost to the Dark. There is no coming back from it this time for me. My fate has been written." He looked away as he finished, but I caught the flames flare in his eyes.

I didn't believe he was lost permanently. There had to be a way to reverse it. "You're not a loss. My aura broke through earlier. It can do it again."

"No, you don't understand." He shook his head. "My heart is dark. My soul is dark. Light no longer lives in me." He looked defeated.

Before I responded, the door flew open. My neck tightened with the anticipation of killing the vampire sauntering into the room. My hands bound in shackles prevented me from forming an energy ball, but summoning magic was still an option. Sucking in the damp air of the dungeon, I prepared to cast a control spell. My eyes locked with a sea of green halting me in the middle of the spell. *Nick.* Relief washed over me only to fade away with anger and Darkness.

"Hell's Fire!" I shouted willing it to surround Sorin and me. Sorin blew out a small puff of air to extinguish the wall and tempered my anger.

"Let her go, Nick. She will turn dark, and you will lose her forever if you keep her here," Sorin pleaded. I looked at my father. It sounded like they had this discussion before.

"You do not command me!" Nick advanced and roared directly into his face. I bore my eyes into him. He turned to me, and I feared him for the first time. His eyes were dull and lifeless like he had cast all his humanity away. "My beauty."

His breath brushed against my cheek, and he touched my hair. I strained to lean away. *What the hell is wrong with him?* He took out a key and showed it to me. "I will let you go if you promise to be good, my beauty."

I looked to Sorin, desperate for an explanation as to why Nick was not Nick. My father blinked almost imperceptibly. Tears flowed down my cheeks as I rolled my head back to face Nick. *Was this the real man standing in front of me?* Drunk on power, the clouded green eyes staring back at me prevented our connection.

He put a hand around my waist and pushed me back against the wall with his body pressed against mine causing slack in the chains. The relief welcome, but I feared what his plan was. He unlocked the first shackle and admired the bruising on my wrist. Without a word, he placed a gentle kiss on it. His behavior earlier didn't match his reactions here. *Was it an act earlier?* He repeated it on the other wrist. *What is wrong with him?* He was vicious and gentle all at the same time. Taking my hand, he led me away. I formed an energy ball in my free hand ready to knock him on his ass, but I squashed it when I saw Sorin shaking his head.

Nick ushered me toward the door. I counted five guards stationed on the other side and took it as a compliment, but maybe it was more for Sorin than me. Nick placed his hand on a panel at the next door, and it opened to an elevator. The doors closed with us alone.

"Of course, you vampires would have an elevator to your dungeon," I said, letting the bitterness flow from me.

Nick smirked at me. A small glint of light in his cloudy eyes. *Maybe he was in there somewhere.*

He pressed me against the metal wall. It reminded me of the night before my last birthday when he was taking me home. He focused on my eyes. A twinge was all our special connection offered. It was a fraction of the intensity. I welcomed it because it meant he might be in there.

His hand caressed my cheek as the elevator stopped. He pulled away before the doors opened. It left me empty.

Nick led me past guards who smirked at us, and my resentment grew with every step. He shut the door to the King's chamber and turned to face me. I saw a glimmer of what I knew as his real self there. He sped toward me pushing me into the wall. Most of the air in my lungs forced out. Dust drifted down around us. He kissed me hard on the mouth. His vanilla whiskey scent wrapped around me. It took everything in me to push him back. I slapped his face.

"You don't get to kiss me after avoiding me and throwing me in a dungeon."

His green eyes cleared, and we connected with a powerful electrical surge. I gasped.

"You need to teleport out of here now, Brie," Nick said desperately.

This personality belonged to my Nick. A knot formed in my throat. I was so relieved he was still in there. "I'm not going anywhere until you tell me what the hell is going on here."

"We only have a few minutes before it comes back. When everything feels wrong and you do not know me, remember I love you. Teleport now." My Nick kissed me gently, and his love warmed me. I didn't want to leave him or my father here.

"What do you mean before it comes back?" I asked.

"You need to go, Brie." The fog clouded his eyes again, and he was a shadow of himself again. The idea of doing it ripped me apart. I needed to figure out what was wrong with him., and that couldn't be done from the dungeon of the Vampire Castle. I thought of the library teleporting away, leaving my heart in the Vampire Castle and without any more answers than when I arrived.

Grandmother waited for me on the couch. She appeared as if she was waiting for me at least, and I was relieved to see her. I ran to her collapsing. She patted my back as I lay in her lap with my eyes wide open. All the books in this room and no answers to be found. Comprehension eluded me.

"I don't understand," I said.

"We live in the supernatural world, Granddaughter. Things don't always make sense immediately to us even with all the tools at our fingertips," she said. "Your mother and brother are on the way. Prepare yourself."

Brandon and Mother burst through the door. They both wore the same confused expression. Fighting with them sounded exhausting. Mother sat beside me taking my hand.

"He's alive?" She asked her voice no more than a whisper.

"He's alive." I squeezed her hand and watched the tears of joy pour from her eyes.

"Thank God," she cried out. "Let's go get your father," She looked from me to Brandon.

"He doesn't want to be rescued," I answered, knowing it would rip her apart on the inside like it was me.

"What do you mean he doesn't want to be rescued? Don't be silly. Of course, he wants to be rescued," she said, her voice laced with denial.

"No, he doesn't. He's using Hell's Fire to prevent it." Afraid to tell her everything because I might lose her too, I chose my words carefully.

"You can summon Hell's Fire so I don't see the issue," she said.

"It doesn't work like that, Mom," I said.

She pulled her hands away from me.

"Your precious vampire is responsible for this. Why didn't you stay there with him?" She stormed out of the room. It reminded me of being a child and feeling betrayed by her, but we were different now. *I was different. Stronger.*

Brandon never said a word, but his wrinkled forehead told me he didn't side with her even though he would comfort her. I was glad she would have him because all my energy and time were required to try to figure out a solution.

"She doesn't understand. Don't hold it against her," Grandmother said.

I gave her a half-hearted smile.

"Nick is power drunk," I said, hoping answers would come by telling someone. "It consumes him like the Darkness consumes Sorin."

"He has to find his own way, Brie. You can't choose his path for him."

"I know, but he was there for me. I don't know how to be there for a split personality." I shook my head. "The dark is reaching for me every chance it gets. The pull of it is maddening."

"It's always going to want to claim you. You know this." She confirmed what I had already figured out.

"Do you think vampires have souls?"

She sighed. "I know there are different beliefs as to whether they do or not. What do you think?"

"I think Nick has a soul. I'm not sure they all do." I looked down at the floor. "I ended two vampires today with Hell's Fire out of rage. The power nauseated me as the Darkness consumed them."

"You think you sent them to Hell?" She raised an eyebrow.

I nodded slowly fighting back tears at the thought.

"You don't control who goes to Summerland or Hell or Heaven for that matter." She assured me. "Meditate." She stood, kissed the top of my head, and left me alone.

Being alone resulted in thinking, and I didn't want to do

that right now. I wandered around the Great House, but memories assaulted me on every corner, especially at the chapel. I ended up sitting on the spot on the green in the back where I tackled Nick during my bad levitation experience before our first battle. I sighed and sent a prayer up for guidance. I pondered what Nick had said because everything felt wrong every moment he wasn't by my side and Sorin was held captive. I tucked my knees up to my chest wrapping my arms around them. I pictured Nick's arms around me and the love in his eyes in the moment before he pressed our lips together. Warmth generated in my core and spread through my body. He loved me. He couldn't fake the warmth between us or the bond. *So what happened?*

I switched my focus to what he didn't say. He never told me what the 'it' was that was coming back. I leaned back onto the grass looking up at the stars making their appearance for the evening. I inhaled the cool night air letting the sweet scent of damp grass fill me and allowing its healing properties to take over. *What the hell is it? Sorin? No.* He must have meant the drunkenness the power possessed over him. There were no spells to remove an obsession with power. Each person had to fight their way to their own fate.

A shadow moved toward me, and Cal's figure emerged. I sat up waving him over to have a seat with me. I welcomed my oldest friend's company. He was probably the one person who understood how I felt.

"You look knackered." He smiled as he sat down, sadness in his brown eyes. "It's ok to say that to my queen, right?"

I laughed. "It's perfectly fine to tell your friend she looks tired. Considering I feel like warmed-over French fries."

He laughed. I recounted the day for him, and he listened without judgment. My stress dissipated as we talked, but my worry didn't.

"Do you think Sorin is controlling him?" He asked.

"No, I don't. Sorin is a prisoner. They beat him." I swallowed through the lump in my throat. "Nick never desired power, but he is saturated with it now. As soon as Stefan died, something in him changed. I've never seen power drunkeness like that happen so quickly."

Cal studied me. "You should understand changes better than anyone."

"My birthday gifts don't change me. It's different. His was like a power awakened in him. He wasn't even the same person," I said.

"Don't give up on him too quickly, Brie. I can't recall ever seeing a love as true and pure as what he has for you. You are his soul."

"He told me that once." I smiled at the memory. "I feel like I'm not strong enough to save them both."

"Remember how much Nick loves you when you face him." He looked me in the eyes driving home his point.

"You've seen something?" I recognized the knowing look.

CHAPTER
FOUR

C al hesitated, but I held his gaze. I shared his resistance to dispense his visions but if it helped me understand how to reach Nick, I had to know.

"I'm not sure my friend will want to hear it, but my queen needs to prepare," Cal said, his tone soft but serious.

My heart sank in on itself.

"Nick is preparing for battle, and my vision was of his victory. He will come here, and he knows the secret passages. Many witches will perish and few vampires die." He paused and looked off like he debated on whether to continue.

My stomach twisted up in a knot and I braced for the worse. *Whatever Nick's plan is, I'll talk him down. If his plan is to take me, I'll go to save the lives of witches, even if he's turned into someone or something I can't love.*

"He will personally execute Sorin for the death of Stefan."

My heart slowed and became heavy in my chest. I rocked back on my feet.

He wouldn't. My hand moved to my throat to soothe the

tightness. *He knows how much time I lost with Sorin.* I met Cal's eyes.

He blinked back the sadness pooled in his brown orbs.

His vision was much worse than mine. *How in Hell's Fire am I going to fix this?* My fingers slid down my throat to my ancestral necklace with the hidden vile of Vampire Death. *Could I if it came to it? If Nick made me choose. If Nick tried to kill my father, could I end my fiancé first? And would it be enough to save the witches that will perish if he invades the coven?*

I didn't say a word. *What was there to say? There's only one thing I can do that can stop all of this.* I walked to the wall where the oldest books were stored and waved my hand in front of the section I needed. The shelf creaked and groaned as it exposed the book I sought. Dust swarmed in the air, causing us both to cough. Only a portion of The Blood Moon Prophecy was written in the books provided to us. A vision had shown me this, and I never divulged it. I was never alone enough to research it and seeking out this path acknowledged a part of The Blood Moon Prophecy linked to the Darkness of magic. I hadn't even shared it with Nick because I never intended to go down this path. My options exhausted, the choice made itself. *Accept the Darkness. The power I need to end this can only be found there.*

The book flipped open and glowed in a soft orange, the color of a Super Moon. It floated a few feet away as it waited for my final decision.

"Brie, this is not the answer." Cal stepped in front of me. The Darkness pulled me even as I looked into his eyes. I blinked back my tears and swallowed down the pain of the loss it would bring. *Not that I will feel it after Darkness claims me.*

"This is the only answer." I wanted to call on Light to protect me, but I would be a hypocrite to do so. I embraced my friend. "Find a way to bring me back." A tear spilled over at the corner of my eye and blazed its way down my cheek. "Go. I'm not sure what will happen."

Cal didn't budge.

Even as events pushed me to the worst choice I could make for my own soul, he stayed loyal. Sadness for all I'd lose on this path bowled over me like an avalanche. I wiped away my tears.

"I command you as your queen."

Cal dropped to his knee with his head bowed. The sign of respect a last gift. He rose, and said, "I'm only leaving because my Queen commanded it of me as her subject. As your friend, I promise with my life to bring you back from the Darkness." He squeezed my shoulder and left me alone to my fate.

As soon as I touched the book, it pulled me forward. Fear morphed into relief to not have to fight the constant tug any longer. The case swung around leaving me standing in Darkness. I closed my eyes against the painful hold that enveloped me. Hell's Fire sprung up in a circle around me providing the only light as I looked at the book.

For he and she will be brought together in Darkness to bring about Hell on earth. I blinked at the words on the page. *What am I about to do?* If I had listened to Sorin, I wouldn't be standing here right now. I ignored his guidance and the words of the prophecy when I chose my love and Light, and my choice came with a price. *I'd pay my price.* I sucked in a deep breath, but the heat I inhaled didn't relax me. *Damn this inhuman world!*

I grabbed hold of the book with both hands as I relinquished myself to the Darkness. I breathed out, letting go of my resolve against the dark. Hatred for myself was swallowed up. My pink aura fought every inch, and the Darkness stung and burned through it. Calling out to Light to fight passed through my mind, but I let it go without a command. My pink aura convulsed as the dark aura swallowed and squeezed it out of existence. Numbness replaced the guilt I carried. Anger twisted into rage like an inferno in me, and I wanted to inflict pain in the worst ways for Darkness to devour. My eyes blazed from the inside, and I had no doubt they now mirrored Sorin's. I reached my hand out to the Hell's Fire ring around me, and it no longer burned my flesh. Darkness crept through my body, and I knew I needed to leave the mansion before it completely took over. My desire to feed Darkness with pain would drive me to hurt those I love. There was one person who would understand. I thought of the dungeon and Sorin.

When Sorin's fiery eyes met my own, he closed his and heaved a sigh. Hell's Fire no longer prevented me from rescuing him, but my original plan dwindled to the recesses of my mind like the faded feeling of love. *Pain. Anger.* My soul writhed against the Darkness as it corrupted a path through to the farthest points of my limbs. Heat rose around me and encircled me in Hell's Fire. When the fires encased me, they fueled the anger brewing within me. One by one, my thoughts for my friends and family flickered away and died in a place within me I could no longer reach. Inflicting torture and gaining power claimed my focus. I narrowed my eyes on Sorin and curled my lips up as my head tilted to the side. The foreignness of the movement lost to Darkness in the action.

"See, Sorin. I am your daughter." My voice was harsh, even for me. I walked a deliberate straight line, leaving only inches between us. I was aware but not fully in control and suspected that would fade away in time.

"Don't do this. Call to the Light. It can still save you." His voice cracked on the last word.

"Call the Light?" I laughed, a hollow sound from my normal laughter. "Calling the Light is the last thing I plan to do." The last of Light drained from me. I left Sorin in the dungeon still shackled and teleported to the throne room. *I'll be the one calling the shots now. Not Nick.*

Nick's mouth gaped open. Being near him felt right. *Love.* Darkness sucked it away. His men moved toward me.

"Tsk." My lips pursed. I raised my hands out to my sides. Hell's Fire shot from my fingertips. The flames followed invisible lines to the vampires advancing in my direction. The power was like a drug, and I wanted more. I spun in a circle to watch. The fire engulfed Nick's guard and turned them to ash. It pleased me to watch them suffer and end an ultimate vampire death. Darkness drank in every death.

Strong, recognizable arms wrapped around me. My heart constricted and Darkness consumed it. The electric touch erupted as he spun me around sending us both airborne. I landed on my back. The impact forced the air from my lungs. Vampire dust filled my nostrils with the scent of burnt death. I gasped for clean air. A thud against the wall drew my attention. Nick's head struck the wall like a diver hitting the bottom of a pool. The crack of his neck echoed off the walls.

The hate in me cleared. Horrified, I saw the man I loved on the ground by my own hands. *Goddess. What have I done?*

I ran to him. My vision blurred from the tears. I laid my hand against his cheek. He should come back right away, but he wasn't. Terror took hold. I stroked both sides of his face and kissed him. "Light. I need you now." I called to it with barely a whisper, but it didn't respond. Regret filled every part of me as I looked at Nick with his neck bent in an awkward position. The broken vertebrae were visible under the skin. My fear grew.

"Come back, Nick. Come back to me." I cried out.

My hand grazed his tattoo as I went to shake him. A charge shocked me so hard that it sent me backward. His tattoo glowed like mine had the first night it appeared. Not a trace of doubt remained in my head that our destinies intermingled in more ways than we could have imagined.

But Light never responded and Darkness claimed me. It crept back in like a snake in the garden. It burned through my body. Nick stirred on the floor as he came around. My moment of relief was sucked up like a vacuum by Darkness. Our eyes met for the briefest moment and I knew I had to leave in the same way he had me leave when he was lost. I teleported back to the dungeon. I grabbed Sorin's arm and teleported back to my library before Darkness had its full hold on me.

My pink aura fought to keep the window that opened

while I fought Nick. The fight was fleeting, but it gave me some time.

Mother, Brandon, and Grandmother stood with the healers beside Sorin. He was in bad shape, but he would recover. I snuck away to the library to wallow in the mess I'd created alone.

I fucked up. Not just a little. It rated an epic on the scale of fuck ups. I walked to the table, and a shock met me when I touched our ancestral book. If I had light left in me, I'd be able to touch it. Fingers positioned over the book, my heart pounded. I lowered my hands down and met the sting of energy. I jerked back. Sweat beaded on my forehead. Incantations prevented my touch because my soul aligned with Darkness. The opposite of the ancient book I held earlier which required a commitment to Darkness. As intoxicating as the Darkness was, and it was very exhilarating, my inner voice told me it wasn't right for me. The excitement and power offered control, but they lacked the completeness of the Light. Even as I thought it, Darkness dimmed the recognition of it with fire and promises of power.

I grabbed the book and held onto it as long as I could. The current knocked the Darkness back for a moment of clarity. I clutched my chest against the pain building. *I hurt Nick.* My stomach churned. Tears spilled down my cheeks.

Darkness pushed my remorse aside filling every crevice of my body with burning hate. My pink aura battled the dark aura in a painful duel. My eyes heated up like a stove burner. Darkness staked a fierce claim in my body. I didn't want to remember the pain I caused and surrendered again. In my soul I recognized the longer Darkness stayed in me, my chance of ever being free of it reduced exponentially. Darkness blotted away my ability to care about the consequences.

I crossed the room to enter the hidden one on the other side. The dusty mirror reflected a new version of me. A smirk drew across my face. My eyes no longer blue. The flames, larger than Sorin's, engulfed the pupils. My hair no longer blonde and pink. The tinted locks turned a red to match the fire in my eyes.

"Hello, gorgeous. I'd always wondered what I would look like as a redhead."

Voices carried through the door, and I knew they were looking for me. I started to transport, but the yelling drew me in for Darkness to feed. I moved deeper into the room, not wanting to disclose my location.

Mother rounded the corner. "Brie—" She gasped, Grandmother positioned beside her with eyes wide.

Nick stood just behind them. He took several steps toward me. "What have you done?" His voice was full of concern.

Hell's Fire flew up between us partitioning me from everyone else. Fear radiated from them and fueled my strength. I sucked it in like air.

"You look well." I eyed Nick. His health was restored, and he looked sexy as hell. I licked my lips.

"You don't. Let me help you." He stood close to the fire.

Grandmother hooked her hand around his elbow. "Step back, Nick."

He looked over his shoulder at her and gave in to the gentle pressure she applied. His eyes found mine.

A twinge quivered in me and wanted more, but Darkness

shot fire from my hands to reinforce the wall between us. *Power*. Power like I'd never imagined literally at my fingertips. *Oh, the things I can do.*

"Remember the prophecy. You are on a dangerous path," Grandmother said, her tone stern.

"Fuck the prophecy. I can decide my own destiny."

"Darkness is leading you and the ones you love to death." She stood tall letting go of Nick's arm. Her hands swirled in the air and energy gathered around her. The pale blue light blasted out when her hands came toward me. Hell's Fire rose to meet it, but the orangish-red glow was extinguished. Grandmother collapsed.

Darkness wanted vengeance, but a different kind of Darkness closed in on my vision. Breathing became difficult. Pitch black wrapped around me like a straitjacket and tugged me to the ground.

)) ● ((

Goosebumps prickled my skin. My eyes tried to focus as I woke up on the floor of the dark room. *Cold.* I reached my hand upward to call Light, but it did not respond. It didn't answer a soul consumed by Darkness. The burning inside me had eased, and I was filled with one thing. *Regret.* The mess I made played like a bad movie in my head. I crumpled into a ball pulling my knees to my chest. The cool stream of tears caused shivers in my already chilled state. Shame wound from my toes up through my spine and spiraled around me like a snake smothering the last of life from my soul. *I was no longer the Queen of the Witches. I won't be welcome in the coven any longer. My family won't trust me. The one that hurts the most is I will never be Nick's wife. No wedding. No waking up together. No inhumanly long life together.*

I placed my hands, fingers wide, on the floor beside me and sought out the only thing I had left. Warmth traveled up my arms stirring the burn of flames in my eyes. Light abandoned me as I had abandoned it. Darkness was my only consort now.

Flames bolted up from the floor to the ceiling encircling me and filling the void. Strength returned to my body, and I stood to take in my surroundings. My despair melted into nonexistence.

They put me in the fucking dungeon. I will not be anyone's prisoner. The door would be easy, but I didn't need it. My thoughts went to my apartment. Heat swirled around me and carried me to my home.

I sealed the door to prevent any unwanted visitors. *Family. Ex-family. Ex-coven.* "I can't believe they put me in a dungeon." My voice roared and rattled the windows. Darkness scorched me from the inside and blackened my soul. Power flared inside me, and I wanted nothing more than to unleash it. I enjoyed the strength at my fingertips.

The balcony beckoned me. I looked down at the empty pool and held my hand out. I waved it back and forth. Waves sloshed over the edges. Not satisfied, I needed more. My hand fixed in place, steam rose from the pool. Bubbles rolled like a boiling pot. I sucked in a deep breath reenergized from exercising my strength.

They could try to stop me. My family. My coven. They would lose. My power grew every second since I gave into it. I'd never again be anyone's victim.

Power. Lucious power. Warming power. Strengthening power. I had it all, and I wanted to hunt. A quick glance at the clock told me it would be an hour until Club Red opened. Plenty of time to get ready.

꒰ ꒱ ● ꒰ ꒱

I took my own car to the club. Something I had never done before out of fear, but I had nothing to fear with Darkness at the helm. Hell's Fire obliged my call to conceal my witchiness from the vampires with a surge through my body. *Witchiness. Nick's word.* I shook my head and got out of the car.

Ian, the doorman, let me past the line. I waved to Mike as I passed the bar. No liquid courage required tonight. Darkness and Hell's Fire gave me all the reassurance needed.

The dance floor contained the normal offering of drunk humans as a feast for the vampires. The human's pathetic existence was ignorant of the power around them, and they were in my way. I paced around the edge of it watching for a vampire who wanted to tempt fate. A hand grasped my elbow hard enough to bruise. *Vampire.* I spun around to see what idiot the appendage belonged to.

"Ella." I forced a smile and inclined my head. Burning her with Hell's fire would be delightful.

She took my hand and pulled me to a quiet corner booth. She motioned to the seat. I rolled my eyes and sat down.

"Brie, you shouldn't be here without your bodyguards. Every vampire knows who you are. You are a walking target."

"I assure you I am capable of taking care of myself." I met her eyes, imagining what she would look like as ash.

"What's wrong with your—"

"Eyes?" My head fell in an exaggerated tilt. "Let's just say I could burn this club and everyone in it to the ground and walk out of here unscathed."

"Hell's Fire," she whispered.

"You're familiar." I smiled.

"First Nick, and now you." Her hands covered her face.

A twinge stabbed my stomach when she said Nick's name. Nausea waved over me causing a temporary coolness. I swallowed hard against it, and the warmth crept back to me.

"Well, you're not going to be able to help Nick until we fix you." Ella waved her finger at me.

Fix me? I'm perfect. "I don't want to be fixed. I'm powerful. I'm in control. And I want to hunt." I looked her up and down. She was strong and capable. I could use someone like her on my side.

She shifted in the seat but stayed her ground. *Impressive. I see why Nick thought he might marry her once.* She snapped her fingers in front of my face. "Meanwhile Nick is losing his battle for control, and his humanity will be lost forever unless you help him. Something broke him out of it earlier, and he went to look for you. When he came back, he was worse than he'd been. I didn't recognize him at all. He'll be another Stefan and the vampire clans don't need another power-drunk tyrant."

I failed to see how that was my problem. I could end them any time I wanted. *One little call to Hell's Fire and poof.*

"Why do you want to help him after the way he treated you? Not like you were a saint in the matter, but he was pretty cruel to toss you aside like he did."

She met my gaze this time. Solid. Firm. Committed.

"I think you know why."

"You're still in love with him."

She scooted away from me. My suspicions confirmed. An ache formed in my chest, but Darkness gobbled it up like the weakness it was.

"What makes you think he's going to listen to me?" I clasped my hands in front of me.

"Because he loves you, and you already reached him once."

How in the hell did she know that? I'm burning the bitch. A crack in my dark aura broke like a lightning strike, and the ache for the love I'd never have pierced the small sliver. My heart yearned for what would never be. Darkness could own every part of me except that piece. It could suppress my love for Nick, but it would always be there waiting for a chip to break through. *Maybe I could save him, even if there was no saving me.* I stuck my hope like a wedge in the door of Darkness.

Darkness chewed on my hope, planting new thoughts on how to gain power. *If I can't help him, it puts me in the right place to end him.*

My eyes cooled. The flames must have retreated... for a moment. "Fine. What do you want me to do?"

Ella's face relaxed. "Come with me."

꒰ ꒱ ● ꒰ ꒱

"They aren't going to let me in, Ella." We stopped a short distance from the gate of the castle and hid out of sight.

She made a swirling gesture with her finger. "What if you swish us into my bedroom?"

"You have a bedroom at the castle?" My eyebrow arched upwards. The wedge I had in place slipped and the peek of Light in my aura dimmed. Jealousy shocked my system with coolness. *Darkness.* I pushed back against it. My silent request brought warmth though not enough to fully quench the chill of an emotion eaten by Darkness.

Ella stiffened and grabbed my forearm. "Stefan made Malachi and I move back to the castle before he died."

I glanced at her hand on my arm and back up to her. She released her hold.

And Nick hadn't thought to tell me this. Anger festered in me, and flames circled my feet. Ella jumped back. My heart pounded against my rib cage. A deep breath filled my lungs, and I focused on the small wedge of hope to save Nick. I snapped my fingers, and the flames disappeared. The mark was visible with the scorched circle surrounding me.

"Sorry. I have trouble controlling it." It was a lie with a fake smile not showing any teeth, but I'd already damned my soul, so what did it matter. "Give me your hand." I held my own out to her.

She studied my palm. "You're not going to turn me to ash, right?"

"No." *Not yet anyway.*

She took hold of my hands

"This might be a little uncomfortable." The swoosh enveloped us. *Ella's bedroom.* I expected it to be feminine, but it wasn't. Her room had few decorations and the only color was from a handful of red accent pillows on the bed.

"Not bad," she said, landing on her feet. Good for anyone on their first time.

I inclined my head her way. "Let's get to it." *The sooner we save Nick I can put an end to her.*

"We should wait until Nick is in his chambers."

"And I guess you know exactly where those are?" I crossed my arms over my chest to keep from burning her to a crisp.

She fidgeted with the hem of her shirt like a teenager caught having sex by their parents. "Yes."

The one-word answer bothered me. She had been strong when we met. She tackled me outside Malachi's when she thought I was an intruder. She'd been strong every time our paths crossed, but her slouched shoulders portrayed something different today. The Darkness dampened my empath abilities, and I couldn't tell if she was telling the truth or not. I'd have to watch her every move.

"Screw it. Let's just go there now. We can hide in the closet or something." My hand extended, I waited for her to take it.

"He's in the King's chambers, and it's—" She took my hand.

"I know where the King's chambers are."

The wind swirled around us carrying us to Nick's suite of apartments in the castle. Nick wasn't there. Bile rose from my stomach up in my throat until I tasted it. I swallowed hard.

"I hate this place. I hate every inch of this castle." Memories of my captivity at the hands of Gaius, Nick's deceased brother, and later with Stefan hammered at the wedge and threatened to knock it loose. I pushed them back as much as I could. "The closet is over here."

I pulled Ella toward it. "How do you..." her voice trailed off.

"Yep. Not something I want to go into right now unless you want me to burn this castle to the ground."

Ella remained silent.

The darkness covered us when I shut the door. I closed my eyes and relished the peace it brought to me. Her vampire eyes could see expertly in it, and the Darkness was part of me. I let my dark aura reach out and explore. We didn't need any extra light to find our way around it.

"What are you going to do to break the spell on Nick?" Ella whispered.

"Spell? You think it's a spell? Isn't he drunk on power?" I

whispered back. *Who would be powerful enough to cast a spell like that on Nick besides me? My father, but he wouldn't do that. There weren't many witches or warlocks powerful enough to wield that kind of magic.* If it was a spell... If that was the case, his action hadn't been his own. A twinge of regret tapped on the crack in my dark aura, but Darkness took it away.

"No, I don't think it's the power at all. I think Alastair is controlling him."

The traitor. How had I not even thought of Alastair? I'm such an idiot. Of course, he would be involved. He'd helped Stefan wage war against the witches. His own damn kind. I'd been a fucking blind fool not to have seen it.

"You're sure Alastair is here?" Flames flickered at the end of my fingertips. I folded my fingers into my palm to smother them.

"Yes, he is serving as an advisor on Nick's council, just as he did for Stefan."

"Fuck." I shook my head. "Of course, he is."

Alastair was the most powerful warlock behind my father. He rivaled my power even. Any spell he cast on Nick wouldn't be easy to break. If he used a blood spell, it would be even harder given vampire nature and the need to consume blood.

"You can break it can't you?"

"I'm sure as hell going to try." Flames tingled my palms. I clasped my hands together to extinguish them.

Dark magic enhanced blood spells. Alastair was dark. Not that I had doubted it before, but I knew for certain now. *Would I be able to break it with dark magic now?* My thoughts turned inward to contemplate how I could use my bond with

Darkness to break the spell. Sacrificing Ella would satisfy the craving of Darkness, but it wouldn't help break the spell. *I can't burn it out of Nick, because hello... vampires turn to ash.*

The bedroom door opened and closed. Anticipation fluttered in my stomach. Footsteps echoed on the hard floor. *One person.* The gait was Nick's. One characteristic that hadn't changed. I put my hand on the knob to ease the door open.

"You can come out, Brie. I know you're there. I always know when you're close." His melodic voice sang to open the wedge and reinforced it. Darkness still had control, but the wedge was firm enough that I didn't have the overwhelming desire to hurt him. *At least not to make him suffer.*

I stepped out of the closet with Ella in tow. The skin between Nick's eyes bunched together at the site of both of us. He looked at me and leaned back against the desk with his arms across his chest.

"Ella, what are you doing in the King's chambers?" His voice was like venom toward her.

She cowered behind me. It surprised me that she was afraid of this version of Nick. I didn't like it much myself, but she wasn't one to show fear. My tattoo itched matching the irritation I had and Darkness fed on her fear.

I lifted my chin and forced power into my voice without pulling out the wedge holding a place for light in my aura. "I brought her with me."

"And why would you do that?" He narrowed his eyes at me.

"She knows her way around the castle," I said.

He stepped toward me, more seductively than menacingly. "So do you."

"Why didn't you tell me Alastair was serving as your advisor?" I moved toward him. My magic skated over my skin ready to merge with the dark aura.

"When was I supposed to do that?"

"Oh, I don't know. Maybe when I texted you or maybe when I saw you. Or a novel idea would have been for you to call me." Hell's Fire bubbled over the surface of my arms ready to unleash its wrath. To hurt Nick again would be like putting a dagger in my own heart, and it narrowed the wedge in the Darkness of my aura.

"You should have known that wouldn't be possible," he said. His eyes were cloudy, but not as much as they were the last time. He turned his head to break eye contact with me.

The mark on his neck, hidden at most times by his shirt collar, was unmistakable. *Wiccan.* Alastair had cast a blood spell for sure. The symbol resembled a combined X and spiral. A journey and partnership. Or in this case, it allowed Alastair to control Nick's path.

Flames gathered at the tips of my fingers lying in wait for my command. Since I no longer commanded Light, I'd use Darkness to rid him of the spell. It could end him and kill me, but it was the only tool available to combat the complicated blood magic. *Darkness, yield my warning. Protect him from this. If you do not yield to my warning and he dies, I will go with him.* I envisioned a simple spell to focus on the mark and remove it. *And hopefully not turn him to dust. I can do this.*

"Darkness, I command you to release him from this spell." Hell's Fire zeroed in on the mark, but the symbol reflected it back to me. The force knocked me on my butt. The sizzle from my shoulder where it made contact stunk of burnt flesh. I studied the area. The Darkness couldn't heal itself. Meaning it couldn't heal me like the Light could. My shoulder burned like a hot poker was stuck in it. I refused to cry out and bit down on my lip until Darkness ate the pain.

Nick was on top of me before I could sit up. His hands firmly grasped my throat. *Fuck. That backfired.* I clawed at his hands, frustrated Hell's Fire didn't remedy the situation. The hold was tight enough I couldn't even speak. Ella grabbed him by the shoulder digging her nails in till blood pooled on his white shirt. She tossed him back. I gasped for air choking it down.

"You need Light, Brie," she said, over her shoulder. She delivered a kick to Nick's chest knocking him back.

Light had left me. Light had been drowned by the Darkness. I couldn't let Ella die for my failed attempt nor could I kill Nick for being controlled by someone as evil as Alastair. *How do I let go of the Darkness?* My tattoo itched again. It started glowing. I stared at the light radiating from it.

"Light I choose you over Darkness. I erred in my ways thinking Darkness was my only chance. I was wrong. I call to you Light. I embrace Light. I choose Light." A whiteness glowed around me bathing me in golden brightness. I inhaled Light like it was air I needed to breathe. *Thank you.* Energy coursed through me as my pink aura fought the dark aura, widening the wedge like a partial eclipse. The magnitude of my mistake weighed on me, but I'd have to deal with it later.

"Light. Cleanse the mark of Darkness from this vampire." My voice full of power directed the energy to Nick's neck. The symbol lit up like a sparkler. It traced a path until it was erased.

Tears pricked my eyes. *Goddess, I'm sorry for the wrongs I've caused.* Nick would be free of Alastair's control. My eyes were heavy.

Nick landed on his knees in front of Ella. Blood ran from his nose. Not sure if it was from damage inflicted by Ella or from the power Light had yielded. Ella backed away to stand beside me. I stared at Nick, waiting to see if it had worked. The fresh pink skin was visible where the mark once was. Nick moved in slow motion as he turned toward me.

His hand reached up for his neck, and his eyes widened. "How did you know it would work?"

I slid into the floor with relief and exhaustion "I didn't. I hoped."

He crawled across the floor and buried his head against my chest. Warmth spread through me. His touch, the real him, opened the box Darkness had stuck our love in. Anguish for what I'd been prepared to do for Darkness would haunt me forever. But Nick was free now, and that mattered most to me.

"That symbol Alastair put on you should have killed a vampire. I don't understand how you are alive, but I'm so thankful." Tears spilled down my cheeks into his hair. "Are you really you?" I whispered.

"I am." His body shook against mine.

He wrapped his fingers around my forearms. His thumb stroked back and forth as his hands inched up my shoulders. Fingers pushed my hair back. His thumb caressed my cheek.

My eyes fluttered into his gaze, my lids heavy with a weary ache.

"The flames are gone from your eyes," he whispered. Our lips met as he drew us together. His caress was pure love, and it stirred desire in me.

I wanted to say how much I loved him, but I couldn't. The universe had found a way to make me fulfill the prophecy despite my choices, and I had to let Nick go.

Darkness would be back. It wasn't permanently gone. It stirred in me ready to explode at the first opportunity. Nick's love took up the space occupied by Darkness, but it was temporary. I suspected Sorin's battle had been a similar painful journey, and I understood his decision to leave. To stay meant breaking everyone who loved me until there was nothing left of them. To leave gave them a chance for safety and happiness.

He pulled back staring into my eyes again.

Connection. It was still there. And it was fleeting.

"How?"

"I called to Light." Even as I uttered the words, the Darkness crept back inside me. The burn started in the center of my body and spread outward. "I have to go." I averted my eyes from him but met Ella's. The embers sparked to life. No matter how many times I called the Light, Darkness would return until it eventually scorched my soul. *Just like it did for my father.*

Her lips tight, she nodded.

"You're not going anywhere." He nuzzled my cheek.

I closed my eyes and drew in a deep breath. Sadness and regret settled deep in my belly. The choice had been mine, and if I hadn't, Nick might not be himself now. "It's over, Nick."

I scooted away from him not looking in his direction. My back turned from him, I focused on Ella. The shuffle as he scrambled to his feet siphoned tears from me. My heart wanted him, but I couldn't be with him until I eradicated the Darkness in me. *If I could.* The wind rushed around me to carry me away. *Alone.*

Grandmother was on my mind, and I found myself standing over her bed. The room was dim except for a night-light in the bathroom. She was sound asleep, but she stirred as I sat on the edge of the bed. Guards shuffled about on the other side of the door. *Why is no one in here with her?*

"Brie?" her weak voice drew my attention. *Is she groggy?* I worried if she was okay.

I held her hand in mine. Hers was cold, and I placed my other one on top to warm it. The Darkness only allowed me a few minutes before it would take over again. Tears soaked my cheeks, and I feared they would only stop when Darkness took over.

"I thought you might come. I told everyone to leave me alone." She gave a frail smile and stretched her hand up to my face, wiping away my tears. "Don't cry, granddaughter. I'll be fine. My energy is depleted, but it will return."

Her words bounced off the inside of my head. They didn't resonate in comfort as they should. They nagged at me, telling me they weren't true. I held my hands over to heal her.

She grasped both of my wrists. Her hands guided mine into a prayer position. She held them tight together with hers. The strain on her face was evident by her creased fore-head. Silver in her hair glistened.

"Save your energy for your battle. You'll need it soon enough. Lock yourself in solitude. Meditate. Call Light to your side. Fight the Darkness, Brie."

Darkness bit at my insides. It wouldn't be long before I succumbed.

"I'm so sorry, Grandmother. I thought I could control it." I choked out the words.

"Sssh. Everything happens as our destiny dictates. This is your path. Now go before the Darkness seizes you. Go to the secret room."

She knew about it. Of course, she did. I bent forward to kiss her cheek. Her skin was cold against my lips. I stood up. "I love you."

"I love you too." The whoosh of air around me carried me to the secret room off the library.

The pages stood open to the prophecy. Darkness claimed a new part of me with each step forward. It scalded me like a punishment for my actions. "Light, I need your help." Flickers of pink pushed against the dark aura around me, delaying the inevitable result.

I bent over the book. "She determines whether Light or dark reigns." I swallowed hard. I'd failed in the worst way possible. "She being me." I flipped the page and ran my finger down to the passage I recalled. "Darkness cannot be ignored any more than Light. Both must be embraced to balance the scales, but the choice must always dominate with Light."

"You know the answer," Cal said.

I startled at the sound of his warm voice.

"How long..." my voice trailed off because it didn't matter. He knew the truth. He saw the choice. "How do I fix it before the Darkness consumes me again? It's like I lose a piece of my soul every time it does."

His voice was even and calm, but he took careful steps toward me. "I've read it a dozen times. The ultimate battle might be symbolic. Not saying there won't be physical battles, but the ultimate battle could lie within you."

I sighed. The desire to fall into a ball on the floor and cry for days was stronger than any other, but I pulled my shoulders back and stood tall instead. If my destiny demanded I be strong, then I would be.

"I need help." Those words were so hard for me to say. My pink aura weakened against my dark aura. The burn spread through me. The battle was lost for now. Darkness claimed me again. The inevitable takeover frightened me. The Light in me withered with each touch of angry tentacles tempting me to do things the real me wouldn't contemplate.

"You need to go, Cal. I don't know what the dark version of me is capable of, and she's almost back."

"I'm not leaving you, my queen," he said, his tone firm.

"She's dishonorable and vicious. She'll say hateful things and physically harm you."

"She is still my queen." He squeezed my hand in a quick motion. I'd left us all vulnerable, and the pain of that made a never-ending meal for Darkness.

"No, she is not. She is evil at her core, and I'm lost in the dark." My skin tingled with warmth and expanded into a full burn while my insides went cold. Darkness gained control and the coolness of a tear on my cheek was almost painful.

"Darkness," I whispered. It wasn't a command, but it responded just the same. All the pain and struggle I had inside me was wiped away and filled with anger and strength. I turned my back to Cal. "Leave me." My voice echoed off the walls.

"Not on your life."

"It could be yours if you stay." I faced him. Hell's Fire blazed in my eyes and spit to life at my feet.

"You don't scare me. I know. I know your deepest thoughts, your worst fears, and your visions." Cal stood firm. He was spectacular if not stupid to stand against me in all my power.

I studied him. His dark hair a little messy like he'd been running his fingers through it, but his brown eyes were firm and his stance confident. It seemed a waste to burn someone so fearless. "So, you do. Does that make you an ally or an enemy?"

"You are my queen. Ally, confidant, and consultant is what it makes me."

"You'll have to prove that to me." *I could have him torture and kill, Alastair, his own father.* The thoughts of what I would have him do elicited a snicker from me.

"I think I have proven my allegiance multiple times. Most notably when I chose you over my father."

His words hit a memory in me, and nausea oscillated at the truth of his statement. A sliver of pink came forward like a spear piercing my armor. It ripped into the dark aura around me, but the dark tamped it down. My stomach wrenched, and I grabbed it.

"Are you okay?" He stepped forward.

"I'm fine." I held my hand out to keep him at bay. "Never better." Darkness spun around me to offer strength and fury. I regained my composure and stood tall again.

His forehead wrinkled at the sight of my eyes. He took a hesitant step back.

"If you're going to stay, you're going to help me with a plan to kill Alastair. He wants control of both the vampires and the witches. I'm the only one who will have that power." I smiled at him. The flames in my eyes burned in a dance at the return of the Darkness.

"Yes, my queen."

The redness in his eyes didn't escape me. *Weakness.* His softheartedness for his father could be the end of him. *What a shame. So be it.*

SEVEN

Fire coursed through me and warmed the emptiness until it pushed away. The pages of the ancient book of Darkness flipped to a shadowed mantra for control of vampires and witches alike. Blood required from powerful representatives of each. *Blood.* The key to so many of the dark spells. A twinge of pink aura reminded me of the blood spilled in the field months ago, and I seesawed between it and Darkness. The dark aura gained control, and I didn't even fight. *Power. That's what I need. Power and control.*

"You do understand that I plan to kill your father?" I said, keeping my voice soft but serious. I faced Cal.

"Yes, my queen. I do." He clasped his hands in front of him. "And I'm still here."

"And you would be willing to kill your own father out of allegiance to me?"

"You are the queen. There is no higher allegiance." He cleared his throat. A notable difference in the sparse way he spoke now versus how he spoke to the disgusting nice version I once was. His words were chosen with care. *Could I trust him? Could I trust anyone?*

"We'll see." A knock on the hidden door startled me. "Did you tell someone we were here?"

"No," Cal said. His eyes widened.

"Brie? Open the door," Mother said.

I cringed at the sound of her voice. She cared about herself, so no doubt she was here to ask for a favor.

"Go away, Mother." My voice roared off the walls and through the door.

She matched my tone. "I'm not going anywhere. Open this door."

"You're going to make a demand of me? Go search in the bottom of a bottle for your answer."

Her gasp was audible on this side of the door. My laughter echoed around us.

The pink aura chipped a small hole in the dark, and a tiny pang of guilt landed in my stomach. It billowed up my torso and touched my heart. I could fight the dark aura.

"Light," I whispered.

"Yes, call Light." My mother's voice a whisper itself with the barrier between us. The fabric of her clothing scraped against the door with a hiss against the wood. *Why is she still here? What does she want?*

The pink aura worked from the inside out pushing the dark away. A pink bubble engulfed me. Like the other times, it wouldn't last. Darkness made me its Queen, and it didn't intend to let go.

"I'm losing this fight." I waved my hand in the direction of the door. It swung into the room. My mother sprawled out in front of me, and I dropped to my knees, exhausted from the battle. I wanted to give into the dark to find relief, but I held on as long as I could.

"You must continue to fight." She crawled to me and put both hands on either side of my face. "You must."

"Don't be here when the Darkness comes back. Hate builds and takes over. I will hurt you." I pulled her hands from my face and turned to Cal. "You shouldn't be here either. You need to lead the coven no matter how much I fight you. Find Brandon. Our twin bond is probably pure chaos for him with the bitter feelings I have while buried in the shadows. He'll need some help to process that."

"You need to lead the coven. They are not going to believe in anyone but you," Cal said.

"I can't," I said. "I'm broken."

"We're all a little broken." Cal extended his hand in front of me. "We don't have to be perfect to lead. We just must do our best."

I grasped his hand. "I'm not sure my best is good anymore. Good for me or good for the coven."

He pulled me to my feet and helped my mother up.

"None of us are a hundred percent good, Brie. We all have a dark side. We decide as to how big a part it plays in our lives. My father has allowed it to consume him. Don't do the same."

Hadn't I already done that? I felt shame for the me that planned to make him kill Alastair.

"I made the decision the first time I called to dark. No matter how many times I call to Light, the Darkness is always going to be there. I surrendered to it so easily. I'm no longer your queen." A mix of guilt and despair pitted in my stomach.

"You can't give up, Brie." Mom said.

"You don't understand what it's like to have your insides burning and all feelings burned out of your soul. Or your skin to burn and everything inside turn cold." Tears rushed down my cheeks. "I need to renounce my status." I wiped the tears away as my resolve grew. "I can't rule the coven as a queen aligned with Darkness. It would mean our end. I'd have us in a battle with the vampires in a week."

"Don't say that. Do you understand what you are saying?" Mom's tears flowed.

"Queens do not renounce the crown. There is no exile like Sorin had. They must die in battle or die when their chosen successor is ready to ascend," Cal said.

Fuck. I can't even do the right thing now. "If I haven't chosen a successor, who will become the leader?"

He shook his head. "Your closest living relative."

"Sorin?" I'd been absent and didn't even know if had fully recovered.

"Yes, if the ancestors bless it. They haven't blessed a warlock in centuries though. Sorin would have been the first if he had fulfilled his place," Mom said. "But that's not going to happen. You are not going to die."

"Will the coven accept him is what I need to know?" If I could find a spell to draw the darkness from him, he'd be free to rule, and maybe that would atone for my mistakes.

"They're not going to be very accepting of someone who went into exile, because they were consumed by Darkness," Cal said.

"What about a current queen that is consumed by it? I can't be any better." Once the witches understood the Darkness in me, they were going to want to burn me at the stake anyway.

"It's not going to come to that. You're going to overcome, and we are going to help you before they find out." Mother took my hands.

"How?" I asked, desperate for a glimmer of hope more than someone's words.

They exchange a look. It was the kind of look when someone pitches a last-ditch effort that has no chance.

My hope dwindled, and my anger rose. Darkness answered pushing back against the pink.

"Go on." Mom nodded to Cal.

"I had a vision of a ceremony that would restore the balance. Dark and Light would live equally in you. I researched it in the book the prophecy is in, and it is indeed a real ceremony."

Hope quivered in my heart. I would be me again. New tears formed in my eyes. I could be with Nick again. "What are we waiting for? Let's do it before the bastardizing dark comes back."

"We don't have everything we need here." Cal's eyes flickered to my mother.

"It's never simple. Is it? Level with me."

"It requires a—"

"Sacrifice. What kind? Let me guess. Love?" If this required love, it would erase all hope for me, but I'd do what needed to be done to make things right.

Cal cleared his throat and looked at my mother. She

nodded to him.

A foreboding pit settled deep in my belly.

"No, love isn't required. It must be a selfless sacrifice." He cleared his throat again and shifted his weight. "The volunteer must give their life freely. A vampire life."

I sank to a new level of self-hatred for the mess I'd made. *I can't believe they would even suggest this option. Fuck no. Never.* Anger built in me that had nothing to do with Darkness, but it taunted it.

"Are you really standing here asking me this? You want me to ask Nick to sacrifice himself so that you can save me? If you knew me at all, the me without Darkness knocking on my soul, you would know that was never going to happen."

"Brandon has already left to see Nick," Mother said, her tone cautious.

Rage erupted in me, and the Darkness wound its way back in through a crack in the pink.

"Are you fucking kidding me? You sent my brother to ask my ex-fiance to die for me?"

"Brie, if he agrees—"

"We're Blood Bound, Mother. Do you know what that will be like for me? It will be like losing my soul. Do you honestly think I will even want to fight the Darkness if Nick is dead?" I took a step back from her. Darkness readied to vomit out of me, and I needed distance.

"You must do whatever it takes to bring peace. You knew from the beginning a sacrifice of love might be the cost. Our destinies never ask us if we choose them. They choose us." Mom's voice boomed with authority like I'd never heard from her before.

"He'll do it, and I'll be left here alone." My voice was weak and hoarse from the magnitude. I didn't even try to get to a chair. My body dropped to the floor where I stood. He would do it whether I asked or not. He would choose to sacrifice himself if it meant saving me. My heart told me it was true, and I would do it for him. "Do I have to be here for the ceremony for it to work?"

My eyes trained on the floor. If it required me to be here, I could remedy that.

"No," Cal said.

They'd help him whether I was here or not then. The decision was made without me. I'd had no say in my own future. My love would die because of my horrible decision.

"There's one more thing," he said.

"It doesn't matter." There was no winning here. If the ceremony worked, I'd be without Nick, and I don't know what that looked like. It seemed like my life was over either way.

"The ceremony must take place during a Blood Moon."

"Of course, it does." I laughed one of those crazy people laughs. It began soft and worked into a full-blown laugh. The room went out of focus. "I give up. I give myself to Darkness or death, whichever takes my soul first."

"That's not an option," Mother said. Her hand connected with my cheek.

The sting radiated from just below my eye to the corner of my lip. Revenge fluttered on the tips of my fingers, but I didn't care enough to go after her. I closed my eyes thinking of the pain and Darkness. Darkness would choke out any of it if I just let it.

"Choose Light, Brie. Choose Light."

"I can't. I won't. You took my choice away from me when you sent Brandon to secure Nick's agreement. I'm taking the path left." My decisions were mine and I owned them but going behind my back when it came to Nick was theirs. Darkness latched onto me, and I welcomed the burn.

"Nick wouldn't want you to give up. He will do this for you so that you can achieve the peace for both of our people."

"You're right." I opened my eyes, knowing but not caring they could see the flames.

"How was he when you saw him?" Cal asked. He tried to distract me with thoughts of Nick, and I could play along.

"He'd been marked by your father with a controlling spell. Not sure why it worked instead of killing him, but I'm sure your father does." My words launched like daggers at him, and I didn't have the energy or desire to care. It made me want to call Darkness even more to put a wall between me and them.

"I'm not my father's mistakes, Brie. You know this," Cal said, his tone offended.

"I'm going to sit with Grandmother." I walked out the door without looking at either of them. "Cal, shut the door when you leave."

I detoured to the grassy area where I'd laid under the stars with Nick. The grass stood up perfectly in the spot where we had sat. I squatted down and ran my fingers through it. Soft and full of life and promise for the future. My fingers wound in it. *One tug and the roots would pull free. One tug and the roots would pull free! Could a magical tug free me from Darkness? Could it free Sorin?* I teleported to Grandmother's room to check on her but with no intention of staying.

She looked worse. Much worse. Her skin was so pale and paper-like.

"You've been crying. They told you their plan?" She sighed.

"Yes. Has it ever been done before?" The pit in my stomach hardened at the mention of it.

"Not in my lifetime, but it is said to have been done with a great huntress a thousand years ago. She was supposedly as blessed as you." Her voice was still weak.

I nodded, remembering the folklore we were told. "Ariana. I thought they were children's stories."

"There's always a hint of truth, especially in the stories we hand down. We change names and details as they go through generations to make them more palatable for children, but there are portions of history in them."

"I have an idea I want to ask you about." I paused. "What if we did like an energy slingshot to pull the Darkness out of me?" Darkness flared in me like it staked a claim to fight. I bit down on the inside of my cheek and tore a chunk away. The healing required focus and energy, but it only bought me so much time.

She patted my hand, her eyes apologetic. "You've read the prophecy. It might work, but you can't completely eradicate it from your being. The ceremony Cal found is your best chance with the power of the Blood Moon behind it."

"I can't let Nick die for me, Grandmother." Tears threatened. My heart sped up against the pang of the possible loss. Darkness leached onto the pain and sank its teeth into me.

"It's not your choice. It was never your choice. He must decide."

And he would. He would decide to sacrifice himself wholeheartedly. He'd already been willing to do it several times.

"Can't we at least try it my way?"

"Of course, you can. I don't want you to get your hopes up though. You need the kind of power that is only available when the veil is thin." She seemed supportive but cautious.

"Like when someone dies."

"Yes." She arched her eyebrow at me.

"So, if I did a handshake with death it might work." I'd studied the art of near-death magic, but I'd never practiced it. The ritual scared the hell out of me, but not as much as the thought of losing Nick forever. It only took one skilled witch to lead the ceremony, and there was one in this room. The only one I knew that had practiced it. She could guide us on how to do it.

Grandmother squeezed my hands. "Taking you to the brink of death is too risky. The coven will not be willing to put you in such peril."

"But we don't need the entire coven or even the council. Would you do it?" It pained me to ask in her weakened state, and I wouldn't if there was another option that didn't require Nick's death.

"Would I take the risk if I was you or would I perform the 'slingshot' as you called it?"

"Both."

She gave me a sad smile. "I would do whatever I thought necessary to protect the ones I love."

"Hmm. Exactly what I want to do. I love you, Grand-mother." I bent over her and kissed her forehead. "I'll check on you later," I swallowed hard. "Well, unless the Darkness punches through."

"Fight with Light, Brie."

I smiled at her and closed the door. Teleporting to my suite would eliminate facing people, but my gut told me I could keep the Darkness at bay longer if I didn't use magic. It worked for Sorin for years. *Like my entire life practically.*

I strolled down the halls inhaling the sweet scent of sage mixed with wood polish. Not quite as refreshing as cool night air, but it was a close second or maybe third after beach air. I could restrain from practicing magic for a little while until I found the right witches to help me slingshot. I didn't know who yet, but I'd find someone.

The guard practiced outside the window, and I paused to watch. I missed the physical part of hunting. Not the killing. Except when Darkness ran the show. Dark aura craved pain and death. I shuddered at the dark thoughts playing in my mind. The dark aura singed as it made another chink in my pink armor. Sorin dealt with this, and I can too. I sucked in a deep breath and let it out slowly. I stepped out into the courtyard to connect with nature.

)) ● ((

TIME OUTSIDE REJUVENATED ME. I was more in control of the Darkness after being connected with the earth.

Footsteps clamored down the wood floor in a hollow

echo toward me. I spun around to find Cal red-faced and out of breath.

"Your..." He took a deep breath, grabbing his knees. "Grandmother."

"My grandmother? What?" I dug my fingers into his shoulders.

"She can't breathe." He fought for his breath.

I didn't think twice about teleporting. No matter the cost.

Mother was there. Sorin had come from seclusion. Brandon had returned from his meeting with Nick. They were all there.

A stench assaulted my nostrils despite the candles and sage burning in the room. I knew the smell. The rot of death. I'd smelled it the day Cecily announced me as her successor.

No. This cannot be happening. I will not let it happen. I denied the scent.

"Move." I pushed them aside. "I'll heal you, Grandmother. You should have let me before." My heart raced, seeing how blanched she was.

"No, you hold on to the Light. You need it more than the world needs me. I've lived a long time, and it's my time to move forward."

"I need you." I paused, steadying my hands over her.

She placed her hands on top of mine and pushed them down. Her grip was tight enough that I couldn't move them.

"Grandmother, please."

"Stay on the side of Light." She took a couple of labored ragged breaths. Her chest stopped in mid-breath. She was gone.

The loss was immediate like my chest had been cracked open and hollowed out.

"No..." I bowed my head against her rib cage. A light filled the room. A glowing light and it wasn't me. A golden ring surrounded Brandon. Grandmother gifted him. I'd shed so many tears, but these tears were a mix of sadness for her and joy for him.

Grandmother's eyes dulled, and I slid my hands from underneath hers. "Goodbye, Grandmother." My hand hovered over hers as I considered an attempt.

"No," Sorin said. His voice was hardly audible. He took my hands in his and pulled me up off the bed. His arms went around me in an embrace. "You know the consequences."

"She wouldn't be coming back from Hell."

"No, she wouldn't, which is why you need to let her go." I'd cried more in the last year than in the last ten years put together, and I was all cried out. Anger replaced the sorrow I should've felt. Darkness both fueled and fed on it.

"I'm so mad right now," I whispered against his shoulder.

"It's the Darkness. Remember your grandmother's words. She wanted you to be on the side of Light."

"I need to be alone—" It was harder to keep Darkness at bay with the grief and everyone else here in the room. The weight of it was too much for me.

"No, you don't. I was wrong to leave, and you would be too. Stand up to the Darkness."

"I don't have any strength to do it. My last bit of strength passed on."

"She'll always be with you. You need to go to your brother. He's going to need your guidance."

I nodded and looked for Brandon. My twin had been there for me so many times, and a gift could be a curse while you learned how to manage it. I could do this for him. Mother stood with her arms held out, and I dodged her to go to my brother.

"When they said she asked me to come back, I didn't realize..." He pinched the bridge of his nose. Tears came down either side of his face.

I bear-hugged him to me. He cried in heaves and sobs. I wanted to cry, but everything inside me had gone numb. I considered what I should say.

"She had a plan for you, or you wouldn't have received her gift."

"I can't even think about that right now. She's gone." He pulled back and slumped against the corner.

I looked over my shoulder to Sorin for help or guidance, but he was deep in conversation with Mother. My gaze came back to Brandon. He mourned. I should be mourning. *Why can't I feel? Lost. Confused.* My breath hung in my throat. I teleported to my secret room, leaving everyone else behind. Seclusion was my choice, and I understood exactly why Sorin had chosen it so many years ago. I didn't have to care if anyone was around. Darkness punched a giant hole in my pink armor.

My hands rested on the book representing the ominous side of our race. We'd professed to be keepers of peace, but we were responsible for the vengeance the vampires dealt. Yet, Alastair sought to control them. *How am I supposed to fix this?* I laid my head on the book with my nose in the spine. *Maybe the book with snap up and smash my head.*

I leaned back from it. My right hand hovered over the page, "Show me." The pages flipped in haste at my command.

"Only when balance is achieved will The Queen find peace for all." Underneath the words, the details of the ceremony leaped off the page at me. *Freely given blood from a vampire. Drained and burned with Hell's Fire and extinguished by Light.*

"How are they planning on burning his blood with Hell's Fire without me?" I didn't have to answer my own question. *Sorin.*

His struggle with Darkness was even worse than mine since I brought him back from Hell. They weren't only sacrificing Nick. They were going to sacrifice Sorin too. Thunder rumbled in the background at my displeasure. They had to know I would find out, and I would be angry.

I slammed the book shut, and the pedestal rocked back and forth. By the time it stopped, the burn of Darkness tried to sneak in through the hole it punched in my fragmented pink aura. It could drive a semi through it, but it tested like it wasn't sure. I could let it have me, and I'd be powerful enough to stop them. The dark version of me wouldn't give a shit though.

The delicate dance between Light and Darkness exhausted me. This entire day had been more than I'd ever thought I could handle. I wanted peace.

"Light," I whispered. "I need you." My pink aura danced in delight to welcome the power of Light to me, but Darkness walled around it. I fashioned my mental wedge into place. The strength and resolution filled me. No one was sacrificing themselves for me.

EIGHT

The familiar whirlwind swirled around me. I closed my eyes. My gut told me where I would land. I squinted through my lids before opening them. Of course, he'd be in Stefan's throne room.

"Brie," he said. A satisfied smile crossed his face.

Darkness, Hell's Fire would be great right now. We could just burn the bastard. He was my last chance to save Nick though, so death for him would wait.

"Alastair." I crossed my arms in front of me and focused my eyes on him. "You're alone? Stefan would've never been so stupid."

His smile widened. A genuine one. Genuine evil. "Stefan didn't have the power I have."

I could incinerate him where he stood and fought the urge to roll my eyes at his smugness. "What will it take for us to have a truce?"

The last thing I wanted with him was an armistice. But he was a warlock, and the offer should be made.

He laughed.

"Aah." He nodded. "They must have found the spell in the Fire Book. I bet it was Cal." His gaze dropped to the floor, and he rubbed his chin. "You're here to save Nick." He winked at me. "We can make a trade."

He manipulated me to get me here. "I'm not helping you make your vampire-witch army."

"Once the Darkness consumes you completely, you will without me having to do anything."

"So, you're just biding your time until I can no longer come back from Darkness? That's going to be a long wait." It wouldn't, of course. Darkness was part of me.

"I don't think so." He laughed again. "Guards!"

Did he really think he could hold me here? "I can teleport before they get in here."

"Then you wouldn't know whether I was going to kill your boyfriend or not."

My heart raced, but I forced my exterior to remain calm. Besides, he needed both of us for the ritual. "He's my fiancé."

"Didn't you break up with him?" He smirked and took a swig of amber liquid. "So, he's your ex-fiancé. If you want him to live, you will want to stay."

I opened my mouth to argue, but his gaze turned toward the door. I followed it.

The guards entered the room not to apprehend me. Instead, they escorted Nick. He followed them like a zombie. His eyes darted to me and back to the front of the room. The quick action convinced me he still had Alastair fooled he was under his control.

Panic shook me to the core, but I reminded myself that

Alastair needed both of us. Nick was safe for the moment, and he was himself. He'd fight if it came to that. I tried to teleport to Nick, but nothing happened. *Wrong time to go on the fritz powers. Or had Alastair cast a spell in the room that prevented me from using them?*

"I have no interest in confining you in the dungeon, Brie. I want to help you find your potential," Alastair said.

"Darkness has eaten your soul." Disgust rolled off my words. "You're a sick man."

He shook a finger at me over his glass and took another drink. "No, I'm a man with a purpose."

There was more to his plan than the manipulation he used to get me here, and this was a chance for both Nick and me to hear it. "Why do you need me? You're powerful. You know how to perform the ritual."

He smiled without answering me. My command of Hell's Fire seemed the obvious answer, even if he didn't confirm it.

My eyes moved to Nick, but he wouldn't make eye contact with me. His head hung and his gaze focused on the ground.

"I'm waiting for your answer," Alastair said.

I looked him in the eye ready to give my reply. Not only would I say no, but I would burn everyone loyal to him in this room with Hell's Fire.

He nodded to one of the guards. The guard took out a lighter and held it close to Nick's hand. He struck it.

The smell of burnt flesh wafted around me. An energy ball formed in my hand on instinct, and I flung it at the guard. My energy wasn't blocked, so maybe he hadn't cast a spell.

Alastair stopped it centimeters from the guard's face. "Squash it. I will not have you killing my guards."

My hand went up to summon the ball back to me. It shrank in my hand. My fist closed around it, extinguishing the light.

It would have been easy to send it toward Alastair, but if I wasn't successful, I couldn't handle the consequences. He wouldn't punish me. He'd punish Nick. Darkness found a nick in my pink shield and squeezed through the crack. My eyes ignited, and I closed them against the ache.

"Make sure he gets to his room," Alastair said, waving off to the guards.

Nick's lip curled up at the corner in a snarl.

Afraid he would growl or worse, I shook my head in a very small jerk.

His mouth fell back to the expressionless position it had been. The emerald green eyes that could mesmerize me were now flat. He stepped toward the door, and the guards flanked him.

"Don't fight it. Let the Darkness in. Let it grow in you." Alastair stood close enough to me that I could smell the sourness of his breath. It reminded me of spoiled milk. The kind that had curdled.

"There will never be a day I do not fight it." My resolve weakened despite my words. *Wouldn't all this end if I just gave in?*

"Oh, there will. Cal had a vision of you as the Queen of Darkness."

The shadows of Darkness might have broken my internal lie detector, but even without it, I could tell he told the truth.

Darkness possessed a part of my soul, and I feared its permanent hold. The charred smell still hung in the air. A cruel
reminder of how the kindness in me shriveled against the
burn of the evil festering me.

The bastard was right. Hate bubbled under the surface. An
energy ball would be so easy to summon. My eyes narrowed
on him.

"If you harm me, the guards are under a spell to kill Nick.
Maybe you don't care about him anymore? That would make
you my ultimate dark queen." His laugh was like thunder in
my ears.

Nick was the only one it seemed could bring me back.
Well, Grandma did, but she left me. *Maybe I didn't deserve
love. I spent most of my adult life avoiding it...until I fell in love
with Nick. Had we ever been good for each other?* Darkness made
it harder and harder to remember what Nick's love was like.
My memories twisted in my mind like an abstract painting.

"Come, Brie. Give into it. You feel it there waiting to
break through. Let it loose."

I gave in the tiniest bit to the Darkness, because I wanted
to see Alastair flinch. My feet moved in deliberate steps in his
direction until I was nose-to-nose with him. I looked into his
eyes. Mine flamed. I could see them reflected in Alastair's
pupils.

"Do you have any idea how powerful I am? The limitless
power I yield? I could destroy you and all your little followers
with a clap of my hands. You will never control me."

He drew back in the smallest way, but it was enough for
me right now. I mustered a wicked smile and walked past
him toward the door. Two of his vampire subjects blocked it.

"You really don't want to mess with me, assholes." Hell's Fire formed a knee-high circle around me.

"Let her go. She'll be back." Alastair dismissed the guards with his hand.

"Oh, you better believe I will, but it won't be to serve you." I turned to one of the vampires. "Boo!" I yelled with flames radiating from my hands.

He stumbled backward against the other guard. They tumbled to the ground like dominos.

My head fell back, and laughter rang out. I strode out of the room. Darkness grabbed hold deep inside me, ready to make me its queen.

I passed a window of the castle and glanced out. I figure on the other side caught my attention. *Grandmother?* I ran to the window, but she was gone by the time I got there. It couldn't have been her. *She's gone.* The hole grew inside me from her vacancy. Darkness took advantage, consuming the emptiness in me. I turned my back to the window and slid down the wall. My head rested on my knees.

Fire Room. Fire Book. The gush of air filled the space around me, and I didn't have to open my eyes to know I was in the Darkness of my room. The Fire Room.

Teleporting worked fine. It had to be something in that room. I left Nick there. *Stupid. Idiot. What have I done? Did he still need Nick for the spell if I let Darkness in? He's afraid of my wrath. Or is he? Fuck. Screwing up seems to be my middle name.*

My pink aura grabbed hold during the confusion and pushed the dark aura back. A deep breath filled my lungs. I needed help from the book. Or the books. My eyes went to the Fire Book. *Hell no.* I got to my feet and pushed the door open.

The office was full of people. My family. Friends. They were all there. Joy filled the cracks in my aura, but it didn't stop the thoughts they were here to confine me in a different way from Alastair.

"If this is another intervention, you can stick it up your—"

"No, a message came. Nick is a prisoner of Alastair." Sorin squeezed my shoulder.

"Yes, I know. I'm going to take care of that." I was far less confident than I portrayed to them, but I would figure out a way to rescue him.

Sorin stood in front of me, blocking out the rest of the room. "Alastair is demanding we surrender the Fire Book to him."

I expected this move from him and shook my head. "No, we can't. He wants me to make his army, and that's not happening."

Sorin studied me. Worry wrote a book across his face.. "He said he would trade Nick for the book."

"It's a lie. I just left there. He told me Cal had a vision of me as the Queen of Darkness, and he wants that to come true." I located Cal and stared at him.

He averted his eyes. It was true, but I didn't blame Cal for keeping it to himself. I would have done the same.

"He thought you would say that. His note says his plans have changed. See for yourself." Sorin passed me the hand-written note on fine linen paper. Nick's stationery. The bastard used Nick's personal stationery.

I read through the letter. Sorin had recapped it well enough. "It's a ploy. He's playing games like he has been."

Sorin met my eyes. "You understand he is threatening to kill Nick?"

Cal walked toward me but stopped about halfway.

"Do you think he has plans to let anyone I care about live? Do you think any of you are safe?" I looked around the room. "Maybe Cal because he's Alastair's son, but I wouldn't hold my breath on that either."

Cal stepped back.

My emotions bounced back and forth like a yoyo thanks to the constant feuding between my pink aura and the black aura that wanted to consume it. My big mouth wanted to eat my foot. My brain was like scrambled eggs. I ran out of the room to escape, to breathe, to calm the storm inside me. I made it down the hall and came to a stop in front of the door to my suite. The hairs on the back of my neck stood up, pausing my outstretched hand. Someone followed me. A glimpse of her was all I saw. She disappeared around the corner. *Grandmother.*

"Grandmother!" I chased after her.

She beat me around every corner. Just out of reach each time I caught sight of her. The hallway dead-ended.

"Grandmother!" My voice bounced off the walls. My hand pushed against the wall at the end, but it didn't budge.

I took a few steps forward, and a breeze tickled my arm. My eyes closed and a smile crossed my face. Even in death, she led me where I needed to go. I reached over and pulled the loose stone from the wall. It came out with little effort.

A small wooden box rested inside the hole. The lid

clicked open, and a key sat on a soft pillow. I picked it up and placed the carved box back in the hole. The key glinted in the light as I turned it over in my hand.

The wall shimmered in front of me, and a door appeared. A door with a lock about the right size for the key. I slid it into the lock, and the tumblers clicked over. The door creaked open. Excitement coaxed me forward, but hope for answers drove me.

A small space waited on the other side. *Who knew the mansion had so many secret rooms?* More secrets like everything else in this coven.

The door closed in a slow soft motion. Light flickered on the walls. All of them. I spun around watching them come to life. It looked like videos. Four random women. Witches. They were in varying straight of dress from centuries past, but they shared a resemblance.

The witch to the left began to speak. "If you are here, then the time of war has arrived. No doubt you are being tested in ways that make you wonder if you will survive. I wish we could guarantee that, but we can't. Lives will be lost. There may have already been some lost that you loved. You must remain strong."

The next one started. "You were chosen and gifted by many of us. No one will match your strength, but it will come to you at a cost. Darkness will forever be a part of you. Its strength will rival the Light within you. You alone have the power to find the balance. First within you and then for the world."

It took to the third witch to realize these women all

looked familiar. My heart swelled at the sight of them. They all looked like me. *My ancestors.*

"You are the only one who can walk a special line between human, vampire, and witch. Your power to heal will be quicker, and you will notice your power less draining as time moves forward. This is a gift, and like all gifts should be treated with respect. Abusing it will shorten your life span. Be conscious that you need to live a long life to fulfill your destiny completely."

The blurry picture of the final woman cleared. *Grandmother.* Tears filled my eyes, and I walked to her picture on the wall where the hidden door was. My hand traced her face. Her much younger face.

"Granddaughter. I'm sorry I left you before we had this talk in person. I trust your Greats filled you in with the specifics. The only thing I will add is to always be yourself. Trust in the Light. Follow the Light. Believe in the Light. You are the Light, and I love you."

"I love you too," I whispered. The lights disappeared. The room was once again dark. "I will do my best to stay on the side of Light." I'd said it a dozen times to myself and others, but my determination renewed in the wake of their special messages. "I don't know how I will do it, but I will do it."

I patted my hands around the wall until the door opened. It closed behind me. I slipped the key into my pocket in case I needed to come back for a reminder. My spirit renewed, I was ready to figure out how to rescue Nick without giving into Darkness or Alastair's demands.

Down the hall, I stopped at my room. My necklace had been left on the dresser, and I needed the relic around my neck as a constant remembrance of the past and the future that was my legacy. My fingers instinctively traced the scroll-work until their search yielded the location of the vial.

Everyone was still in the library when I returned. All eyes were on me. They remained silent either from fear or respect, and I'm not sure I deserved the latter after the way I acted earlier.

"I'm not giving Alastair the book, and I'm not letting Nick die at his hands. Does anyone have a good idea for making that happen that doesn't require a shit load of magic? I don't want to teleport to the vampire castle without a plan again so help me out here."

Finally, they all started flipping through books.

I sought out Cal and stood next to him. He smiled like there were no wrongs between us, but I'd wronged him.

"Hey, I feel like I keep apologizing to you for stupid things I say. I'm sorry, Cal."

"I deserved it. I did keep some of my visions from you. I shouldn't have done that," he paused. "Especially to my friend."

"Friend not queen?" I raised an eyebrow at him.

"Both, but mainly my friend."

I hugged him.

"Let's save your boyfriend."

"Fiancé." I corrected. "Maybe ex-fiancé if he's not as forgiving as you."

"Fiancé. There's no chance he wouldn't forgive you. Maybe we're making it too hard. Just teleport in and out with him like you did Brandon."

"You think it would work twice? And last time something

happened. I couldn't teleport when we were in the same room, but I could from the hall. I don't know if I can trust it to work there."

"You have teleported in there a lot. Maybe a perimeter spell is cast there in certain places." He rubbed his chin like Alastair.

I cringed a little at the movement.

"Maybe there's another way," he said flipping the pages of the book in front of him. "We'll find an alternative."

》 ·》· ● · 《 · 《

Sorin and Cal hadn't left my side, despite the fact they must both be bone tired. Darkness refueled me every time I became fatigued. Sorin wouldn't use it, and Cal didn't have it. *How are they still on their feet?*

"I'm worried about you," Sorin whispered in my ear.

"I'm good now," I said, turning to face him. "What about you?"

Flames danced in his dark pupils. Small but still visible. He'd been dealing in Darkness for years.

"I'm fine," he said. "Your eyes are clear for now, but it is a battle you must always be aware of. The cost is everything you love."

Goddess, I understand. My journey and his are similar but not, and it was the differences that worried me. "I'm in a better place now. More in control. I had some help."

His brows furrowed. "Where did you go? You didn't make a deal, did you?"

I patted his arm. "No, nothing like that. I found a special message left for me. Specifically, for me."

A small tight smile formed on his mouth. "You found the Moon Chamber."

"Moon Chamber?"

"Where our ancestors speak. The door moves so it's never in the same place twice. It appears when our leader or their successor needs guidance that can't come from here."

I slipped my hand into the pocket where I placed the key and poked around. It was empty, but my pocket didn't have a hole. I was confused because I knew I put it in that pocket. No key.

"Was Mother there?" He asked, his tone soft.

"Yes." I smiled at the memory of the younger Grandmother who appeared. "A much younger version."

"What I wouldn't give to hear her voice again." He stared off into the distance.

The pain between us was mutual. "I understand. She was ready though. She told me, and I don't know why, but it gives me comfort that she was. Have you figured out how she gifted Brandon yet?"

Sorin pulled me into a hug. "No, and he is frustrated. I told him sometimes it takes time to understand the gifts."

Grandmother sent me to the meditation room to understand my gifts. I wonder if Dad suggested that to him.

"She told me to be true to myself and follow the Light." I paused, contemplating my next words. "I'm scared, Dad. I'm not sure I know who my true self is anymore, and I don't want to let her down. I don't want to let you down. Or the damn world. I don't want Nick to sacrifice himself. It's so

overwhelming, and I'm not sure what step is the right step."
It gave me relief to say the words out loud.

He wrapped his arm around my shoulders. "What do you
think Mother would tell you to do?"

I looked down at my fingers. "Meditate."

"Then go meditate."

"I don't have time right now. We have to get Nick back
and figure out how to stop Alastair." I tamped down the
burn building in me. Darkness wanted me confused. It
made it easier for it to find the cracks in my aura to seep
into.

"You have to be strong for everyone, but you can't be
strong for them if you don't give yourself time to process it."

"Evidently, I'll heal, and my power will rejuvenate faster
now. A gift." I snorted.

He nodded. "There's a reason for your gifts. They have a
purpose. Do you know who your ancestors were?"

"No, you know all that was kept secret." The elders were
wrong for keeping our family history from Brandon and me.

"Hidden in plain sight. Let's look at the Vladislav book."

There on the pages were the faces of those I'd seen in the
Moon Chamber. *Grandmother. The rest I'd never met. Great
Grandmother. Great Aunt. Great Great Grandmother.*

I pointed to each of them as we looked through the book.
The resemblance between them powerful and strong. All of
them were surprisingly tall like me. Same eyes. Same
features as mine. *Before Darkness.* They all had the same dark
hair. I had my mother's blonde hair. *Before Darkness. Red
streaked now.*

"They were all highly gifted. Your great-grandmother

was killed by a vampire in love with her. I never got to meet her." He blew out a soft breath. "Until the Moon Room."

"Grandmother told me."

"Really? She never spoke of it to me. The council knew, of course. The records were sealed, but I was allowed." He cleared his throat. "This is your Great Great Grandmother, and she was a queen. Powerful but not as much as you."

"Why is her death listed as a mystery here?"

"She was bold and brave like you, but she was captured. Vampires tried to turn her, so she killed herself without an heir. The Elders thought it would be best to leave that out I suppose."

I ran my fingers over her picture. I understood that sacrifice. *I'd make the same to not become one of them or help them.*

"I'm sure they planned to use her. She gave a sacrifice few could do and deserves to have her story told so that we can all learn from her lesson."

"She may not want it told. That's a pretty horrible end for a coven queen. Something you should think about, Brie."

It was, but I'd pay it more than once if I could to save those most important to me.

"You're right. When I heard their words, it was like a final shift took place in me. I thought I understood before, but it's like a renewed understanding came from the bond I have with them. It made me stronger. I'd choose death over becoming their puppet too."

He lamented. "The Darkness is always going to be there since you embraced it. It will continue to look for any tiny opening to worm itself in and take over."

The flames grew in his eyes like just speaking of Darkness fanned them.

"Have all the Queens battled it?"

"In some way, most do. The Darkness is drawn to power." He paused and ran his fingers over the page. "Our bloodline seems to be a magnet for it."

I closed my eyes for a moment and thought of Nick, and my chest ached. *It will never be right for us. I'll always have to choose my coven over him.* "We are cursed."

"No, we are gifted, and every gift has a price."

"It's a high price." *Why would he want to be with someone who let Darkness in so freely anyway?*

"A high price to prevent an inconceivable loss."

"Is anyone going to follow me after my crazy dark witchiness?" *I damn sure wouldn't. I don't even know how long I can keep the Darkness at bay.* My skin heated like an ignited burner as if it knew my thoughts. *Maybe it does.*

"Very few know so the damage control is minimal."

"That's a good thing at least." *Will it stay that way though? When my Darkness erupts through, and I know it will, what happens then?*

My stomach knotted with fear. My witchcraft skills were on point. My huntress skills were the best. My leadership skills sucked, and I had a lot to prove still. *Darkness or not, I had a lot to prove.*

"The rumors have spread," I pulled some of my red locks into view. "They hadn't escaped me, but I didn't care while Darkness ruled my world." I cared now that I was back in control. Trust ranked high on my priority list, and I wanted the coven to trust me. *How do I ask them to trust me when I can't even trust myself?*

"Rumors swirl around leaders their entire lives. It's part of the job." Dad hugged me to his side.

"Brie?"

I looked toward the doorway. "Hey, Brandon. How are you doing?"

He nodded in Sorin's direction. "Adjusting."

"It's hard. Especially not knowing what the gift is," I said. "Have you tried meditating? That's what Grandmother had me do."

"I think I know. I didn't want to tell anyone but you though." He glanced at Sorin and back at me. "As my sister not my queen."

I moved close enough to reach his hands. "Always your sister first, little brother."

He snorted. "You realize there are only five minutes between us."

"It's five minutes I'm claiming. So, tell your big sister." I chuckled.

His expression sobered. "I'm pretty sure I'm seeing solutions to problems. The answers come to me instantaneously. Do you think it's possible?"

"We're witches. Anything is possible. What's the answer on how to save, Nick?"

"Brie, you shouldn't ask such questions," Sorin said.

But it was too late to take it back. Brandon's body stiffened. Jaw tightened. Brow furrowed.

My already knotted stomach doubled in and pressed against my chest. The air squeezed out of my lungs. Brandon's worry and fear became my own. I reached for the edge of the table. *No.*

"Brie—"

"You don't see a way to save him?" I pushed in on my stomach.

"I don't see the future, Brie."

"But you don't see a solution either?"

"No."

My lips folded in. I smashed them together to hold back the tears. *Damn it. Damn. Damn. Damn.*

"It doesn't mean he can't be saved," Sorin said.

"No, it doesn't. I'll find a way." My voice quivered and betrayed the confidence I tried to exude. Darkness licked at my spine and offered a path. "Let's have everyone stop looking for that solution and start looking for a way to defeat Alastair."

"Why don't you just give him the book he wants?" Brandon said.

"That book is a bible to Darkness. I'm not sure any good can come of it. Even the spells to end curses require some kind of twisted payment."

He nodded.

"I need to make an appearance before the coven, but I need to be able to give them a plan. Is Ella here? I know she trains with the vampires stationed here about this time."

"I saw her walk in about ten minutes ago."

"Good. I need to talk to her. Can you work with Cal and Dad to figure out a plan?"

"Of course. Are you sure you don't want one of us to go with you?"

"No, I'd rather do this on my own," I said over my shoulder.

I rushed to the training area and located her standing in a corner. She observed but didn't do any of the training today. *Unusual.* She looked like her best friend had turned on her.

"You didn't stay at the castle today?" I leaned against the wall by her.

"Obviously not." She rolled her eyes. Her strong persona returned. I liked her better this way.

I inhaled a deep breath and tried to think of a way to tell her what Brandon had shared. *What I knew in my dark heart before he even answered me.* I bit down on my lip to hold back the tears and spilled it. "We can't seem to find an option to save Nick."

She pressed her shoulder into the wall and faced me.

I stared out at the yard full of soldiers. "You know I'm not going to accept that option any more than you would. I'll have to put Alastair down like the rabid animal he is before he ends Nick."

"Whether you are asking or not," she said. "Of course, I'm with you, Brie. You saved Nick once. You can do it again."

I faced her. "If Alastair turns me, promise you will kill me before he can use me to create that wretched army."

Her eyes glinted, and she turned toward the army in front of us.

I gave her the freedom she needed to take out the competition. *Stupid.*

"Nick would never forgive me if I let you die much less killed you myself. Let's take that treacherous bastard Alastair down." She pushed off the wall. "I'm assuming this is a you and me mission. When do we go?"

"At least we agree on something. Alastair is a fucking bastard. Meet me in front of my suite in about 30 minutes."

☽ ☾ ● ☾ ☾

A CASUAL OBSERVER might think we were two women seated on the couch having girl talk... until they heard the conversation. We conspired to take out a high-ranking coven member. A traitor. Not sure how much that would matter to the rest of the covens around the world, but mine had suffered enough loss at his hands. It would not suffer anymore.

Our plan sound from all angles we could come up with. My heart hoped we could get Nick to safety. Since we weren't sure if I'd be able to teleport once inside, I would be bait instead. A distraction to keep Alastair occupied while Ella got him back to the mansion.

"Nick will be furious with you."

He would, and he might never forgive. *I'm not sure I deserve to be forgiven. He'd be better off without me and my Darkness.*

"That's why you will need to go straight to Brandon. He'll calm him down. It's a gift of his, and it kind of does its own thing."

"How will I get back in..." Her voice trailed off.

"To kill me if it comes to that?" I asked. I wanted to

believe it wouldn't, but my gut told me this was it. I accepted it the moment I spoke it into existence.

She nodded.

"Brandon can cast a transport spell. It works a little differently than teleporting. The side effects aren't as bad, but you have to be specific with it. You'll have to give him a very detailed location. Someone has to have been to the location before for it to work properly."

"And he will believe we are going to save you?"

"Yes, I'm his Achilles heel, because of the damn Protector bond. He will not even think twice about it."

Ella studied me., her forehead wrinkled. "Are you sure about this, Brie? Nick's already dead. He would take his end for you."

I shook my head. *No way in Hell's Fire would I let him.* "I can't believe you'd even ask me that."

She softened her voice. "I've known Nick a lot longer. I know how he thinks."

"Trust me. So do I. Let's hope it doesn't come to that." *But it will.* I'd wanted to ask her a question for a while, and I blurted it out. "Have you ever thought there is something different about Nick? He's different from other vampires."

Ella tilted her head like she debated on whether to answer. "I have noticed this too. He smells different. Not offensive, but not like a vampire."

I stood up and walked over to the table. I picked up my cup of tea off the map and took a sip. "There must be something to that. He's tattooed by a prophecy like me."

"And you're willing to sacrifice yourself for him? For a vampire?"

I closed my eyes and thought about our first kiss. The electricity passed between us, and I knew he was different. *We were different. Forever changed from one kiss.* I placed the cup on the table and met her gaze. "For Nick. For the love of my life. My only love. Yes, I would."

"I underestimated you on many levels."

I laughed. "Most people do. Hell, I even underestimate myself most of the time."

"When do we leave?"

"There's a full moon tomorrow. My power is stronger, so we'll go then." *And the pull of Darkness will be stronger.* I didn't want to use it, but I would to stop Alastair.

"Will Alastair's be stronger too?" She asked. I wondered if Darkness gave him the extra power boost it did me. If it did, we'd be a closer match in a fight.

"Unfortunately, all witches will be which means he will, but I'm hoping my dark shadow gives me an advantage."

"I'll need to power up tonight."

My face scrunched up even though I tried to fight it. "Sorry."

"Don't be. We all have our problems." She patted my knee like an old friend. In another life, maybe we would have been friends. "Can I ask you a question without offending you?"

"Since there is a very good chance you will have to kill me tonight, I'd say ask now if you want to know something."

She leaned back and draped her arm across the back of the couch. "How can you be with a vampire with an obvious disdain for them? How many have you ended?"

"More than I can count, Ella, and I'd do it again to save

lives. Just like I'm going to kill a powerful warlock to save humans, vampires, and witches." I didn't feel guilt, which I suspect was what she was after.

"But it seems odd you'd choose a vampire as your mate."

"You don't choose who you love. He saved me when I needed it. He saved me more than once. Out of love, we can do magnificent things, and my love will save him now as will yours."

She looked solemn. I wasn't looking for her approval or anyone else's on this decision, but I needed her help.

The conflict within me regarding my duty was real. I'd done some risky rescues in the past, but this was the first time I didn't have a backup plan. Sacrifice lived at the top of my list. The difference was there had been a probability I might die. I'd been ready to die. This time there didn't seem to be an alternative.

"Tell everyone I'm going to meditate. Then, I'll hear the plan they have come up with to take out Alastair. We'll play along, but we'll teleport after they are finished."

"Sure. It's a plan."

The door closed behind Ella, and I crossed the room to lock it. The rug already positioned in the spot I liked, I took a seat cross-legged on it. My lids closed, and my focus shifted to my goal. *Save Nick. Kill Alastair.*

I joined Brandon and Sorin in the library. Brandon's eyes, ringed in dark circles, met mine. He needed his strength. *I can send healing energy to him.*

Sorin squared up in front of me. "I know what you have planned, Brie. Cal saw it." His tone was enraged. The flames in his eyes danced.

My own fiery eyes burned, but I kept my voice calm. "Then you know you can't stop me."

His nostrils flared. "What about your renewed commitment to fulfilling your duty?"

"My duty is to stop a war and save as many lives as I can. This will accomplish it." *My burden. My decision.*

"Damn it, Brie." The flames in his eyes flared until they blotted out his pupils.

I recognized what it meant. It happened to me when Darkness found a hole it could widen. I needed to make them believe I would go for their option to keep them both calm. "What's your plan then?"

"We'll storm the castle," Brandon said.

"The Vampire Castle?" I stared at the both in disbelief. They had to know better. "He'll see you coming long before you get there."

"He'll know if you teleport or transport in too," Brandon said, his voice tired.

"Would you prefer him to come to us again?" I asked.

"No, I want him dead now," my brother said. He and I agreed on that point.

Sorin pinched the bridge of his nose and closed his eyes. "Then we will need to use the Fire Book. It's the only option for quick results that don't mean a suicide mission on your part."

"There are always sacrifices with the spells from that book. I'm not sure it's any better than my plan but let me hear it."

Brandon and Dad exchanged looks.

"Out with it." I motioned for them to continue.

"We need Hell's Fire," Sorin said.

"Which you and I can conjure." I nodded.

"A lot of it. It will take both you and Dad to do it," Brandon said.

Dad made a circular motion. "We would have to surround the entire castle with it."

His idea intrigued me, but the power to do a ritual like that had a large cost. "You realize I may not be able to come back which I can live with. What about you? You are deeper in it than I am. Is there any chance you will come back?"

Brandon's mouth formed a half-hearted smile. "That's

where I come in. I'll be the anchor holding your humanity in a fixed state."

"Both of us? Two powerful witches?"

"Yep. I'll anchor you as long as it takes," he said.

Dad formed two energy balls, one orange, and one white. "It's a combination of spells from the Fire Book and Light Book." He smashed them together into one and they blended. Then squashed them.

"And you see this as a solution, Brandon?" *Could it really work?* Ella and I might not have to sneak away after all.

"Yes, it can work if we maintain a balance."

"And if the anchor bond fails?" I asked.

"We will be the sacrifice for the Fire spell." He paused. "All of us."

My stomach sunk in on itself. Brandon had taken the successor bond when we first found out about the prophecy. There would be no backing down for him. He and I shared that same stubbornness. I let out a sigh, knowing I wouldn't win an argument. "And what will circling the vampire castle in Hell's Fire gain us?"

Sorin shifted his weight. "It's the energy required."

"For?"

"Extracting the power from any witch inside the circle. Alastair would be powerless," Sorin said.

The plan had merit. I didn't like the risk, but it would yield the right results.

"I was looking forward to avenging the lives lost because of him, but if we can take his power without killing him, that would be a better punishment to make him live like a human." Darkness lapped at the disdain in my words.

Dad flinched, and I wondered if Darkness found a meal in his thoughts. "Letting him live powerless is a much better punishment."

"Where will his power go?"

"The casting circle," Brandon said.

"So, one of us?" Darkness drooled for that kind of power. It urged me to commit to it.

Dad shook his head. "No, your mother."

"She's not powerful enough to handle it," I said. Power like that would drown her. I don't think she could hold it.

"She is, and she will," he said.

"Can't one of us do it?" Father and I were used to that kind of power and Darkness wanted me to have it.

"No, we have to summon the fire, and Brandon has to anchor us. She's the only one."

I stared up at the ceiling as if I would find better answers there. "I wish Grandmother was here."

Dad pulled my chin down. "She would tell you this is your best chance."

"Yes, I'm sure she would, but I'd be more confident if she were the one opening the circle."

They exchanged looks.

I crossed my arms over my chest and wished it was a warm hug from Grandmother.

"We have to trust each other, or the spell will not work. I thought things were better between you and your mother."

I did trust her more, but I didn't trust her ability to contain that level of magical energy. "They are. Just not that good."

"You need to go spend a little time with her and sort it

out then and make it fast. The ceremony must be done during the --"

"Full moon. When our power is at its highest. Don't they all?" I spun around on my heels. Might as well get it over with.

"Where are you going?" Brandon asked.

I shrugged. "To find Mother. Where else?" I'd been somewhat estranged from my mother most of my life after her failed binding spell that I thought was to take my power. She hadn't tried to steal mine and my twin's power though. In her mind, she was trying to protect us, but she failed at that too.

I stopped at the chapel on my way to find her. It was a place of good and bad memories. Bad seeing Sorin lying in state. Good when Sorin came back. Good crossing the threshold with Nick and the amazement that radiated off of him. I placed my palms flat against the door and pushed. This would be a bad memory in the making. *Grandmother in state.* Darkness readied to blot out my pain, but I held steady.

My chest expanded taking in a deep breath. I walked down the aisle. Her body came into view. Such a contrast from Sorin. He'd still had color in his flesh. Grandmother's dulled in comparison. A soft grey shimmered on her skin but not the natural color Sorin had been. He'd been protected by me. Grandmother didn't want that. My family didn't let me give it to her. *Not that I knew how I did it with Dad.*

Gold tapestry with a crest covered the altar beneath her. Her body was suspended above it as was the custom. She looked like a queen with the traditional purple and gold brocade of the royal families. Our family crest adorned her garments but smaller than the one on the tapestry.

I reached my hand out to hers. My heart hoped for warmth like when I'd touched Dad. *Cold.* The coldness of her hand was like a gut punch, and a sob shook me to my soul. She was really gone. No more hugs. No seeing her smile again. No more wise words. No more laughs or trips together. She moved on to a place I would probably never see.

"I miss you already. Thank you for all you did for me. All the cooking. All the guidance. And most of all, all the love you gave me. Rest well." I leaned over and kissed her cheek. "I will do my best to make you proud," I whispered. "I might not succeed, but I will try to find my way back to the Light in your honor."

Tears forced their way through my closed eyes and flowed like a broken dam. I didn't fight it this time. The sorrow saturated me like the wetness on my cheeks. My heart was tormented by the loss. It was an empty ache that would remain for some time if not forever.

The tears slowed, and I wiped the last of them away.

I paused at the door for one last look. One last little bit of hope doused by the reality of a pale grey sheen of her skin. I shut the doors to the chapel without a sound, but they seemed even heavier on the way out.

Mother was in the library. She looked up when the door banged shut. I didn't see how I could ever have a relationship with her that even came close to what I had with Grandmother, but my family urged me to mend our brokenness in some way, so I would try.

"I never spent much time in this room." She patted the seat next to her.

I plopped down on the couch beside her.

She ran her hand over my cheek. "You've been to see your grandmother. She was so proud of you."

I swallowed against the lump in my throat and focused on the ancestry book in her lap. "You never talk about your family."

"There's not much to say." She closed the book and set it on the table.

"We've never met them. Don't you want us to know where you come from?"

She turned her head away, resting her mouth against the top of her fingers. Her hand patted my knee with a few quick pats. Then she turned back to me. Her eyes had a hint of moisture.

"No, I don't want you to know."

"Mother, what could make you feel that way?" Part of me wanted to console her, but we weren't in that place. Instead, I squeezed her hand.

"My family wasn't exactly respectable. Pure bloodline, but they were schemers. Always looking for the next payout," she said, her tone embarrassed.

That little bit of information was more than she had my entire life. "Are they in the area?"

"No, they were living in central Europe the last time I heard from them. I wouldn't be surprised if they were arrested by a local coven."

If my eyes widened any further, my eyeballs would pop out of the sockets. There had never been a hint of scandal about her. The coven had been good at keeping secrets. Why would they keep this one though?

"Why were there never any whispers about you? Seems like there would have been rumors." *Or were there and I just didn't notice because I preferred my solitude?*

"I left home when I was fifteen and came to live at the mansion. Your grandmother made sure I had a safe place, and she was the only one who knew the truth."

"Not even Dad? She took it to her death?"

"She did and not even your father. She always said it was my story to tell." Mother had a small smile and nodded her head. "She even gave her approval when your father and I fell in love. She could have said no, but she didn't."

Grandmother had a soft spot for Mother. I'd known that, but I'd assumed it was because of Dad. Grandmother had saved her.

"Mom, I don't know what to say." I grabbed her hand. She was broken inside like me. A nagging bit of guilt knotted in my throat. "Did they ever come to look for you?"

"No, they considered me a traitor to the family when I ran away," she said, her demeanor loaded with self-deprecation.

"That's awful."

"Kind of how you felt about me though." She looked at me like she was asking an unspoken question.

Shit. For someone who didn't believe in regrets, I had a lot of them coming my way.

"I can't tell you how much respect I have for you now. Thank you for sharing such a painful part of your life with me." It was a start for us.

"I wish I had earned it without you knowing that, but I feel relieved having shared it with you. You deserved to know."

My trust in her grew. She had much more perseverance and strength than I had believed. I looked forward to a time when we could be more in each other's lives.

"Will you tell Dad and Brandon?"

"I will after we get through this war." She smiled. "I don't want to be a distraction as we go into battle, and I think it would be for your dad."

"You are much stronger than I ever gave you credit for, and I'm sorry I didn't see that before." *She'd tried to shield us from something she had no reason to be ashamed of. This family needs to learn that we do better if we just give each other the truth instead of trying to protect each other with secrets.*

"You don't know how much that means to me, Brie." She wrapped her arms around me and hugged me tightly to her. "I'm sorry I ever made you feel like you couldn't depend on me. I won't let you down casting the circle."

I hugged her back, and it was different this time. My wall was gone, and I accepted the love she offered. "I know you won't. I trust you."

For the first time, I did trust her. My internal lie detector agreed. My gifts were rallying in the wake of my conscience decision to choose Light. Darkness was still there, and it wasn't easy to hold back. Light supported me and Darkness tore me down.

"I'm going to sit with your grandmother for a while." She patted my leg as she stood up.

The moment between us was over, and I hated to see it

end. I wasn't sure we'd get another chance with the war on us. I looked up at her and saw tears in her eyes. "It still doesn't seem real."

"It's going to take a while for it to sink," she agreed and wiped her tears away.

She left me alone in the room. I used to enjoy being alone, but it unsettled me now. I wanted my loved ones near me. The one I wanted to be close to the most was a prisoner, and all I could do was wait. Wait until the full moon. A Fire spell and a Light spell. My whole family at risk. Nothing about this was good, and a pit formed in my stomach.

I meandered my way to my office. My butt sank into the leather chair, and my head rested against the back. The visions from my meditation session popped like the pictures in an album. Alastair would have a choice to make during the full moon. For his soul, I hoped he'd choose correctly.

My eyes traced a path around the room and settled on the hidden door. I stood and paced in front of it. *What if they missed something in the spell?* Everything about the ritual had to be perfect, or we would all die. The need to double-check became obsessive in me. Resolve took hold, and I opened the passage. An unwanted welcome waited for me. Darkness warmed me with each step. I closed my eyes and called Light into my mind and heart. Without uttering the words out loud, Light came at my request and reinforced me against the dark aura's search for a crevice to invade.

The small narrow hallway took me to the Fire Book. *Time to read the spell for myself.*

I positioned my hand over the book and thought of the spell to absorb magic. The pages flipped to find my desired spell. This incantation demanded a lot from the witch casting the circle. *My mother.* A fragile person wouldn't be able to maintain a circle with this kind of power or the circumference it would encircle. Then again, my mother wasn't fragile like I had once thought. She'd been strong enough to leave a life with a family focused on crime. She was fierce.

The spell was one of the few I had seen that required a full moon, and I guessed it was because it bridged Light and dark. Many incantations are enhanced by the power generated from one, but only a handful required it. A fact alone that caused a twinge of nausea in my stomach. The circle could consume the one who cast it if they lost control of it. The biggest risk was at the time it was closed when the power absorbed transferred to the new host. A missed step and they'd both die, Mom and Brandon. Sorin and I would be protected by Hell's Fire and Darkness. The risk couldn't get much greater for my mother and brother, and I had to decide if I'd let them go through with this or do things my way.

ELEVEN

A state funeral while on the precipice of a war. Only witches would dare do something so bold in order to uphold tradition. I stood in front of the mirror clad in black from head to toe. Black was my color of choice, but the weight of it today sat heavily on me. *Grandmother's service.* We could have left her in state until after the full moon, but we didn't know if any of us were coming back and the Elders insisted on a state funeral.

A knock at the door signaled it was time.

"My queen," Cal addressed me.

"My friend." I stepped into the hall to join him. He too was dressed in all black. Dark circles rimmed his eyes, and I couldn't hide mine with makeup. The long hours in preparation for the battle ahead took a toll on all of us.

Cal took my arm in his, and we walked together toward the chapel. "You'll enter last. The guards are already stationed to make sure there are no disruptions."

My private guards staggered a respectful distance from

us. "She was so loved. I can't imagine anyone causing a disturbance." Except maybe Alastair, but even in his twisted ways, I didn't think he would disrespect Grandmother in such a way.

"It would be about getting closer to their famous queen not to your grandmother."

I nodded. Absurd as it sounded to my ears, I'd learned I had admirers who wanted to be like me or tell me what they know about me. It was weird given how much I valued my privacy.

Today was about Grandmother and celebrating her life, and I didn't want anything to interrupt the reverence of her memorial. I opted to observe as many of the traditions as possible in her remembrance. *I'd do my best to honor her with my mind, my heart, and my faith. To honor her with the dignity she deserved.*

Cal nodded. "It's full. I tell you only so you are prepared."

"Exactly the preparation I need." I sighed. The days of hiding and blending into the background were long gone. I'd wished to be normal so many times, but my normal was leading the coven through good and bad. For this moment in time, that meant I revered my grandmother as the leader she was and for the contributions she made to this coven.

"We'll come in the side entrance, so you don't have to make a procession down the main aisle. The guards will announce you."

"No." I held up a hand. "No announcement. Just let me enter my grandmother's funeral without any fuss. Any grandeur should belong to her today."

"As you wish."

We reached the door. I inhaled, hoping for a cleansing breath but none was to be found. It was pain that entered, and I knew if I wanted to get through this service, I had to hold it in.

"Please wait, Your Majesty, while I advise them of your request." He disappeared.

Left alone and I didn't want to be. I fidgeted with the handkerchief my mother had given me. The pattern in the fine lace edge reminded me of the scrollwork in the necklace Grandmother had given me. My hand went to my neck and caressed the metal. My fingers found the hidden vial of Vampire Death. She was in every part of me that was important.

Cal reappeared. "It's time, Brie." He cleared his throat. "I mean, Your Majesty."

"Brie is always better to me, Cal," I said, stepping inside the door he held open. I let out a breath and straightened my shoulders, tucking all my grief away until later.

My seat was obvious at the front on the end in the place of honor with Brandon in the spot held for the protector. My parents were seated to the distant right on the pew. *Tradition can suck it.* I walked to the front.

"Mom. Dad. You need to take your seats."

They stared at me.

"Now, preferably, before the entire room starts talking."

Brandon stood to wait for us. My parents gathered themselves and moved to the end of the row.

Brandon slipped in next to them, and I took the seat next to him. State funeral or not a family should be together to support each other on a day like this, and I wanted them close.

"Dad is going to lecture you for that," Brandon whispered in my ear.

I patted his knee. "Let him try." I pursed my lips together.

Two elders spoke and then Dad. I heard bits and pieces of what they said, but I spent most of the time in a haze of denial. I knew it was true, but it didn't make sense for her not to be here.

Sorin introduced me as not only the queen but her granddaughter.

I stood behind the podium and faced the audience. A fog still over my thoughts, the first few sentences of my dedicated speech stuttered out as rehearsed. I read her name, and the internal cloudiness dissipated. My eyes stared at the words on the cards. Unable to continue, I placed them face down on the podium. My hand went to my throat, and I swallowed against the knot there. My heart swelled with pride as I thought of who my grandmother was and how she continued to learn, even if she was the wisest person in the room. And she often was.

"My grandmother filled up a room with her shining spirit. Despite losing her parents at a young age, an act that would have closed off most people, she had a large capacity for love. That love went beyond her blood family to her extended family. Many sought her guidance and none more than me. That is the legacy she leaves us. Her love and her gifted guidance. We can all honor her by showing love and compassion to all. Witches, humans, and vampires."

Murmurs and whispers created a dull roar in the room.

As soon as I put the scripted cards aside and spoke from my heart, I expected this reaction. Sometimes tradition and expectations, take a backseat, and this was one of those times. To present Grandmother as a list of accomplishments, because who she was, amounted to so much more than that.

I stood behind the podium and made eye contact with as many as I could.

A hand grasped mine. My eyes fell on it and up to the owner. *Brandon.*

He led me back to our seats. I was relieved to have the speech behind me, but I dreaded the finality of this goodbye.

Once we were settled, the attendees filed past us nodding. Some had red eyes. Others wept openly as they approached Grandmother's body. The room emptied except for our family.

Sorin stood guiding us to our points around the altar she floated above.

Grandmother looked peaceful, and I think she would have been proud. "Dad, I—"

"Not now, Brie."

I nodded.

"East, South, West, and North. Guide my mother in the afterlife so that we might meet again." He closed the circle. Simple. Grandmother would have approved. He stood in place for a long time before signaling we were ready for the pyre. The ultimate act of honor for a witch.

Dad guided Grandmother's body down the hall and out the door to the sacred area. No one was allowed in it except for funerals. He positioned her over the meticulously constructed pile of wood. I'd attended two before Grandmother and found them unsettling, but they were meant to be a gift. The thought of burning my grandmother caused my stomach to roll, but I would not interfere. She deserved the honor of a high-ranking royal funeral.

"Fire." His single word was a whisper. "We stand until it's done. Until they gather the ashes."

The delicate tender burned in a deliberate and quick fashion. It didn't take long.

I wanted to look away. The smell. The site. It was more than I needed to say goodbye. Respect held me in place. Tears spilled down my cheeks as if I hadn't cried before.

"We need to prepare for the full moon," Sorin said, turning away once the ashes were gathered. "They will notify us when she is in the mausoleum."

"We can prepare later."

"We'll prepare now. In the library." He stormed passed us.

)) ● ((

I'D TAKEN the long way to the library to gather my thoughts. I'd made up my mind. My family couldn't take the kind of risk that came with this spell. The ritual required such precision that any minute infraction could cause us to fail. "We continue to look for other options. This is a last resort."

"We are out of time, Brie," Sorin said. "Brandon will anchor us. Your mother will cast the circle. Final."

"I'm your queen. What I say is final." It was a cheap shot, and the Darkness in me craved more. It taunted me to dish out jabs, but I stormed out the door of the library and marched straight to my beloved courtyard. The place where peace came to me more often. *Damn it.* Sorin's plan was sound. It was right. It didn't make me like it. To commit to something that could endanger my family, all that I have left, caused pain in my heart. *I will not let them risk everything. That is my job. My duty.*

We still had two days to figure it out. Two days to find a solution that didn't put them directly in the fire. *Literally Hell's Fire.* In the meantime, Sorin said we should be working on the bond that will tether us to Brandon. I had a bond with him. Sorin needed to work on the damn bond. He's the one that left us.

There it was. It bubbled up again. I thought it was settled, but I still carried hurt from his departure during our childhood. I smeared the tears across my face with the side of my hand. Even with him in our lives at present, I still held abandonment deep in me. Blamed him for the wrong turns I made. Those decisions were mine. *Own it, Brie.*

"Can we talk?" Sorin's voice came from behind me. His tone was gentle and soft.

I took in a deep breath and wiped my face of the fresh tears. "Of course." I gestured to the bench under a favorite tree of mine.

"I know you still have resentment for me. We have made progress, but you still hurt," he said, his tone much softer than earlier.

I stared out at the green grass not surprised he could read me. We were so similar. "I don't want to. I don't know how to stop."

"It's justified, Brie."

"No, not all of it. I blamed you for bad decisions I made, and that's not your fault."

"In some ways it is. If I'd done my duty, you wouldn't be here."

"This is how it was meant to be. I've accepted that fact."

He wrapped an arm around my shoulders. "Do you know what my first gift was?"

"No." I twisted to look at him and saw a sad smile on his face.

"Healing, but I couldn't heal myself then. It was so draining when I used it for others." He paused. "I almost gave up on magic."

"All of it?" It surprised me he'd want to give up a gift like healing.

"Yes. Little did I know then that I would have to give it up one day to save my family."

"Is that what you are telling me to do now?" *I could do it. I really could. Would it save them though?*

"Not at all. I'm not telling you to do anything. I want you to understand my sacrifices. They were my own. I made those choices with the information I had, and it was done with the best intentions for my family. I didn't think about the coven. I thought about my family."

His decisions were similar to mine, but with a different outcome. *Or was it? We were here.* "The full moon will be a Blood Moon."

"I think we are all aware of that and that it means your powers will peak."

"I have to choose between love and Light. That could be

Nick or Brandon or Mom or you." The truth of the impending decisions ahead was like repeated gut punches, and I couldn't avoid or defend them.

"Undoubtedly, it will be a choice for you," he said. "And for me."

"I want to forgive you, Dad. I do. Why can't I let it go once and for all?" I felt desperate as I admitted it to him.

"Stop beating yourself up. You will when you are ready. I still haven't forgiven myself."

I understood then. He hadn't forgiven himself for his choices, and I still needed to forgive myself for my own bad choices. Until then, I wouldn't be able to forgive him. "You should. It's been long enough. You've paid your price you didn't have to pay."

"Maybe one day. Maybe after we get Alastair in check," he said, his hopeful tone seeming genuine.

I leaned over and rested my head on his shoulder. "I do love you, Dad. I just get angry."

He wrapped his arm around me, and his head settled on mine. "I know you do, and I love you. As for the anger, we have a long line of bad tempers and grudge holders."

"That figures." I giggled. "Grandmother never seemed to have a temper. How'd she do it?"

"She did. She had the ultimate control over it by always seeing the good in someone or the situation." He gazed up at the sky as he remembered like she would be able to hear him.

"I'm too much of a skeptic."

He chuckled. "You can blame me for that. I caused those trust issues."

"Nah. It's my personality." I swallowed hard. "And other things."

"Brie, bad things happen to good people every day. Don't let that eat at your soul. Your soul is good like your grandmother's. Find your peace. Then, it will all come into focus."

Grandmother was on a different level far above me. I could try an entire lifetime and never achieve the goodness she possessed.

"How does one find their peace?" *I'm not sure I'd even recognize it if I did find it.*

"Soul searching, my dear. It takes the best of us time. Your grandmother told me I was looking in the wrong places. It took me twenty years to figure out what she meant."

"I hope I'm not as stubborn as you."

He chortled. "I hope not too."

My mind drifted to what awaited ahead of us. This war would strain us all in ways none of us had experienced. "Do you think we'll win?"

"I don't know. I'm hopeful."

"Me too."

I almost told him about the first time I was kidnapped when I was young and a bigger risk-taker. I smiled at that. *When had I become so risk-averse?* But I wasn't afraid of risk for myself... only my family. Part of me wanted to tell him so he would understand me better, and so he would understand how Nick saved me and what he means to me. I closed my eyes and buried my head in my father's shoulder.

"We all have secrets we keep in our soul, Brie. I don't know what yours is, nor do I need to, but you need to find a way to reconcile it. If it is keeping you from your peace, you need to free yourself of it."

One word popped into my head. "Revenge isn't an option." *Gaius was ended. Stefan was ended. There would be no revenge for me.*

"It's not about revenge. The soul heals when you work through your past injuries."

"I don't know how to work through this one."

"Talking about it usually helps. If not with me, then maybe Nick or Brandon. Or even your mother." Mother had bared her secrets to me, but I wasn't quite ready to do the same.

"Nick knows, but who knows if we'll ever get the chance to talk again or if he'd even want to talk to me at all." I paused. "He knows every ugly part of me, at least before I let Darkness claim me." He'd love me anyway. He'd told me he would. My chest ached for him.

"I doubt he sees any part of you as ugly. It's obvious he loves you, and that's why it weighs on you. You love him and don't want him to see any cracks in the veneer. Do you doubt his love?"

"No, not at all."

"Then you should have figured out that those that love you, your family, your friends, your future husband, we all love you because of your flaws. Your flaws are who you are."

"Flaws are a sign of weakness and brokenness." *Reminders of my mistakes.*

"No, Brie, they're not. They are a sign of strength and, more than that, they are a sign of humanity." He kissed the top of my head and stood up. "You need to be kinder to yourself."

He left me alone on the bench.

Be kinder to myself. What does that even mean?

Humanity piqued my interest. Witches were born witches not human. What did we have in common with them? We lived longer. We had powers. They had free will like us. They loved as we did. Maybe we were more like them than we were taught.

I wound my way back to my room and curled up on the couch. More than anything I wanted to see Nick.

)) ● ((

THE LIGHT in the room rippled. Nick sat on the couch in our room. My eyes were bleary, I couldn't focus on him. A book propped up on his knees. He closed it and placed it on the coffee table. "Do you want to come to sit with me?" He patted the seat next to him.

I nodded and dropped onto the couch beside him.

He slipped his arm around me.

I laid my head on his chest. The comfort warmed me, and I relaxed into it.

"Do you want to talk about it?"

I closed my eyes and shook my head. My face was buried in the material of his shirt. My hand a fist full of it. Tears flowed down my cheeks.

"She's gone. She's really gone." I stuttered the words through sobs. Emptiness spread through my chest.

Nick pulled me into his lap and tightened his arms around me. "Let it all out."

My pillar was gone. The woman who mothered me when I couldn't trust my mother would never hug me again. She'd never listen to me without judging again. My emotions emptied out of me through wails until there was nothing left to spill. As hard as it was to let go, the relief was harder to accept. It felt like a betrayal.

"Sorry. I'm sure I look frightful right now."

He put his hands on either side of my face and looked into my eyes. "Brie, you are beautiful, because it starts from the inside. Your brain. Your soul. Your heart. Never apologize for being the authentic you."

"Says the man who always looks perfect." I fiddled with the buttons on his shirt.

"You know that's not true. You see me as more than that. Don't you?"

"Of course, Nick. You are my rescuer."

"But do you see me, Brie?" He demanded.

"I see someone who would sacrifice himself for me. Someone who knows what he wants. You didn't let being a vampire define you. You found you."

"Only after I found you did I find myself," he said, his voice soft with love.

"You are a hero to your people and mine. You are my hero. That is who you are." I put my hand over his heart. A heart that didn't beat. Hadn't beaten in 250 years. Yet it somehow still did in a way.

"I'm undeserving of that, and you know it. I did terrible things before you came into my life."

"I've done terrible things too. Our flaws are not weaknesses. They make us human."

Nick's eyes sought mine.

It might not have been exactly like Sorin put it, but it was close enough.

Nick's hand pulled my face to his. He crushed my lips with his. His lips separated mine.

I sighed when he pulled away.

"You've never referred to yourself as human before."

"If I'd known it was going to get that kind of reaction, I would have done it a long time ago." I smirked.

"What changed your mind? You've always said witches aren't humans."

"Sorin reminded me how much we are like them today."

"There is so much about you that is human. I hope you do see that, Brie."

"I see it in you." I smiled at him.

His lips curled up in agreement.

I sat up on the couch in the dark and patted around on the sofa for Nick. He was nowhere. Coldness wrapped around me, and emptiness filled the space. I was alone, and the ache of his absence returned.

"Nick?" Then it hit me like the entire library in my office had fallen on me. It crushed me. Nick wasn't here. We'd never have that moment. *Next time we see each other, it will end with one of us dead. This wasn't real. It was just a dream.*

CHAPTER
TWELVE

)·)·●·(·(

The nearly full moon glowed brightly in the sky. My head rested against the frame of the window while I studied it. There was only one connection in my life stronger. *Nick.* I missed him with every fiber of my magic, every piece of my pink aura, and every part of my heart right into my tainted soul.

"It draws you to it." Brandon squeezed my shoulder.

"They all do, but the Blood Moons sings to my soul." My eyes remained on the moon. "Both my pink and dark aura reach for it. There's power in it." My tattoo marking glowed as if it agreed. There was a tug of war around me between the auras, and it could be painful at times. Darkness was ready to drink in the pain.

Brandon's hand brushed over my mark. "I'm not going to pretend to understand it, Sis, but are we going to talk about Nick's mark?"

"We don't know what it means. Stefan knew something, but he's gone. Alastair probably knows, but he's a bastard.

There's nothing in the books or the prophecy on it." My frustration became hard to keep in check the more of me Darkness claimed. The power of dark magic was all-consuming, and I was just trying to hold on to what was left of me to fulfill my destiny. I knew the mark likely meant something linked our destinies, but I was at a loss as to what the key was.

"What does your gut say?"

"I haven't had time to focus on it." Not entirely true, but enough that it wasn't a lie.

Brandon's voice softened. "Or you're avoiding it because you're afraid of the answer."

"You know me too well, brother. And there's some truth to that. I am afraid." The thing I feared most had already happened. I'd lost Nick forever. Only one of us would survive, and I'd lost him either way. Darkness heralded that thought and wanted more, but I denied it.

"Are you afraid he'll be stronger than you?"

"No, he's already that." I smiled. "I'm afraid it is going to be the reason we are drawn together, and all the happiness I feel is going to come crashing down around me." The weight of the truth I uttered settled in the bottom of my stomach. The heaviness was like ten tons sitting there. *And the fate was sealed.*

"Have you talked to Nick about this?"

I glanced at him to see if he was serious. His face looked firm as if that wasn't a ridiculous question. "Not sure when we've had the chance between my surrender to Darkness and his power-drunk state before Alastair imprisoned him."

"True, but we will free you both from the trap of this

prophecy. And when you are free, the problem will still be there. If you don't even know what the mark means, you can't move forward."

I nodded and met his gaze filled with fear and hope. It nearly broke me to see those raw emotions on my brother's face, but I couldn't afford to break. If let the emotions in, then I'd lose control, and we all needed me in complete control Our lives depended on it. "It's either going to bind us together or tear us apart. I know it in my innermost soul. Neither one of them is something I want. If he's with me, love should be the reason. Not a mark. I'm not sure I'll survive if it tears us apart." I paused and focused back on the big moon in the sky. My body was tired from all the struggles. "I don't have enough strength to tackle it today.".

"You're tired. Mentally and physically. It makes you vulnerable, and you need to be strong."

I shoved my shoulder into his. "When did you get so wise?"

He blinked, and the glint in his eye reminded me of Grandmother.

He pulled me into a hug. "Your eyes are glazed over. Maybe you need to get some rest. I'll do some research and wake you if I find anything."

"I'm good. I just saw a hint of Grandmother in you," I smiled. "You and she shared a lot of traits so it fits."

His smile started small and grew across his face. "I want to do her memory justice."

"You will. If anyone is capable of doing her justice, it's you, Brandon."

"Then you need to figure the tattoo thing out. Let's walk

through what you know." He pulled out his phone and opened the notepad.

I glanced at the moon. *What did I know?* "It's a countdown. Like mine."

"Same countdown?"

"I don't know. Maybe." I shrugged.

He typed into his phone. "End of days. Like yours. It must be."

"Doesn't it seem unlikely two people would be marked with the same warning?"

"Not to mention a vampire," Brandon added.

"Exactly, but I wouldn't say that to Nick."

"No, that would be uncool."

"And he never wanted to be vampire so humanity is his link to life." I studied my brother. *What was he looking for in my words?* "Honestly, I wanted to be human at one time and have human problems. I wouldn't have ever had Nick if I was human so I'm glad I'm not." Human wasn't my destiny, and I'm glad. To have known a love like that wasn't something I'd traded... even if I lost it.

"But you want to feel human," Brandon said earnestly.

"I want to feel normal."

A small brief smile crossed his lips. "That ship sailed a long time ago. Normal is not for us."

"It is. It's just a different type of normal. Normal for us is waking up and not facing death, Darkness, and destruction." I shook my head and half-laughed.

Brandon smirked. "Is that ever going to happen again?" His smile faded.

I matched his seriousness. "I hope so, brother. I hope so."

"I'm going to the library for research. You need some rest."

"Sleep is not my friend these days."

Worry lined his face. "Try."

I hugged him and headed down the hall to my room. The lights were off, but I didn't need to turn them on to know it was empty. I knew Nick was Alastair's captive, and the absence and fear it caused created a pool of agony in my gut. I missed Nick with every particle I was made of. *What if we are never together again? Could I live with that?* Darkness liked my thoughts too much, and I had to push them to a far corner and tuck them away.

The empty bed garnered a frown from me. I had no intention of crawling into the bed alone. My feet carried me out to the courtyard.

I gazed up at the familiar light. The healing powers strengthened me.

"Moon, moon so bright. Living life to find the Light. I see you in my soul tonight." I closed my eyes and imagined Nick there with me.

"That's beautiful. What's it from?" His hands on my shoulders a comfort. It seemed real. I wanted it to be real.

I squeezed my eyes together tight afraid he'd disappear. "My grandmother used to say it to me. It's a witchy nursery rhyme thing."

"Sounds like part of the prophecy," he whispered against my ear.

I leaned back against him. "It is. I was being funny."

"Some things aren't a joke," he paused. "Like how much I love you and have missed you." His breath tickled my neck.

Goosebumps ran down my arm. My eyes flew open. I spun in his arms. "You're real."

I squeezed his arms and ran my hands over his chest, not trusting he was really here. My heart flipped an erratic dance in my chest.

He smiled. "Dead but real." His arms wrapped around my waist and pulled me close.

Relief washed over me. "How..." I struggled to finish a thought. "When?"

"Secret passageways and some good friends. Alastair is a warlock. He'll never have the loyalty of all vampires." He leaned his face close and brushed his lips across mine.

He's real. My knees buckled, but he held me in place. Desire stirred in me from his touch.

"I love you," I whispered against his mouth. "But Nick... I'm not the same person. Darkness has a hold of me." I didn't want there to be any secrets, and he probably suspected. I wanted to be honest with him before I gave in to the passion inside me.

"Then I'll love your dark side too, Brie," he said. "You can't just walk away because there are challenges. Didn't we already figure that out together?" He kissed my cheek.

We had discussed it, but that was before Darkness claimed me. Before I experienced the intensity of its draw and the strength of its demand. I rested my chin on his shoulder. "I don't want to walk away, but if Darkness consumes me totally, I won't be who you fell in love with."

"You will always be who I fell in love with, and I will always fight for you." He lifted my chin until he brought our lips together.

"All I care about at the moment is that you are here and safe," I said.

Tonight, I'll enjoy this time with him, and tomorrow we will face the reality.

$$) \;) \; \bullet \; (\; ($$

I PROPPED myself up on my elbow to look at him. My hand rested on his chest. "We need to tell the others what we know about your tattoo. Brandon has that same intuition that I do, and he thinks they're linked too."

He rolled over on his side and ran his fingers into my hair. "It's not a stretch considering how similar they are. Do you think we should figure out what it means first?" His lips brushed mine, and the familiar vanilla scent that was all him filled the air around me.

"We barely know what mine means, and we have two books that reference the prophecy."

"Mine has to be in there somewhere." His lips pressed against the sensitive spot under my ear.

A moan escaped from me. "You'd think so." My voice came out breathless.

His mouth devoured mine, and his weight pushed me on my back. The sheet slipped down exposing me below the waist. He slid his hand to my hip and skimmed back up my side to cup my breast. My back arched into him.

"I missed you," he whispered against my skin. His lips wrapped around my nipple.

"Nick." His name came out a throaty moan. "I missed you."

He chuckled. His hard length pressed against my leg. Heat built in my core. His palm moved down my belly. Nick nipped my ear as his finger slid inside me, and my body arched again. He looked into my eyes and our special connection took over. It sizzled between us. My body blazed. He added a second finger to the motion, and I came undone. Darkness crept into the opening and powered me. It wanted control, and I did too.

I flipped us over, so Nick was on bottom. I took him in my hands and positioned myself to take all of him. His hands roamed over my breasts and twisted my nipples. I dropped down in a swift motion and rode him. His hand slid down until his thumb reached my clit. He punished me with slow circles while I bounced up and down on him.

Darkness drove me to move faster. His hardness made me fill full. I wanted to be closer to him. Darkness wanted to control the pleasure.

"Brie," he said. "Come for me."

I moaned. "Nick." I did as he asked, and he exploded inside me. I collapsed onto his chest.

Nick brushed the hair out of my face and pressed a kiss to my forehead. "That was..."

"Hot." I raised up and smiled at him. Darkness retreated with the pleasure.

He cupped my face with his hands and pressed our lips together. "I'll take ten lifetimes of that."

"Me too." I giggled.

He tucked me into his side and wrapped an arm around

me. "When we go on our honeymoon, I hope you know I don't plan to let you sleep."

I laughed and slapped his chest. "Well, I guess it's a good thing Darkness likes to power me up when I get tired." My words hung thick in the air like my dark aura. Darkness was always going to be with me. *Can Nick accept that?*

"We'll purge it from you somehow, Brie. We'll find a way." He pulled my hand to his lips and placed a delicate kiss on my knuckles.

"Of course," I said, not wanting to spoil the moment. He answered my unspoken question without even knowing it. The flames in my eyes flared. I'd have to enjoy whatever time we had together and say goodbye when the time came, just like my father had before me.

THIRTEEN

I snuggled in bed with Nick, but I averted my eyes and avoided looking directly at him. The flames hadn't abated despite my efforts to pull my pink aura to me. I trailed my fingers across his tattoo. It glowed when I touched it, similar to the reaction mine had. The Darkness in me wanted more connection, and I knew that was an omen...a bad one.

"This is out of my depth. We need Grandmother." I inhaled a deep breath and let it out slowly.

"She chose Brandon. I imagine he will successfully fill her shoes. Let's go see him," Nick took my hand and pulled me into a hug.

I rested my head in the bend of his neck. "I have no doubts. It takes time to understand our gifts though. We don't master them overnight."

Nick kissed the top of my head. "He's a fast learner like his sister."

"What do you think it is?" I asked. "based on what little Stefan did tell you?"

"He thought it was a key to vampire rule. I don't believe that." He pulled me tighter to him.

"What if he's right? This whole prophecy we've thought we beat is still at work."

He pulled back to face me, but I kept my face down. His finger crooked under my chin and lifted. My eyes cast down. "Look at me, Brie."

I look up and met his gaze. The flames were softer, but the burn told me they were visible.

"You never have to hide from me, my love." He kissed the tip of my nose. "We will beat Alastair. We will figure out what this tattoo means. And most importantly, we will cull the Darkness from you."

I wanted to believe him, but if Sorin couldn't rid himself of it, I had little hope for myself. This was borrowed time, and I needed to focus on saving Nick. "A mark like this should have killed a vampire," I said. "So why it didn't kill you? A non-witch isn't supposed to be able to carry the power of that kind of gift."

Nick wrapped his arms around my waist. "We don't even know if it carries any power."

"It does. I can sense it. I can't tell you what kind of power though other than it's strong." *And Darkness likes it. A lot.*

"How long have you known?"

"As long as you have." I smiled up at him. *No one can carry a mark like that and not experience the power rolling off of it.* "Mine feels like an iron shackle around my arm."

"I thought I imagined it."

"Have you tried to do any witchy stuff?"

Nick's forehead wrinkled. "No, I wouldn't know how."

"I think it's how Alastair controlled you. He used the power in you from this mark to control you by channeling it through his mark on you."

His nose wrinkled up in disgust. "It came from deep in me. Painful at times."

"Because he had you do things you didn't want to do. When we resist, that's how it feels. Pain from our souls to remind of us our duty."

"No offense, but it's easier to be a vampire than a witch."

The flames in my eyes intensified. I cocked my head to the side. Darkness pushed forward. "You like not having to think about your actions?"

He studied me like he was gauging what I meant. "Tell me you don't believe I'm like that."

I focused on my mental wedge and tried to pry open a bigger space for my pink aura. "I'm sorry. I didn't mean it that way. It was a careless thought."

His voice lowered. "I remember everything I've done since becoming vampire. The good. And the bad."

"I know you do. You didn't give into the all-consuming lust of the vampire world." *Like I did with Darkness.*

"No, Brie. I did for a time. It wasn't who I wanted to be. I didn't want to lose the human in me, and that was stronger. The life I had sustained me until I met you, and you became the life I wanted."

He was the life I wanted too. His love made me want to be whole.

That's why he thinks he can fix me. Banish the Darkness

inside me. I wish it worked like that for me. I leaned forward and kissed him. "You are amazing. Do you know that? You talk about my strength, but I am weak compared to you. Strength grows in you every day, and it keeps me going."

He shook his head and pulled away. "No one sees me like that but you."

I took his hand and laced my fingers with his. "They do. You just don't see it."

"I'm not the leader you are, Brie."

"No, we're not the same. You are better in so many ways. You're levelheaded and consistent." I shifted off the bed.

"You take risks that yield great results."

"And some pretty big fails." I curtsied in front of him. "Dark witch queen at your service."

He pulled me back into his arms. "But we are better together, my love."

"That we are." A twinge shuddered through me. I loved him, and that's why I would have to leave. We might have been better together, but he was in danger as long as I was nearby. "Show me your tattoo again."

Nick's eyebrows scrunched together.

"You're not getting shy on me. Show me the tattoo, Mr. Domenico. I want to touch it again."

"You can touch anything on me you want." The corner of his mouth turned up, but his shoulders were stiff with tension. He pulled his shirt up and gestured for me to touch him. I pressed my palm flat on his pectoral, covering the tattoo. Light glowed between us. I glanced up at him.

His brows scrunched together. "Why does it do that? Are you doing something to it?"

"I'm not doing it," I said, trying to tune myself to the vibration.

"Well, I'm not. So, who is?" He asked, confused.

I took in the detail of the mark. It was as similar as it was different to mine. "I think it's the magic in your tattoo. This is a witch's mark remember."

"Shouldn't it burn me or something?"

"Or something." I laughed. "I think it's protecting you from my magic."

"But the auras went around me."

"They weren't a threat. I'm trying to sense the origin of the tattoo, but it's blocking me." I pulled my hand away.

The glow disappeared. "Why would witch magic block the most powerful witch?"

"I'm really gifted, but I'm not the most powerful. That's Sorin," I said. Darkness shoved thoughts in my head on how I could become the strongest, but I pushed them away.

He grimaced. "You're going to ask me to let your father touch my chest. Aren't you?"

"Yep." I smiled at him.

"Did you get anything at all?"

"Not anything that would help. It's old. How old I can't say, but I could feel something very old at work." I touched it again and closed my eyes to focus on it. "It's tied to a family. Not mine." A zap from the tattoo pushed back on my probe. "Ouch." I shook my hand.

"What happened?" Nick grabbed my hand and ran his thumb over my palm.

"I was about to get the family name when it shocked me.

It doesn't have anything to do with my family. Some other witch wants to protect you besides me."

"Jealous?" He smiled.

"Should I be? Are you letting other witches get that close? I could put my mark on the other side." I ran my hand up his stomach and over the other pec.

His voice deepened. "I'd let you mark me wherever you wanted. Yours is the only one that matters to me."

"Smart answer." I smiled at him.

He took my hand and led me toward the door. "Come on. Let's find Sorin. You won't let it rest until we do."

"I love how you know me."

He winked at me. "I love you."

☽ ☾ ● ☾ ☾

DAD GOT past his shock at seeing Nick here. He studied Nick's tattoo and grabbed some of the oldest books in the library to look for answers. He pressed his hand against it, but it didn't glow like it did when I touched the symbol. "Brie, this isn't a mark I made, nor have I seen it before. The fact he's still alive means it was meant for him. That's all I can tell you."

"You're the most powerful witch on the planet. You can find out," I said, unable to hide the disappointment in my voice.

"Patience." Sorin leveled his gaze on me. "You need to grow some. It will reveal its meaning when it's time."

"Everyone was all over mine. Why aren't you concerned about one on a vampire? It has Blood Moons," I said. "It's on a vampire. My vampire." The Blood Moons alone convinced me it was related to mine and the prophecy.

The flames in his eyes flared. "Are you not feeling unique now or are you that concerned?"

My eyes flared in retaliation. "I don't give a fuck about being unique. I want to make sure my fiancé isn't going to turn into a pile of ash because of a damn prophecy tattoo." I pushed my hair off my forehead. Sweat beaded on my brow line. "Tell me he's not wearing this mark because of me."

I glanced at Nick and frowned. He was kicked back watching us like the championship tennis match at Wimbledon.

"Didn't we just talk about this? Stop being so hard on yourself. Nick has his own destiny. It may or may not be related or even intertwined with yours. Stop trying to force everything to fit in a neat little box you can carry around. It's never going to work."

"How did you protect your family?" I paused. "By running away."

He took a step in my direction. His voice softened. "Stop with the digs. You want to control everything, and life isn't like that."

Darkness. He was right. I was a control freak without it, and it encouraged me to be more so.

"I'm sorry. I'm on edge," I said, remorseful. "It bugs me how old the tattoo felt when I tried to sense the origin."

"Old how?" Sorin narrowed his eyes at me.

"Like old."

"And it offered protection to him?"

"Yes, at least it felt like that to me. It shocked the shit out of me." I looked at my palm, but the zing had left no visible reminder.

"I do remember a time when children of important families would be marked with protection. It fell out of practice because it wasn't needed anymore." Sorin flipped through one of the books. His interest renewed, almost excited.

"So, someone old marked him?" That didn't seem likely since there hadn't been any old witches near him.

"I don't know. They'd have to be near him."

"No one was near me when mine happened."

"Yours was already there from the day you were born. It remained hidden and dormant until the time came for the prophecy to be revealed."

I ran my hand over my mark, and it warmed under my touch. "And his couldn't be the same way?"

Sorin rubbed his chin. "I don't see how. He was born human. During the time he was born, witches wouldn't have made themselves known to humans. The risk would have been too great, and a human wouldn't survive a powerful mark like that."

"A vampire shouldn't either. Maybe there were some witches in Nick's earlier life."

I turned to Nick, who was still quietly observing my dad and me. "Do you remember any witches besides me and Alastair getting close to you?"

He shook his head, almost like he didn't want to get involved in the conversation. But he was the reason we were here.

Sorin studied the old book. "The Blood Moons are interesting. That does make me wonder if it has something to do with your prophecy."

Finally. He was getting my point.

He glanced between Nick and me. "But we would have known. There would have been something in the texts to link them together."

And it's gone.

"He's not like other vampires. Don't forget that," I said. "I noticed he was different and other vampires can tell he is different."

"He is a vampire, and you need to remember that." The flames in his eyes danced and grew like something was stoking them.

"What's up with you?"

"My mother's funeral was yesterday. I'm grieving, and I don't feel like discussing your boyfriend's tattoo. I want to be alone, Brie." His attitude switched so quickly that it shocked me, but I recognized the reaction. Darkness had him.

"Dad, I'm sorry. I ..." I didn't know what to say to bring him back.

"It's okay. I need some time to myself." He pinched the bridge of his nose. An action I did when I was stressed. His arms went around me in a quick hug. "I'm going for a walk."

"But you're coming back, right?"

He stopped in the doorway. His hand was still on the knob, but he didn't turn around. "Yes, I'll be back."

The pit in my stomach warned me. It hit me like a ton of bricks. Sorin didn't have control of the Darkness in him like he wanted us to believe. His struggle made him act with split personalities like me. *Would he come back this time?*

I wondered if he would come back each time he left. My insecurities peaked when his behavior became erratic. The very thing he wanted me to be less of. I knew my fate was inevitable the more I saw the Darkness take over him. We were both damned by the Darkness. I leaned back against Nick's chest, and he held me to him.

﹚﹒﹚﹒●﹒（﹒（

M editation at dawn seemed like a good idea this morning. *Why can't I focus? Could be because Sorin's not back yet. Could be because my future husband has an unexplained witch marking. Or maybe because everything is going to shit around me. Including myself.*

Damn it, Brie. Focus.

I repositioned myself on the floor facing East. The direction drew me to align with it today for the knowledge I sought. Incense wafted around me. I inhaled deeply. It filled my lungs and cleared my mind.

What does Nick's damn tattoo mean?

Not the best meditation. Okay. I have a clear blank mind. Clear. Blank. Open to answers.

Light engulfed me, and I welcomed it for the reprieve from Darkness. The warmth it provided was powerful, but unlike Darkness, it strengthened the goodness in me. I didn't have to fight against thoughts of violence and pain. Light transported me into a sea of bright white. No floor. No ceiling. Not floating. Stationary in time and space.

Meditation, although fruitful, could bombard me with too much information to process. If I tensed up, I'd lose the connection so I couldn't brace myself for the images that flooded my mind.

The first snapshot appeared. Nick's tattoo. Light radiated from it as it formed on his chest. His face came into focus. Mouth opened. He gaped at it in what looked like legitimate surprise.

A blur in front of me, and a Blood Moon appeared high in the sky. Past or present I couldn't tell. The moon called to me. Sang its song for me. The tattoo on my arm tingled.

Nick stood beside me. His tattoo glowed. My tattoo glowed. We reached to the sky and blood dripped from the moon. Lightning struck between us. It separated us with a large crack in the earth. Wind whipped around us and pushed us further apart. My heart beat fast even though I knew it wasn't real.

Fire walled up around me. Hell's Fire. Brandon and Sorin stood on the inside with me. Mom and Nick stood on the outside. Nick bowed and walked away. Mom cried on the other side of the wall. Alastair stood in the center engulfed in Darkness. The black aura around him caused a wave of vertigo for me. Liquid covered my feet. I stood in a pool of red. Dread and fear

White light around me and back to Nick. His tattoo. The snakes hissed and pulsed through the artwork. I reached out to touch it, and a snake latched onto my hand. Snakes circled a child. I tried to step into the circle to rescue the child, and one of the reptiles struck my foot. Each attempt to save the child brought an attack from a different snake. Nick appeared in front of me. A blue aura encased him. He reached into the pit and plucked the child to safety. Nick smiled and made a face. The child laughed and reached for me, but the serpents pulled me down into Darkness.

Light whirled around me and pushed me back to reality.

I gasped for air. Never had I experienced visions so vivid or intense. My role tended to be a bystander who watched events unfold. I'd been a participant in this one.

Nick would not be at the battle. That vision was clear. The reason not so clear. *What the hell with the snakes and the child which I couldn't tell if it was a boy or girl? And the blue aura? Vampires don't have an aura. I need to find Gran... No, she's gone.* There was only one other person that would understand visions. *Cal.*

)) ● ((

"Visions don't always mean what we see on the surface. It could mean a number of things," Cal said. He sat in the chair across from me and poured us both a cup of tea.

"I've never had one that felt so..." I searched for the word when no other would fit. "Real."

"It can be confusing when one is so strong. You saw a lot of different things too. It may be a case where you don't know what it means until the time arrives." He handed me a cup, being supportive and sympathetic.

I took a sip. "That's not acceptable. We've gotten into a

habit of that, and we are given these visions for a reason. I don't think that reason is to wait and see."

"It's extremely personal like the one where you saw Nick and Brandon die on the battlefield. Remember how you found no way to save them until the day of the battle? This could be a similar vision."

The reminder of that day jabbed my gut. My father died in front of me, and I was broken by it. So, broken I brought him back from Hell and didn't even know how. "I didn't save them then either. Sorin did and look at the cost."

He sat his cup on the table next to him. "You saved them together. My point is you didn't see him in the equation until the day of. He never appeared in your visions, and you had several of them. This is one vision."

And visions are subjective. "Good point. So, you think there is something outside my view, so to speak, impacting it?"

"I think it's a real possibility. I've seen it with some of my stronger visions too."

I leaned my head back on the chair. "Some gift. I wish I had the control on mine you have on yours."

"It's my only gift, so I've been able to focus on it more. Your gifts are spread a little thinner." He smiled at me.

"You find the bright side in everything. Well, kind of." I smiled back. "Have you seen any of this in your visions?"

"No, these are yours alone. Yours to choose who you share them with and who you don't. If it were me, I'd share them with my partner," he said, without judgment. His friendship meant a lot to me.

Nick was just back and had the mark we were trying to

figure out. He didn't need something to worry about that might not turn out to be anything at all. "He's pretty spent with everything else. I don't have answers, and this would stress him out. He doesn't need that right now."

Cal waited like he expected me to continue. "Don't you think he would want to know? Especially since he was in it?"

"My vision. My choice. Didn't you say that to me a few minutes ago?"

"Indeed, I did, and it is your decision." He finished his tea and placed the cup on its matching saucer. He clearly thought I was wrong in my decision.

I steadied my voice, preparing myself for his reaction to his father's fate. "So, my plan is to take your father down, and that will likely mean his death. I don't expect you to participate, but I wanted you to hear it from me."

He stared off into the library and met my gaze. His eyes had hurt in them but determination as well. "My allegiance is, as always, to you, Your Majesty."

I relaxed. "No formalities between us, and I know it is. You have proven it over and over again. I can't ask you to fight against your father though."

"I'd prove myself if needed," he said, his voice even, but there was pain in his eyes.

"Not needed. I'm going to the library to continue searching for Nick's tattoo. When I touched it, I got the sense it was a pretty old marking. Do you want to go with me? We could your eyes if you have time."

"No, I am meeting with Elders to get my confirmation." He smiled, a bit forced but genuine. The confirmation was their acceptance that he was my second in command. If I was away, he would lead the people. It wouldn't make him a formal candidate for the line of succession, but it did place him in a position to make decisions on my behalf.

"That is a good reason." I hugged him.

We parted ways at the door. He took off down the hall toward the Elders' council room.

I walked two doors down to the library.

Inside, I contemplated the best way to tackle the search. I could put my hand in the air and will to me any books with information on tattoos. An image of me buried up to my neck in books came to mind and stifled that thought.

Guess I'll stick with the old fashion way.

I pulled several books off the shelves and took them to the table. Some of the books Brandon looked through earlier were still there.

The first one held pictures and descriptions of markings made around the time of Nick's human life. I turned pages of drawings. None similar in the slightest to the mark on Nick's chest.

My tattoo only existed in The Blood Moon Prophecy texts. If Nick's was as unique as mine, maybe I needed to try a more distinctive approach. I hadn't seen it in the prophecy text. Other prophecies existed. Some had already happened and others still to come. Some were small and some world-changing like mine.

The door creaked open, and Brandon emerged through it. He looked tired. "Sorry, Sis. I didn't know you were in here."

"No apologies needed." I patted the chair next to me.

"I came back to see what I could find." Brandon slid into the seat.

"I've been doing the same. I don't think what we're looking for is in here," I said. My frustration was evident in my voice.

"Why's that?"

"My tattoo is referenced one time by description only in the prophecy. There are no other texts it exists in and no pictures. Nick's might be obscure too."

"That would make sense. Your prophecy was studied because they think it determines the end times. If his is in a lesser prophecy, they may not be as concerned."

"Exactly what I was thinking. It could have been overlooked."

"How do we go about finding it?"

"I'm stuck there. I've mulled ideas over, but they usually get a big failure stamp across them. I'm open to hearing your thoughts."

He leaned back. "I can't see the solution to this one, but I can share my tactical assessment. We need to hit the one place that might hold an ancient obscure prophecy, and we'll need help. I'll rally the troops and meet you in the vault."

The vault was the room next to the Elders' council room. Under lock and key from everyone except the Queen and the Elders. It held the oldest of texts for the covens. Some were so fragile they could only be opened with magic. A physical touch would crumble them.

I waved my hand in front of the door. The bolts snapped back, and the door creaked open. The room large enough to hold twelve people at most. Many of the works stored here were scrolls. Some too old to determine the age. I pivoted around viewing the materials. *Where to start?*

A dot bounced over a shelf. I blinked and rubbed my eyes not sure if I'd imagined it. It bounced in front of it again. A small circle of white light. Perhaps Grandmother reached out to point me to the answers. *She's still here offering her guidance.* Happiness overtook me.

My head tilted upwards. "Thanks, Grandmother."

I gingerly lifted each scroll from the bin and set them out on the table. Seven in all. *Imagine that. Seven.*

Brandon and Cal strolled through the door.

"We're it, Sis. We couldn't find Mom and Dad," Brandon said a smile on their face.

"By the look on your face, I'm guessing you didn't try their bedroom."

"That would be a no." He scrunched up his nose.

I smirked at him. "I have it narrowed down," I said. "With Grandmother's help."

"Huh?" Brandon's eyebrows bunched together, and he looked around the small room.

"Some other time. These are some of the older ones so use your magic to unfold them with care."

We each picked one to start.

I held my hand out over mine and used magic to unfold it in the gentlest of ways. The words were written in ornate scrolling penmanship. The style ancient compared to what we used today, and I could barely tell the letters it formed. The first thing I recognized was way too familiar. *Blood Moons.*

"Guys, I think this is it, but I'm having trouble reading it. Did either of you ever study the old penmanship in your language classes? Like before calligraphy?"

"You must have skipped that one, because I had two semesters of it," Brandon said.

"Me too," Cal said.

"Good. Then you can decipher all this swirly shit." I motioned for them to come around to my side of the table.

"It's not calligraphy-like. It is calligraphy. Albeit a rare style," Brandon said.

"It's old. Older than any we studied, but he's right," Cal said.

"How old was the writing you studied?"

"It was eighteenth and nineteenth-century stuff."

"So, this was written before the seventeen hundreds?" It was more than three hundred years old.

"I'm not an expert, but I would think so," Cal said.

Brandon scanned the parchment. "Patterns are the key. Look for them, and that will help us figure out letters and words."

My finger hovered over the scroll. "This is obviously a 'B' here and here, and the only words I recognize are two I'd know anywhere."

"Blood Moon," Brandon whispered.

I nodded. "Yep."

Cal leaned in closer. "Capital letters are a little more distinctive. The lowercase letters are harder."

A knock rapped on the door. We all froze and looked toward it.

My mother stood in the doorway. She looked a little disheveled like she had gotten ready in a hurry. "Mom, come on in."

I raised an intentional eyebrow at Brandon. He shook his head but smiled.

"I got the message you were all down here," she said. "It sounded urgent."

Brandon waved her over to the bench. "Yes, looking for info on Nick's tattoo. Have you ever seen this writing before?"

She studied the paper. Her eyes met mine with confidence. "Actually, I have. Your Grandmother had something similar in her family book."

"Family book?" I asked.

"She never showed it to you? I'm surprised. We went over it several times."

Grandmother went shared our family history with Mother but not me. *Was this another of Grandmother's attempts to reconcile us?*

"Can you read this?" Cal asked.

"Let me see." She pulled up a chair.

Her eyes scanned over the writing. Her brows furrowed. "Has anyone else seen this?"

"Not that we know of. Just us," I said. "Why?"

She looked out the doorway and whispered. "Do not show this to anyone else."

"Mom, what did you read?" Brandon whispered back.

"It's been twenty years at a minimum since I've read this style of prose, and I want to be sure. It's different than reading from a family book."

My mind came up with a thousand scenarios, and each one worse than the last. "Just tell me already."

"This word is queen. I know that for sure. As I know this word is king."

"And?"

"The king and queen will burn the Darkness," she said, her voice shook as she pointed to the words.

Cal leaned in next to me. "That doesn't sound so bad."

"Only if they survive their own battles," she continued.

I nodded. The prophecy was as much about our battles within as it was about the physical battles. "Internal. That's what it means."

"Not necessarily," Brandon said.

"She will lead hers. He will lead his. Together and alone," she continued.

"What the hell does that mean? It contradicts itself."

Her finger moved along the page. "It goes on about what will determine when you are together and alone."

"Quit dragging it out."

She was defensive. "I'm not. I'm rereading as I go to make sure I am understanding it correctly," she paused. "He will be her salvation at her darkest hour. She will be his at the end of his reign."

Nick had saved me numerous times. He'd pulled me back from my darkest hours. "Nick's been my salvation at all my darkest moments." *He told me not to hide from him. That he loved me.*

Her voice became gentle. "You may have faced yours, but I suspect Nick is yet to meet his. That's why the tattoo appeared now."

"If his is coming, how do we know what it is?" I asked.

"You'll know, Brie. He'll know," Cal said. "You know your darkest moments so will he."

I dropped onto the stool beside my mother. "He thinks he's already seen his darkest moments. How am I going to break it to him that he has something worse coming?"

She rubbed my back. "With honesty, Brie."

I didn't want it to be true and tried to deny it. "Are we sure this is it? Does it mention the mark on his chest?"

Mother pointed to a sentence. "The Blood Moon Queen shall have her king. His mark a mate to her own."

"Sounds pretty solid," Brandon said, his tone apologetic.

"It does." I studied the words on the paper, deflated by what we uncovered. "Can you all leave me alone? I need to process this."

"Come get us when you are ready to talk through it," Mother said, her tone full of compassion. "Come on boys. Let's give her some space."

Alone in the room, I looked upwards again. "Grand-mother, does it ever stop? Are Nick and I going to face this our entire lives?"

I leaned over on my elbows and put my head in my hands. The pity party lasted long enough for me to take a couple of deep breaths. My eyes focus back on the old text. There was more writing than what Mom had read. It wasn't word for word. *Did she leave something out on purpose?*

Most of the words she pointed to came back to me as I looked at them. She skipped entire paragraphs. *Why? Was it deliberate? Did she not understand the writing?*

I could clearly make out some of the words that repeated from the paragraphs she had deciphered for me.

My eyes searched the room for paper and pen. I worked my way around the room opening drawers and checking shelves.

Score. A drawer had blank computer paper and modern pens. I took them back to the table and started mapping out as much as I could. Blanks remained for the words I didn't know. Each time I figured out a different word, I would go back and fill it in.

I sat back in dismay. The puzzle pieces came into. This prophecy, Nick's prophecy, tied in directly to mine. Because we chose each other, his prophecy came into play. We caused this with our decision, and our prophecies intertwined permanently. We would have to face this together.

The power between us would be like none known in recent centuries, but it confused me. A vampire didn't have powers other than enhanced senses and physical movements. He would rule the vampire kingdom and by my side for the coven. The power there would be enormous for both of us, so that had to be it.

Another paragraph made me doubt my interpretation. If this was right, mine was off. I read a couple of lines out loud.

"His power enhanced by her salvation. His power realized when she sets him free." *Is this talking about the alone part?* I'd known I would have to let him go the moment I accepted Darkness in me, but to see it on paper created an ache in me. Darkness was all too willing to take it from me.

Nick saved me long before his rise to King, but I hadn't set him free, not really. He received his power because another witch murdered his father. My brain hurt.

"Grandmother, I know you expected me to understand

this better than I do. My brain is tired, and you'd probably say I'm making it harder than it has to be."

I closed my eyes to try to focus on the words I'd read. "This is pointless, and I'm officially talking to myself now." A walk to clear my head felt like what I needed. I locked the door on my way out and twisted the knob to double-check it was locked.

FIFTEEN

>>·●·((

I stood in front of the door to my suite. *Our suite.* I sensed him inside, and I hesitated. Not sure why. Other than it meant I'd have to explain to him what I found. *Well, I don't have to.* I couldn't keep it from him though. Cal was right. Nick deserved to know.

He sat on the couch looking every bit as gorgeous as the day I saw him in the club. His emerald green eyes met mine, and I savored the electric connection. The flames in my eyes sprung to life, and I tried to blink them away without success. If I survived the takedown of Alastair, it would kill me to let Nick go.

"Hey," I kissed his cheek and dropped down on the sofa. "Where have you been?"

He stretched an arm out across the back of the couch. "Making phone calls. You?"

"Researching your tattoo."

"Find anything?"

"Actually, I did." I slid down on the couch beside him. "It's old. Really old."

He wrapped his arm around me and pulled me closer. "You already sensed that though. Anything new?" His lips pressed against my temple.

I explained what we had uncovered from the scroll.

"Can I see it? Maybe I can read it. I was born around that time."

"It's in the room next door to the Elders' council chamber." I considered the location and what the coven would say. Especially the Elders. They wouldn't be happy if they found out, but this was about me and Nick.

Nick echoed my concern. "I don't know how they would feel about it me entering a room that close to them, especially one with old texts in it."

"It directly affects you, Nick," I said. You need to see it."

"Yes, but they deserve the respect," he said like he contemplated if it was worth the risk.

"They never even checked on us when we were there earlier. The fact that it talks about your mark, and you link to the prophecy is all the justification I need," I said.

"Okay. Let's do it," he said.

"They already think I ignore them so one more time isn't going to matter at this point."

He slid his hand into mine and brought it to his lips.

I stood up and pulled him with me.

"You're stronger than you look," he said.

"Yes, I am." I smiled at him, but I wondered what made him say that.

)) ● ((

WE DIDN'T PASS anyone on the way to the room. I reached for
the handle to unlock it, but it slid open.

"Son of a bitch." Darkness reached for my anger. I kicked
the door open the rest of the way. "I know I locked it when I
left."

Nick peered inside. "Maybe someone was here after you."

I eyed the empty spot where the parchment had been. I
shoved the stool in front of me, and it bounced along the
ground. "They took the scroll too."

"Who would have motivation to take it?" He turned
around looking at all the old books and documents.

"My mother." My hand rested on my hip and a frown
took over my face as I tried to keep the Darkness at bay.

"Your mother?"

"She saw something in the text that disturbed her. I
figured out she hadn't read the whole thing with us, but I
gave her the benefit of the doubt on it. She gave just enough
of it up to make it look like she was helping." I opened
drawers in hopes it was hidden in the room and slammed
them close.

"I wonder what she saw other than what you translat-
ed," Nick said, sounding confused.

"Me too." I shuffled some of the papers on the desk.
"Shit. She took my notes too."

"Want to go see your mother?" Nick slipped his hand in
mine and laced our fingers together.

"Abso-fucking-lutely."

We made it to the hallway she had chosen for her suite. My guards met us as we rounded the corner.

They bowed before me. "Your father is asking for you, Your Majesty."

Panic gripped me with a memory of him in the mud of the battlefield. "Is he okay? Where is he?"

"He asked that you meet him in the dining room."

I ran toward the dining room with Nick right behind me and didn't slow down as I entered the door.

"Dad, are you okay?" I looked him over for injuries or changes in his aura. He seemed the same, but the Darkness in me was drawn toward his dark aura.

"Brie. Nick. I'm fine." He hugged me. His voice was optimistic. "I wanted to tell you in person I am going on a trip, but I'll be back in time for the moon and the spell."

His announcement made me nervous. *He can't leave now.* "You can't leave now. We still have a lot to do."

He held me at arm's length. The flames in his eyes grew. "Everything is planned to cover all the details. I'll be back in time. I can promise you that."

"We are still looking for alternatives." I reached for reasons for him to stay.

"There are none, Brie. This is how it needs to be, and I need some time to gather strength for what we need to do. You should think about it yourself." His eyes flicked to Nick and back to me. *He knew. He understood the choice I was prepared to make.*

Darkness jolted through my body. "I understand what I

need to do. It's a terrible option which is why we need to find others."

"You're out of time. We're out of time. Trust me on this." The message was clear. He believed this was our only option, and I needed to prepare for the consequences.

I hugged him still convinced even though I didn't want to give up, but I didn't want him to leave on a disagreement either. I wasn't sure if he'd be back as he promised, because I wasn't sure I could stay with my Darkness fighting to be free.

He walked out the door, and a wave of regret hit me. Each time he left, I thought it might be the last time I see him as himself.

Nausea waved over me. A familiar feeling at this point. My ability to decipher what it meant hadn't gotten any better.

"I'm worried about him. More every minute he has to leave to get his shit together," I said.

Nick encircled me from behind with his arms. "He's struggling. I can see it."

I leaned back against him. "It's a shitty spell mix, but that's not what you're talking about."

"No, I meant internally."

I closed my eyes as if that would block it out. "I've noticed it too. We have to give in to Darkness for this spell so his internal struggle will get worse before it gets better. I'm scared of it, and I'm scared for him. I don't want to lose him again." My worry wound around my heart like a vine and tightened.

Nick rested his chin on the top of my head. "He's smart. Let him do it his way. Your strength will help him."

"If only that were true. The battle with Darkness is a lonely battle. No one can fight it for you, Nick." The weight of these battles, Darkness, and Alastair, would change all of us, but perhaps none more than my father and me. He'd leave to isolate himself, but a different fate waited for me. My heart cracked each time I thought of it. I'd name Brandon as my successor as soon as the battle was over. *If I can hold it together that long.* Then, the ceremony would do the rest. The successor bond would be created just as it had for my aunt, Cecily when she named me. My death would come, and the Darkness would die with me. I'd die a dark queen, but the coven would survive. My family would survive. I fought back the tears forming. Nick would survive.

He whispered against my ear. "That goes for many things. My battle to maintain humanity was mine. I wanted it, but I knew I had to make that choice when I met you the first time."

I swallowed down my tears and turned in his arms. "You said I saved you. Is that what you meant?"

"I thought I told you that," he said, his voice soft.

"You did, but sometimes a girl needs to hear it again." I forced a smile. "The scroll hinted at us saving each other, and that is true. You saved me more than once." I laid my hand over his mark. "Your tattoo is correlated to mine. Our destinies are linked."

He rested his forehead against mine. "Was there a doubt it was? I suspected it from the start."

"I didn't want to believe you were tied to the stupid prophecy. It felt like it was a curse."

He cupped my cheek with his hand. "Brie, I've been part

of it since we met. We didn't know the prophecy was looming over us then, but it was still there."

I leaned back and met his eyes. His gaze was solid in resolution, and I couldn't dash his hope. "It makes how we approach things different though."

"It doesn't change us. We are the same people." He almost convinced me, but Darkness tainted every part of me. I'd never be the same person I was when we met.

"What we do impacts so many more people though."

"And it will for the rest of our long lives." He pressed his lips to my cheek. "I intend to make you happy forever."

I smiled, but inside, my heart shattered. Forever would die in Darkness like my soul. "I just don't want to make a wrong step or mistake."

"We are both going to make mistakes. Perfection doesn't exist."

"My mistakes cost lives. Every one of the lives lost is etched on my soul like a scar to remind me." The faces of the witches Stefan slaughtered to get to me haunted my dreams.

"I remember every life I've taken and every soul that died because of me. I won't lie and say you forget those. You don't." Nick's tone sobered. "But you accept that you can't change it, and you move forward to be a better person."

"It weighs on me."

"A lot weighs on you. You are in a position of power with a prophecy hanging over your head that promises more death. It's not the life for someone weak. Maybe the universe thought you needed a partner in crime, and I fit the bill."

I laughed. "You are the best accomplice ever. I wouldn't

want to do it with anyone else," I said. "How do you deal with it? The weight of those who have died around you?"

He paused, looking conflicted. "I've tried to make some sort of amends where I can. Taking care of their families for generations. Following my heart helps too."

"Don't you mean choosing your mind over your heart?"

"No, my heart. It reminds me my actions should be out of love."

I melted into his words. How selfless the love of my life was. "I don't know if I trust my heart when it comes to the prophecy. The prophecy seems to have waged war on love."

"What are you talking about, Brie? You chose love on more than one occasion."

"And there was a cost to my choices." Darkness danced up my spine. *A very painful cost to me and those I loved.*

"There are always consequences to our actions. Those consequences can be good or bad based on our decisions."

"It sounds good until you have to look in the face of the family of the person who died."

"My whole family died. The murderer looked me in the eyes and lied. You look them in the eyes and tell them the truth. That is a small gift you can give them." His fingertips brushed my cheek and tucked a stray strand of hair behind my ear. "The truth is powerful. It heals the grieving heart from the inside out."

"I'll try to remember that when I look in their faces. There are so many now it seems. I want to stop that number from growing where I can."

"And you will do that by stopping Alastair. The spell will see to it that he can't hurt anyone again."

"He's only one of the evils we face. What about the next?"

Nick took my hands in his. His thumbs stroked the tops. "You can't stop every evil in the world today, but you can face this one. Face them one at a time. Deal with each one as they come."

"I'll do my best to do that."

"Now, tell me what else you learned from the scrolls."

"There's not much else. I couldn't decipher a lot of it. As if the phrasing isn't hard enough to understand, I need a secret decoder ring for the script they use."

"Well, maybe I can find you one of those."

"That is the kind of help I needed." I grinned.

"I'm here to help you, Brie. I'm by your side for as long as you'll allow me to be."

Cal met us at the door. He stopped short of running into us. The distracted look on his face worried me. "I was looking for your dad. Is he still here?"

"No, he left a few minutes ago. You're not going to believe what my mother did now."

"What happened?"

My hands shook with anger, and I tucked them behind me. "She took the scrolls and my notes."

"What? Why would she take them?"

"It's a great question that I am going to find the answer to or she's going to be imprisoned." I'd given her breaks because of Sorin, but she crossed a line with this. Darkness burned in agreement.

"Don't overreact, Brie. Hear her out," Cal said.

I sighed.

Cal glanced around the room. "Just keep an open mind. Have you seen Brandon?"

"Not in a while. He's probably in the courtyard training," I said. "Stop in for dinner tonight if you can. We'll be in the private dining room."

He nodded and took off at a good clip.

Nick and I found Brandon first. He merged into our path from a side hall.

"Hey brother," I said, throwing a playful elbow into his arm. "Cal was looking for you."

"Hey, sis. Where are you headed?"

I sighed. "To confront Mom. You won't believe what she did."

"What now?" He crossed his arms across his chest.

I recapped it for him. His eyes widen in disbelief. He'd given her more trust than I could muster.

He was angry, possibly even more than me. "You are shitting me. Why would she take it?"

"I don't know, but we're on the way to get answers. Coming?" I said, still in disbelief she would do this knowing we were about to go into battle.

Brandon's face dropped. "I better find Cal first. I'll meet you there."

We found my mother in the library. It was the last place I expected her to be, but when I sensed her, my powers responded, both kinds. It led us right to her. She sat at the table in the far corner and leaned over the papers like a student deep in her studies. She looked up when we walked into the room. Her back stiffened.

My shoulders tightened into painful knots.

"Mom, we've been looking for you." I stood beside her and looked at the papers and the scroll. She had my notes and some of her own.

After our conversation about trust, this was a betrayal, and I didn't understand why she would do it.

She laid a hand across the papers. "Oh, what for?"

I pressed my hand flat on the table and leaned toward her. "I think you know what we're looking for."

"Tell me and then I'll have a better idea." Her voice tinged with fake cheerfulness.

"You took the text and notes from the room." My tone was full of menace. Darkness lapped up my anger.

"I can't give you the answers you want." She shuffled papers in front of her.

I reached for them, but she pulled them closer to her. Magic could rip them from her arms, but I gave her another chance. Grandmother believed in her, so I wanted to as well.

"You're not doing this to me again," I said.

"This is not the same, and I wasn't doing what you thought I was the first time either."

"You are hiding information from me. Vital information to me, Nick, and the prophecy. If that's not treason, I don't know what is."

She scoffed. "Really? You are threatening me with treason without even knowing what the reason is."

"It looks like it from where I stand." She hid things and covered her tracks. *Is she capable of anything else?* Darkness whispered she wasn't.

Pain flashed through her eyes. "Can't you let me be a

mother who is protecting her daughter? Why do you always expect the worst from me?"

I inched closer to her. "Because you usually disappoint me."

Her chair scraped along the floor. She stood and met my gaze. Her eyes were full of hurt. "I thought we had moved forward, and you understood."

"I thought we had too, but then you ran off with the text about my future husband's mark and my notes about the text. That makes you look pretty guilty."

She lowered her voice. "Just trust me for once."

I gritted my teeth. "No."

"Be reasonable, Brie."

"I am being reasonable by giving you the chance to turn over the scroll and my notes."

The door burst open, and Brandon walked into the library. He moved between us and looked me over. His face was drawn with anger.

His jaw clenched. "What are you doing? Cal said you are threatening to have Mom arrested."

"I told you what she did in the hall. She is keeping vital information from the queen. In doing so, she endangers lives including her queen's."

"You didn't say you were going to arrest her. This is our mother. Do you really believe she would endanger us?"

"I don't know the answer to that which is why I am giving her one last chance." I glared at her around his shoulder.

She backed a few steps away. "Please talk some sense into your sister."

Brandon pinched the bridge of his nose just like Sorin and turned toward her. "Mom, why did you take the scrolls?"

She took a giant step back like she was going to run, except there was nowhere to go. "I can't tell you."

Brandon moved closer to her. "You've got to give us something, Mom. She's the queen. You shouldn't keep it from her."

Mom set the papers down. "You kids don't understand."

"We haven't been kids in a very long time. We are adults. We are witches. We are hunters. We can handle it," I said.

"Secrets destroyed this family once. We're finally getting to know each other again. Don't let a secret put a wedge in between us again," Brandon said.

She shook her head. "It's not so simple. Some things are hidden for a reason. This could change the teachings and history of our coven. Not only our coven but the greater coven."

"Mother, damn it." I threw my hands up in the air. "Just tell us."

"Can we put it aside until after the Blood Moon? I promise I'll tell you then." She begged.

"It's only a couple of days, Sis. We can make that compromise, right?" Brandon said.

I eyed her. Not one to concede. I turned to Brandon. "I will not." I flicked my eyes in her direction and left the room.

The echo of my hard steps reverberated off the wall. My sight blurred from the outer corners in, and I leaned against the wall. The snapshots hit fast of Mom and Brandon covered in blood. Alastair laughing. Nick and I taking our vows. Nick holding a child. The child, a little girl with dark hair and blue eyes, surrounded in dark aura. Nick setting the child down. The child running through Hell's Fire to get to me. Me shrouded in Darkness. Nick standing on the outside of the ring of fire with tears in his eyes. Me cradling the little girl with flames in her blue eyes.

My sight cleared. I back up to the wall and slid down until my butt met the cold floor. *Was that a vision? Such a random mash of pictures. The child. Our child?* Vampires can't have children. There was no way it was our child I saw. *Vampires cannot have children.* I repeated it in my head, but it didn't counteract the nervous roll of my stomach. *Nick's dark hair. My eyes.* I clenched my eyes close. *Not possible.*

A deep breath filled my lungs, and I opened my eyes. Sweat collected on my palms. I wiped it on my pants.

Nick's mouth was moving, but I couldn't hear him.

I tried to stand up, and his hands went to my elbows to help me. My legs shook from the episode. I leaned back against the wall to steady myself and waited for my balance to come back.

Kids had never been in my plan. Between my childhood and my life as a loner before Nick, it hadn't been something allowed into my thoughts. I considered myself broken and unlovable. That changed when Nick came into my life. Love was given freely to me, and I gave it freely in return. *Did I want a kid? It will never happen. Darkness will take it all.*

My lungs ached like they were collapsing inward. I grabbed my chest and bent over. One hand on my knee to steady me. I took a breath trying to force air into my uncooperative lungs. *God help me. I do want to be a mother. Let it go, Brie. You can't*

Nick can't have children. He couldn't be the father. *No, I don't want children without him.* The snapshot of him holding the little girl warmed my heart. He'd be a great dad. He had taken Christopher, the boy vampire who'd helped us when Stefan was our biggest threat, under his wing and taught him how to keep his humanity. Nick had so much love to give, and he spent time with the children of the coven too. They followed him around like they worshiped him. The young ones hung on his every word when he told them stories from his childhood. He was meant to be a father.

When the shit with Alastair finished and if, by chance, we both survived, I promised myself I'd research something to restore fertility to vampires. If nothing existed, I'd approach adoption with Nick. There were orphaned human and witch children that needed parents. The coven wouldn't accept an adopted child as an heir to the throne either. It'd have to be a witch child. A human couldn't live with the queen and remain ignorant of our practices. There would be challenges.

Why am I even thinking about kids? The first part of the vision was Mom and Brandon covered in blood. Who's blood? Mine? Theirs?

The fate of Mother and Brandon and where the blood came from held more importance at the moment than my reproductive ramblings. They stood outside in the vision. Where I couldn't say. It looked familiar, but not enough that I could determine exactly where it was. Sometimes my visions tormented me. Moments like this I hated having them. Information wasn't always a blessing. *I'll keep my eyes open to see if I recognize it. Never thought I'd pray for another vision.*

Nick's voice rang in my ears. "Brie, talk to me. Are you ok?"

I rested my hand on the side of his face. "I am. It's just anxiety. I need to meditate."

I skipped meditation and walked into the private dining room. Sorin poured a cup of coffee at the buffet. He turned around and smiled at me. He looked better than he did before he died on the battlefield.

"Dad, you're back." I wrapped my arms around his neck, surprised to see him.

He stiffened a little but hugged me. "Yes, I told you I would be."

"I know. I don't know why I said that." *Lie.* I knew exactly why I said it. I didn't think he would come back.

He stood up and headed for the door.

"Aren't you going to finish your breakfast?"

"I'm just having coffee. When you are done, meet me in the courtyard. We need to practice the spell for tonight."

"Ceremony."

He looked at me.

"You said spell, but this is a ceremony."

"It's both. Hurry up."

He turned his back to me. Darkness required solitude to fight, and I could see the war inside him.

Part of me wondered if he was angry with me over Grandmother's funeral. My reaction was unplanned, but it was genuine.

I sat alone staring at my fruit, boiled eggs, and oatmeal. The Queen spent a lot of time alone apparently. I dropped the fork down on the plate and stood. My napkin fell to the floor. I bent over to pick it up and noticed a marking on the underside of the table.

On my hands and knees, I crawled underneath and flipped over on my back to stare up at it. My fingers moved across the words as I read them aloud. "Blood Moon entwined. No one shall divide." I sighed. It appeared to be a blessing for Nick and me. "Who put this here?" It hit me there were only a handful of people who knew about Nick's tattoo or that our prophecies were intertwined. "Why would they put it here?"

I scooted toward the edge of the table when something else caught my eye. Sunlight couldn't reach it, but it glimmered like the rays touched it. I reached up to touch it, but it moved away. "Grandmother," I whispered. "Thank you." The glowing ball bounced away. I smiled against the tears in my eyes. "Why in front of my place at the table though?"

Black shoes stood at the end of the table. Only one person wore those shoes.

"Hi, Nick," I said, not moving from under the table.

He squatted down to look at me. "What are you doing? Hiding from your family?"

I laughed. "Not a bad idea at all, but no. You wouldn't believe me if I told you."

"Try me."

"Come under here with me?" I waved for him to join me.

He crawled under and laid down beside me. "What did you have in mind?"

"Look up." I pointed.

He smiled. "So, this is what you've been doing? Carving love poems in the table?"

"No, it wasn't me," I said.

"Who?"

"That's the part I don't think you'll believe. There's a floating ball of energy that I've seen a few times. I think it's Grandmother," I said, my voice timid.

"You think she did this?"

"I do."

His voice had excitement in it. "That's fascinating, Brie. I didn't think witches could take form after death."

"They can't. Maybe it's a special gift for her."

"Are you sure she was able to move on?" He asked, keeping his voice low and calm.

I cringed. "We burned her body in the pyre, so I sure hope so."

He met my gaze. "I don't mean she's earthbound, but maybe her soul had unfinished business here."

"Not unheard of, but I can't imagine she'd ever leave this world with something undone." Grandmother, like other witches, wouldn't willingly pass on with outstanding business.

"Maybe not. Can we stay here though? Maybe it's a sign

for us to stay under this table." He rolled onto his side and propped his head up on his hand.

I laughed on rolled over on my side to face him. "It reminds me of when Brandon and I made blanket forts," I said. My mood was dampened by the ceremony rehearsal. "I have to go practice for tonight. Practice for something I don't believe is the right thing to do." I ran my fingers through his dark hair. "Promise me something."

"What's that?"

"Promise me you won't wait for me like my mother did for my father. Move on if I can't be brought back from Darkness. It's not going to be easy for me to come back if I can at all." I asked him to do what I would never be able to do myself, and my heart shattered at the thought of him loving someone else.

"I can't promise you that. My love for you is for eternity. I told you before, we do this together whether Light or dark." His commitment to me meant everything, but it was a high price to love me.

I closed my eyes. A spell could be cast to get my way, but it wouldn't be fair to him. It would take away his free will. I wouldn't want that done to me, and I couldn't do it to him. I opened my eyes and looked into his. A sea of green welcomed me.

The dependable connection between us powered me up. "I love you, Nick. I won't force you to do as I ask, but I beg you not to wait for me if Darkness takes hold." I grabbed the edge of the table and slid out from under it. Not able to look back, I left Nick under the table and hustled to the courtyard.

"Ready?" Sorin asked.

I took my place in the position for the ceremony. "It's not too late to come up with something else, because I do believe tonight's the best chance to take him out for good. With the Blood Moon's power behind us, we have the most strength we can summon."

"He'll have the Blood Moon power too which is why we need to do this spell," my father said.

"Brandon, stand here." He positioned Brandon between us. Then he turned to Mother. "Katerina, you'll stand back there to open and close the circle outside of the fire."

She took her place, and I choked down my annoyance with her over the scrolls.

"Brandon, you'll want to put your hand here on each of us." Sorin positioned Brandon's hand between my shoulder blades. He moved into his spot on the other side so Brandon could see the proper placement.

Brandon adjusted his hand position. "My fingers have to spread apart to maintain five points."

"Correct," Sorin said. "Go ahead and practice the anchoring incantation. You don't need to say it loud enough for us to hear. Whisper it."

I flinched when the power coursed from him. It was Light, and my dark aura fought it.

"Good," Sorin said. "Once you have us anchored Brie and I will call the fire."

My skin was dampened with sweat.

"We won't do that here, Brie." Sorin looked over his shoulder. "Once we have the fire in place. You can open the circle, Katerina. When we have him trapped, then you will perform the ceremony."

"I have it memorized, so I'm ready," Mom said.

"His aura will filter out, and we can destroy it." Darkness wanted Alastair's aura. It made me uncomfortable here, and I'd have to ignore it when we performed the real ceremony.

Mom and Brandon exchanged a look. Something went unsaid between them. I eyed both of them. The uncomfortable feeling grew with their uneasiness.

I turned my gaze on Sorin, his expression neutral. "And we're sure we can destroy it?"

"It's tricky with the power of the Blood Moon, but we should be strong enough together to do it. Once we have contained the power, Katerina will close the circle."

She focused on Sorin and nodded.

"We'll drop the fire, and Brandon can release the anchor hold. It's important that it happens in exactly this order. Do we want to practice it again?"

"I think one more run-through would reassure me." Brandon's voice wavered.

Unlike him to feel unsure about anything, but I sensed a vibe of uneasiness from him. His shaken confidence told me they were hiding something from me.

Sorin reset us in our positions and ran through it one more time.

"Very good," he said after the second run-through. "If you will all excuse me, I'm going to meditate until time to leave."

"We'll come get you for dinner," Mom said.

"No, I'll meet you when it's time to leave." Sorin pivoted and crossed the courtyard.

None of us had time to respond to him. His struggle

made me wonder if this incantation would be harder on him. I could have followed him and told him about Grandmother's messages. It wouldn't help his issue though, and she might be sending him his own private communications anyway.

I took in a slow breath and let it out at the same pace.

"Is he going to be okay?" I asked no one in particular.

"I hope so," Mother answered.

"Why is the struggle so hard for him?" Brandon asked.

I answered without pause. "He liked being dark. He embraced it completely." I knew because I liked the strength Darkness offered too. It made me feel invincible and unstoppable. "It's freeing. You don't hurt, and you don't care. When you return to Light, guilt sets in, and it's the guilt and realization of your actions that never goes away."

Mother nodded. "He's never been able to let go of the guilt. It causes depression for him."

"That's why he's so withdrawn," Brandon said, his voice sad.

"Am I going to be depressed and withdrawn too?" Sorin and I shared so many experiences. *Is this another one we will?*

"Brie, don't make everything about you."

I jumped at the sharpness in her voice.

"It's a valid question, Mom," Brandon said. He looped his arm through mine. "And you already have been, Sis."

Mom threw her arms in the air. "And what of your father? I need a glass of wine."

"No wine. We all need a clear head for this thing tonight," Brandon said.

"Of course," she said. "I'll see you at dinner."

We watched her walk through the door.

"What chance do we have, Brie? Our father is depressed if he's not dark, and our mother deals with stress by way of booze."

"Well, I already take after Dad, so you've got Mom." I poked him in the side. "Except you don't really drink much."

"I'm serious."

"I know you are." I gave him a side hug. "How many times have you reminded me we are the ones who decide our path? Are you going to make me remind you of the same?"

"Point made." He put his hands up. "I'll go check on her to make sure she isn't hitting the bottle to deal with it all."

"It's a lot of pressure for her. She's never had to perform a ceremony, and we are asking her to do one that could kill us all. We might all need a drink or ten."

"Are you actually taking up for Mom?"

"Hardly, but it has to be difficult for her. Her entire family is gifted by ancestors, and she's not. Yet, she's the one who will be setting the pace tonight."

"You are taking up for her." He smiled.

"Fine. I'm taking up for her. Go stalk her like you planned."

He stuck his tongue out at me like he did when we were kids and followed the path she took.

)) ● ((

Time with Nick seemed like the best thing I could do for myself until dinner time. He wasn't in our room as I expected. I searched around the mansion in all his favorite spots concerned he might do something rash. *But that's me. I'm the one who does stupid things.*

I paused in the hallway when I saw him in front of the chapel. My heart warmed. I'd used my aura to allow him safe passage in there before our battle with Stefan.

His hands splayed out flat against the door and his head pressed between them.

I made careful steps toward him and tried to remain quiet despite the fact his vampire hearing would have alerted him.

"Want to go in?" I put my hand on his back.

He rolled his head to the side and smiled at me. "Yes, I would."

"Me too." I held my hand out to him.

His hand slid into mine. Warmth built between us. My

pink aura, tinged with some dark, spun around me. I sent it over Nick to encapsulate him. Dark aura wasn't prevented entrance to holy ground, but vampires were.

He squeezed my hand. "I like the way your aura warms me."

My heart melted a little more for him. His love for me was unconditional and present. It was his love that gave me faith when the odds were against us.

"You open the door."

He inhaled deeply into his lungs that no longer required air. A leftover piece of his human life. His hand gripped the knob and turned it.

We stepped through the door together.

"I guess we'll be walking down the aisle like this soon." He leaned over and pressed his lips to my temple.

Marriage had been the furthest from my mind until him, and it had never been further from my grasp than today. "Is this a practice run? Cause I like this kind of practice better than what I had earlier."

"It didn't go well?" Worry lines creased his forehead.

"No, it did. The timing has to be perfect, so hopefully, we all do our part." Practice went as well as it could have, and I was a little more confident in our ability to execute it.

"I want to come," he said. "I should be there." Dad had suggested Nick stay behind, and Nick only agreed because I pleaded with him.

"Sorin insists it's just us to minimize distractions. The guards will be at a distance."

"No one knows the castle like I do," he said as we advanced up the aisle.

"We won't be inside it."

We reached the front of the chapel. Nick took my other hand so that I would face him.

"I'm thankful for you, Brie. I want you to be safe tonight. Come back to me." It pained him to sit the fight out.

"I will do my best."

"You asked me to promise not to wait for you if you turned dark, and I can't make that promise. What I can promise you is I will love you until the end of my existence."

"And I will love you until I have no breath left in me." Even when Darkness had the strongest grasp on me, I still loved him. I might not feel it, but it's there.

"I can't wait to marry you," Nick said. His tone was warm and affectionate.

"It's not too late to elope." My voice broke and so did my heart... into a million pieces.

"Your mother would kill me if I wasn't already undead." Nick tried to keep it light, and I chose to follow his lead.

"I do like my dress though."

"So, there is someone who likes dresses under all that leather."

On our first date, his attire included an oxblood red tie and a suit that fit him like a glove. He was so sexy I couldn't keep my eyes off him. "I wore a dress on our first date. A backless one."

He mulled over the memory. A grin crossed his face. "Mmmmm. Yes, you did, and you looked good in it. It hit all your curves. I wanted to rip it off of you in the restaurant."

I laughed. "Ssh. We are in a chapel."

"So, I shouldn't do this?" He bent his head toward me

and captured my mouth in a lingering kiss. His lips turned up into a smile when he pulled back.

"You should definitely do that. More often too." I smiled back.

He chuckled. "I wish I could stay in here while you are at the castle tonight. It doesn't seem right that you'll be there without me. It's my castle now."

"It's Alastair's at the moment." I shivered inwardly. "His powers will be heightened by the moon like the rest of us. He might be able to control you. That's a chance we can't take."

"You removed the mark he carved on me." He ran a hand over his neck where Alastair's mark had been.

"It made you easy to control. It doesn't mean he can't now. There are incantations that allow those who yield enough power to control vampires, and that kind of power doesn't require any marks." The thought of Alastair's forced control over Nick frightened me.

He nodded. "I concede, my love." He kissed the tip of my nose. "I have two things to do with you after he's neutralized."

"Just two?" I thought of a dozen things I wanted to do with him, but the biggest was to love him for our long lives if I got the chance.

He laughed. "Ssh. We're in a chapel."

I took mock offense. "You like throwing my words back at me. What are your two things?"

"First is to make you my wife."

"That is one I'm looking to for sure." *Even though I doubt Darkness will let it happen. Goddess, you might not listen to me, but I am asking you to bring me back to Nick. Please.* "And second?"

His face hardened in a small but noticeable way. "For us to find out what is up with the witch marks and their attraction to me."

"Mom promised she would tell me what the text means after tonight. We might get an answer to your number two first." I didn't know if I'd make it back to hear it or if I'd be lost to Darkness or if I could even trust my Mother to keep her word.

"You'll always be my number one, Brie. Life rarely gives us do-overs. I'm glad you're mine. I don't want to waste it."

I laid my head against his shoulder. "You're my number one too." A smile spread across my face, and I pressed my lips against his neck "I'll see you when I get back."

It was a bittersweet to say goodbye not knowing if I'd see him again. I took a step away and walked him back down the aisle.

I reached for the doorknob.

"Not so fast." He spun me into his chest.

"I told you when we first met I'm the wrong witch for dancing." I laughed. He brought it out in me.

"And I told you I have exactly the right witch." He devoured my mouth with his.

My body tingled alive. "You make it hard for a witch to take care of her witchy business."

"Hurry back, and I'll take care of your witchy business with my vampire ways." He traced my jaw with his finger still holding my hand in his.

"Promises. Promises."

"That's not a promise. It's a threat." A rueful smile crossed his face.

"I like your threats." I smiled back.

He kissed my forehead. "Go before I decide to do other things to you."

Our fingers lingered together as I reached the door and stepped through. He let go of my hand, and it was like we were transported back to reality. Our world had changed enormously since we found each other at the club. It was about to change even more. Afraid I would go back for more, I didn't look back at him as I walked down the hall.

We would save lives tonight. *Sacrifice for the greater good, Brie.* I sent a silent prayer up. *Please let us do the right thing tonight. Please guide us to the path that will be for all that is good. Blessed be.*

$$) \ ) \cdot \bullet \cdot (\cdot (($$

N ot hungry, I grabbed a bottle of water from the dining hall and returned to the chapel alone for a moment to myself. *Just one*. I walked into the chapel and opened to it. Peace came over me. It wound its way into my soul. I took slow steps to the front and sat on a seat in the first row.

"Light," I whispered. It rushed around me and enforced the peace within me. Light strengthened me from the inside out. If only I could always feel this way. *This might be the last time Light responds*. To call to Light tonight would be a disaster for the ceremony. To call to Light would be guaranteed failure. The ceremony needed Hell's Fire and both mine and Sorin's Darkness as a magnet to Alastair's.

"Grandmother, if you can hear me, tell me I'm doing the right thing. I have doubt in my heart. Doubt in my soul." The ball of light I'd seen a few times before appeared in front of me. "It is you." A smile grew on my face. "I miss you so much.

I hope you know how much I love you. I'm not sure I told you enough when you were here."

The ball of light, Grandmother, danced in the air in front of me. "I guess you did know." My smile broadened. "It's not the same without you here. We need you as much today as we did twenty years ago when mother tried to bind our powers." She stilled in the air in front of my face.

"I don't know if I'm strong enough to do this. It's ripping me apart inside. I fought to get back to the Light a couple of times now, and it's harder every time. Darkness has a hold on me now. It's permanent, and I know it is. Just like Dad." The permanency of Darkness inside me discouraged me and spiked my fear.

She hovered in one spot. It reminded me of how she would sit with me and wait for me to figure out solutions on my own. Grandmother was being Grandmother even from the grave.

"You think I can figure this out on my own, but I'm not so sure. It pains me. It could break me. It nearly did."

She remained stationary in front of me.

"What about Dad? He's already struggling. We might lose him to Darkness forever tonight. We thought he was dead, but he showed up alive. Then he really did die, but I somehow brought him back with my aura only he's linked to Hell's Fire, maybe even closer than I am. Now, we might lose him forever to those flames. My heart hurts. Physical pain."

She made a pattern in the air. After a few passes, I could see it was a heart.

My hand went to my heart and tears welled in my eyes. "I wish I could hug you."

She held in place like she waited for me again.

"You're waiting for me to come to the conclusions I need. We reasoned so much out together. I know I'm not alone, but I feel that way a lot. It's isolating to be the queen. The burden of this damn prophecy shit is isolating too. Sorry for cursing in the chapel. I know you wouldn't approve of that."

I stood and walked to the front of the chapel where the altar was. On it, a consecration cross placed for Grandmother's funeral.

She joined me and made circles around the cross.

My fingertips hovered over it unsure if I should touch it.

Her circles faster as if to draw me to it.

My hand laid against the precious metal and gemstone in the center. Blue light shot from between my fingertips. My jaw dropped. I'd seen the cross touched many times by the elders and never had light emanated from it.

Grandmother held still in front of me.

I removed my hand, and the light ceased to shine. My fingers wrapped around the cross, and I picked it up. The blue light returned.

"I don't understand," I said.

She shot in a straight line to the door.

"I can't take the cross from the chapel." I shook my head.

She flew up to the tip of my nose, and then back to the door.

"The elders will not excuse this even for the queen." I frowned and followed her to the entrance, but it wouldn't be the first time I disappointed them. "What do I even do with it if I do remove it from the chapel?"

She passed through the closed wooden door.

I opened the door to where she waited for me. "Okay. Where are we going? I hope we don't meet anyone along the way. I'll look silly saying I'm following a ball of light that told me to take this ancient cross from the chapel."

She took off down the hall.

"Slow down. Some of us don't move that fast unless we teleport."

She paused to wait for me. If a ball of pure energy could have its hands on its hips, it would have. No doubt in my mind.

"You're taking us awful close to the Elders Council room," I whispered.

The light stopped in front of the scroll room. *Ugh.*

"We've been over this tiny room in detail."

She passed through the door.

I waved my hand to unlock it and opened the door. The lights were out and wouldn't come on when I waved my hand.

Grandmother danced in front of a section of wall.

My thigh met the corner of the table with a thud. "Damn it. That hurt. I can't freaking see."

She glowed brighter shining more light to guide my way.

Always guiding.

I made my way to the corner. "What is that on the wall?" I ran my hand over it. An impression like the cross in my other hand. "Is it the same?"

She darted back and forth in front of it.

The impression had the details of the consecration cross. "Why would someone put this here?" I leaned in closer. "It's incredible how perfect the details are."

She paused in front of me and then scooted to the side of the impression.

I held the cross up close to it. They looked like they were made for each other. I shrugged and lined the cross up to the spot on the wall. *It's not like I'm not already torn between Light and Dark. Not much else could happen that would be worse than what I'm already dealing with today.* When I pushed it in, the radiant blue light shined from it and filled the room.

"That's beautifully amazing." I twirled in the light. "Why did we need to do this tonight?"

The blue light focused into a beam. The beam zeroed in on one of the locked drawers in the wall.

I crossed the room and waved my hand in front of it.

The drawer popped open. It overflowed with scrolls and handwritten texts.

"What is this, Grandmother?"

She danced around it avoiding the blue beam.

I pulled one of the scrolls out and opened it, shocked by the number of scrolls stuffed in the drawer.

"The Blood Moon Prophecy." The sentences were legible to me from the deciphering I did earlier. I read aloud the words scrawled across the top. "Is this the original? I thought that was it in the book."

The lights came on in the room. I jerked my head up and looked around, but no one else was there.

I sat on the seat closest to me and began to read. "This doesn't match the book."

Grandmother hovered next to me.

"If this is true, there is much more to the prophecy than

we were originally led to believe." Fear fought through the Darkness in me, but there was hope there too.

She held still.

"Why do witches keep so many secrets? It's bullshit," I said. My voice overloaded with my frustration and Darkness wanted more.

She waited. There was something specific she wanted me to find. Or it was another hands on the hips moment.

"What am I supposed to see here? I don't have time to read this entire drawer."

She didn't budge.

I scanned the document. "Holy shit." I read the paragraph again out loud this time. "The Blood Moon Queen will come to power to right the wrongs of her ancestors. She will unite those thought impossible. Her peace will be a lasting peace."

My hands went into my hair. I stared at the words, not sure what to think. It wasn't all about Darkness. I wasn't all about Darkness. The passage shook me. "This is what the elders don't want to get out. I'm supposed to be righting the wrongs we inflicted on the vampires." I paused. "Those manipulative bastards."

She jumped to the tip of my nose.

"Sorry. My mouth is worse these days. I'm tired and over the lies and concealment."

My eyes returned to the text. "By her side, he shall rule. Her chosen mate, a king in his own right." I sank back. "So, his tattoo is because of me. He liked having his own mission." I read on. "He shall see what she cannot. He will be the light she seeks in her darkest hour. The King shall end the torment from his time." The text confused me, but as I studied it, some hope worked its way into my thoughts.

I looked up at Grandmother, still stationary in front of me.

"He does have his own path. His torment is from the death of his family though. Stefan's dead, but the tattoo appeared around the same time."

She dove down to the text.

"Blood Moon entwined. No one shall divide." I smiled at her. "It's written in the text as part of the prophecy."

She circled over my left hand.

"After we get through tonight, we'll get back to the wedding planning. You were supposed to do the ceremony. It's hard for me to think of anyone else conducting it." My heart constricted. I went back to the text. "All that is broken will be healed or all will be destroyed by the fourth moon of the tetrad." The saliva got stuck in my throat when I swallowed and forced me to cough.

"This is what you wanted me to see. We're on the second moon tonight. Halfway through the tetrad. I have to figure out how to heal all that is broken by the fourth one or it will be the end times. I can't believe the elders kept this from me." *Did they know? How could they not?* "They have a plan I'm sure. We know they always do. They do more damage this way. I'll make them realize it."

She dropped back on the tip of my nose to warn me.

"Keep it to myself. At least for now. Got it. You realize it doesn't make me any better than them. I'll look at it like now I know what they know."

My phone buzzed in my pocket with a text. *Brandon.*

Where are you? Mom is looking for you

Tell her I'll see her after dinner

You'll have to deal with her

I slipped the phone back into my pocket. Dinner was not a priority at the moment.

"Can I tell them after tonight? Mom, Dad, Brandon, and Nick that is."

She didn't move.

"I can always choose to do what I want. I need their help especially without you here. Yes, I said I need help."

She floated next to my cheek and a tiny bit of warmth grazed it.

I picked up another text. "The Blood Moon Queen's gifts will outnumber all those known. Her power a price she alone must pay. If Darkness she seeks, Darkness she shall find. Darkness will claim her to end the fight." My stomach sank and sweat formed on my palms. "So, no matter what I do Darkness will claim me?"

Grandmother moved left to right in front of me.

"This doesn't sound like I have a choice." I skipped down in the text. "Light will find the queen only when the circle is complete." I looked at her. "Meaning I complete the prophecy and right the wrongs. No pressure with this job ever."

I shuffled the contents of the drawer and picked out a sealed envelope. "This one looks a little newer than the others." A letter inside.

To The Blood Moon Queen,

You have been chosen for an impossible task. Our ancestors inflicted harm on the vampires long before you were born. Time passed and peace settled in except for the small group who sought to control the vampire culture. They seek to return to the times where vampires were used to create a dark and semi-controllable race of witches. The consequences of such actions would be catastrophic to humans, vampires, and witches alike.

Surround yourself with people you trust though they will be few. Your family will be key to your success and should be part of your circle. Keep the circle small and watch for unexpected allies. Some will be true and others not.

The path to the prophecy will be difficult and tedious with sacrifices along the way. Undoubtedly, you will lose friends, followers, and loved ones. Do not let that harden your heart to the Light in the world and the good you will ultimately do.

Use your gifts wisely and for the right purpose to stay on the path to success. Abusing your gifts will lead you down the path to Dark-

ness. Darkness does serve a purpose and has a place in the prophecy, but don't let it consume your heart. We are depending on you to walk the line between both Dark and Light.

Believe in yourself. Believe in your strength. Believe in your abilities. Most of all, believe in the love in your heart.

"IT'S NOT SIGNED," I said. "Or dated. The language is different. I wonder who wrote it." It was written with knowledge and education on the prophecy. Someone intimated with texts only available to senior members of the Coven. "It was a past queen."

"It's getting late. I have to meet everyone. Can you come with me?"

She hovered in place.

"I didn't think you would, but I had to ask. They all miss you too. Dad is having a particularly hard time. If you can visit him, it might do him some good." I stood up from the table. "Will I see you again?"

She warmed my check again.

I didn't know if that was a yes or no, but it was like a hug.

"I love you," I said.

The contents returned to the drawer, I waved my hand to lock it. Mother didn't know the scrolls were there, but I wasn't taking a chance. The consecration cross in my hand, I turned to look for Grandmother before I left the room, but she was already gone. I teleported to the chapel to return the cross.

NINETEEN

)) · ● · ((

Silverware clinked against the plates. I looked around the room at Brandon and my mother. Everyone had the same thing in common. They all pushed the food around on their plates versus eating it. The meal felt like a last supper style dinner and maybe it was.

"Anyone seen Dad yet?" I asked.

"He said he'd meet us at the door." Brandon pushed back from the table.

I worried whether my father would be there or not. My faith in myself wavered the stronger the flames grew in his eyes. I saw what I could become. To barely be in control frightened me. The taste I'd had of it showed me I was capable of doing things to hurt the people I love. It, also, showed me I was capable of fighting it. I could overcome it which meant there was hope for Dad. Sorin had overcome it once. He could do it again.

The doors to the dining room flew open. Cal burst into

the private area. "I'm so sorry to disturb you." His face flushed a bright shade of red.

I jumped up from my seat. "Cal, you're not. You were invited. What's going on?" My stomach quivered with nausea.

"The Elders are on their way. They are not happy you are going tonight. You don't have a line of succession." His words came in bursts between breaths.

It enraged me that they would expect me to not go. "Declaring a successor means declaring my death."

He gasped for air. He must have sprinted all the way here. "They want you to name an intended successor. Not the ceremony to formally declare it which starts the death process."

"How did they even find out? We were so careful not to tell them," Brandon said.

"Michael. He had a vision," Cal said.

"Let's go before they find us. Where are they now?" Mother moved toward the door.

"Too late." Cal shook his head. "They're right behind me."

A small tap on the open door drew our attention.

"Michael, how good of you and the Elders to stop in." Mom greeted him with a kiss on each cheek and positioned herself between them and us.

"Katerina," he said. "We are concerned for our Queen. Are you aware of the plan for tonight?"

"Yes, of course." Mother kept a steady gaze with Michael.

"And the queen's participation?"

"I'm in the room," I said. "You will address me."

Cal and Brandon stood on either side of me.

"Your Majesty," Michael said, his tone respectful. "May we join you?"

"You may." I gestured to open seats at the table and took the position at the head of the table.

Michael's calm demeanor made me suspicious. "My Queen, we have concerns with the activities tonight. Your risk is too great. We cannot allow it."

"Let's make one thing clear right now. It is not your decision. It is mine and has been made. If you have seen something other than success tonight, please do share."

Michael's expression did not change. "I have only seen you and your family mixing light and dark magic for use on another witch," he said. "This is not allowed, as you know."

I held his gaze in a long dramatic pause. They would not change my mind, nor would they bully me into hiding tonight. "A traitor to all of us."

"Your participation is our only concern. Should something happen to you and your family, there will be no one to lead us."

"Yes, there will. Cal was confirmed as my second in command. If I and the members of my family are unable to lead the coven, Cal is the most logical choice." I'd planned to name Brandon as the intended successor, but he'd be with me tonight. It had to be Cal.

"He is your unofficial successor?" One of Michael's eyebrows raised in question. The only sign of emotion exposed under his facade of collected demeanor.

"Until my gifts provide an official choice, he is."

"The Elders have not approved this choice," Michael said. "Please reconsider."

Normally, an intended successor would be presented to the Elders. They'd forced my hand, and I didn't regret naming Cal. "Again, he was confirmed as my second in command. I'm sorry if you have an issue with my choice, but I'm not someone who seeks the approval of others."

"My queen, may I speak freely?" He eyed Cal.

Cal's eyes were wider than usual, but his face bore an otherwise stoic expression.

"I'd expect nothing less." I'd already figured out where he was going.

"He's the son of the traitor you are going to eliminate tonight."

I sucked in air to hold in my annoyance. It irked me how they refused to see how loyal Cal was. "Our goal is to capture Alastair tonight, and Cal has proven his loyalty on many occasions. He is not his father."

"He's not a member of the Dallas coven."

My patience started to wear, and Darkness was eager to strike. I drummed my fingers on the table. "I wasn't aware that is a requirement of witches, especially the head of all covens?"

"The Queen's personal advisors should pledge their allegiance to her through the ruling coven."

"I see." I turned to Cal. His face betrayed no emotion. "Is this something you'd be comfortable doing?"

"Of course, B..." he paused and looked at the Elders. "Of course, Your Majesty."

"So, what do we need to do to initiate him into the ruling coven?" I asked, keeping my voice neutral.

"I can guide you through it, My Queen," Michael said, seemingly satisfied.

"Let's get on with it then," I said.

"I'll retrieve the book and return shortly with those that will serve as witnesses."

"We are leaving in forty-five minutes. If you are not back by then, we are leaving anyway."

"Yes, Your Majesty."

Michael left and the elders, who had stood silently behind him, filed out of the room after him.

"Seriously? Is this a delay tactic?"

"No, they are right. It is code for the queen's advisors to pledge their loyalty to her coven just as she pledges to it when she assumes the throne," Cal said.

"I've never heard this."

"I remember it from class," Brandon said.

"Yes, they are all correct. It's more of a tradition than a code though," Mother said.

I bit back the Darkness ready to strike. "So, it is a delay tactic."

"They are trying to force you into doing things the traditional way," Brandon said.

"Are they ever going to accept my way of leadership? I know I have a different style, but it'd be nice to be supported by the Council like Cecily was."

"They didn't always support her. She had a lot of resistance early on in her time as queen," Mother said. "It took her quite some time after your father left to win them over."

"They are Council to the Queen, but they are overseers of Coven Law too. It's their job to make sure the coven is protected," Cal said.

After what I found in the room, I questioned the elders' actual motivation. My trust in them was little to none, but I did trust Cal.

A rap at the door drew our attention for the second time tonight.

"Come in," I said.

Michael returned with the Elders. They all wore solemn expressions for the occasion.

"I'll lead Cal through his pledge if you please, Your Majesty."

"Yes, that would be helpful."

Michael opened a circle in the room.

"I bind you to the circle of truth." He touched Cal's shoulder with one hand and held a text out in the other. "Callum Kingston of the London Coven, where does your allegiance lie?"

Cal's hand shook as he placed it over the book. "With my queen and my people."

"Name your queen."

"My allegiance is to Queen Brielle of the Dallas Coven," he said, his voice confident and strong.

"Name your coven."

"My allegiance is to the coven of my queen. I swear my life to the service of Queen Brielle and the Dallas Coven." The strength in his voice grew with each step of the process.

"My Queen, do you accept the pledge of your follower, Callum Kingston?" Michael looked at me.

Pride in Cal helped me stand taller. "Yes. Yes, I accept the pledge."

"On behalf of our Queen, we thank you for your dedication of service to Queen Brielle and the ruling Coven," Michael said.

"Thank you for your assistance, Michael. If you could leave us alone now," I said.

"Of course, my Queen. I'll close the circle, and we'll depart."

He led the elders from the room.

"Seriously? That little thing was what the fuss was about? How does it prove anything?" I scoffed.

"It's a public declaration in a truth circle. It has more weight than you think," Mother said. "Although, it ideally would have been done in front of the entire local coven."

"Sis, don't be so hard on them. We all want the same thing."

"I wonder sometimes." I bit my lip to keep from spilling the secret contents Grandmother had led me to.

"Brandon's right. We all want peace," Cal said.

"Their way and my way don't seem to match up on how that'll be achieved."

"No, they don't, but that is part of what makes the ultimate solutions great. It's the best of both you and them."

I took in the food on the table and nothing looked appetizing to me.

"I don't think I can eat," Brandon said. "I've cut this steak into small enough pieces each resident of an ant farm could have their own."

I burst into laughter. "Really? Do you have a lot of experience feeding ants?"

Mom and Cal laughed along with me.

Brandon's face turned red. "You know exactly what I mean. You haven't even made a plate."

I regained my composure. "No, I haven't. You're right."

"I'd suggest we circle to calm our nerves, but I think we need to reserve our power for tonight," Mother said.

She needed to reserve hers. Brandon and I would recover by the time we left from a small spell. Neither of us pointed it out.

"And you won't reconsider going tonight, Brie?" Cal asked.

"No, my family is right. This is our chance."

He nodded in acquiescence.

"Cal, I promise you I will do everything in my power to capture him alive." I'd do my best to keep that promise. The pain of losing a parent was life-changing, and I didn't want to force that on him. If Alastair forced me, I'd do what was necessary.

Cal placed a hand over mine. "I'm your subject as sworn before your family and the elders. My loyalty is with you, but I will not lie by saying I don't fear him."

"I understand." I grasped his shoulder. "Someone told me we rarely get second chances in life. I hope you get one with him, my friend." I had little faith Alastair was redeemable, but I wouldn't be the one to steal Cal's faith.

"We need to go meet Sorin at the door," Brandon said. "It's time to leave."

I squeezed Cal's shoulder on my way out the door.

"I can still go with you," he said.

Even if he could go, I wouldn't ask him to face his father in this situation. "No, you are my unofficial successor. You are doing your part by staying here."

He nodded, his face pained.

Mother was on my heels, but I noticed Brandon wasn't with us halfway down the hall. His absence concerned me. I turned to look for him and glanced at Mom. She shrugged. I walked back to the dining room door.

Brandon and Cal were in a tight embrace. Cal pulled back and cupped Brandon's face. He placed a soft kiss on Brandon's lips.

I smiled. *When did this happen?* I crossed my arms and leaned against the doorjamb. It does explain why they were always looking for each other when they weren't in the same room. They looked damn good together. Witches believed in one love, so they would be accepted here for the most part. Too bad the humans hadn't learned how precious love is and to let it happen and evolve as is in one's heart. Brandon and Cal matched each other well. *Not that they need it, but I totally approve. Maybe I'll get another brother out of this.* It does explain why they were always looking for each other when they weren't in the same room. *We all just need to survive tonight.*

"Hmm. Hmm." I cleared my throat.

"Brie," Brandon said, his eyes dancing. "I didn't know you were still here.

"And I didn't know this was happening, so I guess we're even." I winked at them.

"You're not angry?" Cal asked, gauging my reaction.

"No," I said. "Why would I be?"

Brandon put his forehead against Cal's. "We'll do our best to purge the dark magic from him and return your father." My brother wanted to give Cal hope too.

"Come on lover boy," I said. "Dad will be waiting."

Brandon gave Cal one last quick kiss and joined my side.

"So how long—"

"Later, Sis. Now is not the time."

"You're right," I said and looped my arm threw his. "But I expect to hear every detail tomorrow. Every one." *If we're here that is.*

He rolled his eyes, eliciting a laugh from me. "Let's just focus on our task tonight."

I dropped it because he was right. We did need to be aligned and centered like we never had before.

We walked to where Mother waited. A pang of guilt hit my chest. If I had to kill Alastair, I wouldn't hesitate. The hate in me for him was strong. He'd hurt my family to get to me, and forgiveness wasn't easy for me. No, I wouldn't hesitate if it needed to be done. The guilt was for Cal. I didn't want my friend to know the pain I dealt with in my life nor for it to be at my hand. As Queen and a pissed off fiancée and for all the innocents he murdered, I'd do it with vengeance for all he'd harmed.

I studied my brother as we walked to the door where we would be meeting Dad. *Would Brandon forgive me if I'm forced to kill Cal's father? If they are together, he is the one Cal will lean on while he grieves.*

Sorin pushed off the door when we reached the entryway. He looked outwardly calm, but he never raised his head to acknowledge us. Strange even for him.

I watched the SUVs pull up. My nerves and anticipation made me fidget with Darkness. "Dad, are you okay?" I whispered.

"I'm fine." He turned his head toward me not raising his eyes to meet mine. Flames danced in them. They flared enough I didn't have to meet his eyes to see them.

I'd been there and understood how far in he was. "Don't do this."

"We all pay a price for this life. I'm paying mine tonight." He'd let Darkness in as deep as he could and still keep some control for the incantation tonight.

"No, we'll find another way."

"We're committed," he paused. "I'm committed." He raised his head this time and met my eyes. His eyes were solid black like they had been colored in. The only color in his eyes was the orange and red of the flames there.

He'd given into Darkness to strengthen the spell, so I wouldn't have to. My guilt rivaled the brokenness in me the day he died.

"We'll take separate vehicles there," Sorin said.

"I'll ride with you, Dad." Brandon followed him to the lead vehicle with some of the guards.

Mom and I climbed into the other vehicle with my personal guards.

"Taking the autos will prevent him from detecting us?" Mom asked when the vehicle moved.

"If he is expecting me to teleport or a group to transport there, yes. It should give us the element of surprise."

"That's good." She fidgeted in the seat.

"Focus, Mom. I know you're nervous, but this might be the most important thing you will ever do in your life. Concentrate on the task at hand."

"No, the most important thing I've done is give birth to two children who can conquer the world, but they choose to rescue it instead. You and Brandon are gifts, not only to me but to those who don't even know they need to be rescued." She reached for my hand but didn't take it.

"Mom," I paused. Tears filled my eyes. "That's probably the nicest thing you've ever said to me."

"I should have said it sooner." She took my hand and clutched it in a firm warm grasp.

"It's going to be okay, Mom." I squeezed back. "We are going to be successful."

"I'm worried one of these battles we will all not come back." She stared out the window. She didn't have to say who she meant. I worried about Sorin too.

"We're witches battling vampires, so that risk exists every time we clash whether that's a hunt or a battle. We can't let that prevent us from doing the right thing." *And I couldn't let it stop me from ending Alastair if that is what it takes to stop him.*

She wiped at her eyes. "Of course not."

The first part of the vision from earlier flashed through my mind. The castle hadn't appeared in it, so I convinced myself it wasn't tonight. The sun had started to rise so definitely not during the night. *Nope. Not happening tonight.*

The SUV stopped at a distance from the castle. We stepped out of the car and lined up at the edge of the perimeter. A wet grass smell mixed with the stench of death swarmed us, but there were no guards, vampires, or witches, to meet us.

"We'll go on foot from here and get in position like we practiced this morning," Sorin said.

We climbed down the slope in silence except for the rocks knocked loose by our unsure footing. Sorin reached the bottom first and assisted the rest of us. He didn't make eye contact.

"Everyone remember where they should stand?"

I nodded, ready to wield whatever magic needed to succeed.

Brandon stood between us like we practiced.

"We'll be positioned there." Sorin pointed to a small rise several yards ahead.

Mom wiped her hands down her hips. My nerves skittered up my spine like little shocks. I opened and closed my fists to release some of the nervous energy.

"Katerina, we'll need you focused. There is little room for error if any. You'll stand here and wait for the signal." He positioned her in her place and walked toward the rise.

The flush on her face wasn't embarrassment. It was stress. If she breaks, we all break. *We all die.*

"We've got some time, Mom. Take a few deep breaths with me." I said. "In slowly and out slowly."

We took several breaths together until her cheeks looked a more normal color.

"Your father doesn't look good."

I bit my lip to keep from telling her she didn't either. Her hair was not the smooth coif of her style. Her clothes wrinkled in places. She didn't have the usual confidence in her voice either. We were a ragged mess of emotion and stress. *Goddess, protect us tonight and guide us to the right path tonight.*

"No, but we'll have to deal with that afterward. You can't control him. He makes his own decisions," I said.

"You are so much like him," she paused. Her eyes widened. "In the good ways."

"I got it, Mom." I smiled. "I've seen it too."

She watched him and Brandon. "Whatever he does tonight, forgive him."

I cocked my head to the side. "What do you think he's going to do Mom?"

"He'll do whatever it takes to keep us all safe," she said, frustration in her voice. "Whatever it takes."

"Then you should know, so will I," I said. Mom squeezed my hands.

Footsteps meandered up behind me but stopped short.

"Brie, time to get in position," Sorin said.

"Go team," I said, Sarcasm was unavoidable with the thick tension in the air. It was an old defense mechanism of mine.

Brandon gave me one single shake of his head.

"Katerina, remember to wait for the signal." He turned to me. His hand was at my elbow. "It's going to be quite a drain, but you'll need to push through it." He whispered.

"I anticipated it would be. And there's no danger to Brandon or Mom?" I tried to make eye contact with him, but he wouldn't meet my gaze.

"There's always danger," he said. "Stand here." He kissed my cheek. It felt like a goodbye.

If he was worried it didn't show, but his actions distanced him from us like the flames in his eyes burned.

"Brandon, here."

Sorin moved himself into position. "Hands exactly where I showed you earlier." He glanced at Brandon.

I inhaled a deep breath and settled my mind and my nerves. The air around me stirred with energy. It made it difficult to find the spot where I could center myself. I looked up to the full moon. *The Blood Moon.*

The light from the moon glowed around us. The energy ready to fuel us for the burden on our shoulders. I drank in the light. Soaked up every ray. It filled the empty parts inside me where Darkness would live by the end of this ceremony.

"Katerina, be ready when I tell you," Sorin said, his voice barely a whisper.

"I'm ready," she said.

"Brandon, are you ready?"

"Yes," he said. He trembled.

I wanted to send calming energy his way, but I needed it all tonight.

"Brie?"

"I was born for this," I said with confidence.

He nodded. A pulse radiated out from him. "That's only going to knock them out for a few minutes. Time to work."

Hell's Fire sprung from mine and Sorin's fingertips and formed a narrow circle around the circumference of the castle. It stood not quite knee height. We needed more.

I reached inside myself for strength to power the fire. It earned me another inch. *Damn it.* The wall grew several inches, but it didn't stay there. It dropped back down to the previous level.

Hell's Fire bent to my will or so I told myself. A barrier inside me prevented me from fulfilling my part of the ceremony. My fear for my family and my choice for light seemed to be the problem.

I focused my energy on the fire. Hell's Fire. The flames refused to build the wall we planned. My energy drained quicker than I'd anticipated. My knees threatened to buckle under me, and I strained to stay upright.

Alastair had a protection placed on the castle. There was no other answer. A protection that zapped our energy. Not that we hadn't expected something, but not like this.

Brandon lowered his head in a bowed position. Concentration lines crossed his face. He didn't look as weak as I felt.

Sorin stood upright. His eyes open and directed at the castle. The flames in them darted my direction and back to the castle. His aura black, rolled around him like a boiling pot. "Brie, call to it."

My heart wouldn't open to Darkness. I'd chosen light, and my heart didn't want to fight Darkness on that level again. I didn't want to fight Darkness again. I needed Darkness today for the power. Its power would give Alastair to us if we could pull it off.

I gave way to a bit of Darkness, and it followed the cracks to work in. The warmth made me flutter with excitement.

Hell's Fire responded with growth to the firewall.

"I'm afraid. I'm afraid for all of you if I let go." The version of me consumed by dark wasn't a good person. *If I let go, will that version finish the ceremony?*

TWENTY

S orin looked at me with fires raging in his eyes. "Brie, you have to trust Brandon will anchor us. Let go, damn it. Give into it the way we discussed."

He'd relinquished completely to Darkness. His eyes were a reflection of that choice. He'd told me to balance on the edge and not give way to tip over it. He failed there, whether on accident or on purpose. That line could mean the difference between him coming back or not.

If I tipped over, I'd be lost. No doubt in my mind, but everyone standing here with me held higher importance. Everyone we intended to save was the reason we were here. *Sacrifice.*

I let go. In one quick action, I booted my mental wedge that left light in sight. The Darkness slithered inside my protective shell. Fractures of pink disappeared. Consumed by it. Heat swelled inside my body and burned the goodness in me. A sheen of sweat coated my skin. The smoky odor of the fire and the salty scent of my sweat mixed in the air around me.

My mind stayed on task even as the dark aura choked the Light from me.

Hell's Fire.

Fuel the spell.

Contain the magic within.

Alastair.

The tasks ticked off in my head in the same order I memorized them. My priority zoned into Alastair. This was my link to keep me grounded until the circle did its job.

Brandon stood between us. His hands rested one on each of us. The skin usually a pinkish color on his face was now pale. The Darkness in Sorin and I depleted his strength. An anchor's job was just as it sounded. He weighted us down to reality and kept the dark abated. Even the most powerful witches would be drained.

It had been one of my initial concerns.

He closed his eyes in fierce concentration.

A surge passed through me. I focused on driving the fire around the castle. The flames answered and grew higher. Taller than I'd ever seen. I wanted more. Darkness wanted more.

Mother's voice barely carried over the roar of the blaze. "North."

I couldn't see her, but I followed the sound of her voice. She made a quarter turn for each one she called.

"South."

"East."

"West."

Darkness gripped my heart and mind. The evil twisted thoughts pushed me to challenge the circle. Light would weaken Hell's Fire and the strength of the circle. *Can't call to it.* I focused my mind on Grandmother and her words. *Believe in Light.* I could believe in it without calling upon it. Grandmother exuded good. She'd helped my mother. She'd helped me. Her life lived in the Light. Never did she stray to the Darkness. Never was she tempted like I was. Her resolve and strength passed to Brandon.

Brandon was pure like her. Untainted by the Darkness smattering my soul. Reinforced by Grandmother's gift.

Unlike me. My brother had all the goodness. No one would call me pure. The entire coven knew the prophecy and heard the rumors I'd been consumed by Darkness. I relented to the Darkness and allowed it space to take root.

The flames rose higher. We almost had the castle in a fire dome.

"Brie, whatever you're doing, it's helping. Keep it up," Sorin said.

Great. Recounting how I don't match up to the good people around me helps this spell. Of course, it does.

"Light, I can't call to you, so forgive me for letting Darkness loose." I closed my eyes. "Hell's Fire!" I sang to the depths of the Darkness in me. Vibrations shook me. The words came out in a voice that was not my own. Not one I recognized anyway. Heat seared through me, and I opened my lids.

The fire encircled and encompassed the building like a dome. Darkness had me. All of me except the one tiny wedge of pink I clung to. The sliver of hope that Brandon could pull me back from this shadowed abyss.

"Now, Katerina!" Sorin's voice boomed over the flames. I didn't look at him. Darkness chose me. Claimed me. If it spared my father, then my choice was made too.

Mom's hands went up, but I couldn't hear her words over the roar of the firestorm Sorin and I created.

The energy swirling around us intensified. The powerful ceremony worked inside the dome. Alastair appeared in the circle. The incantation drew Alastair's aura to us. Darkness surged around me and collapsed down on me like a fiery wetsuit.

I wanted to look at Sorin to see if he acknowledged what I sensed. A chance I couldn't take to hold the fire in place.

Alastair struggled in the center of the circle. His hand out and rage marred his face. He fought hard against the spell, but Darkness wanted his power. It no longer favored him with so much strength in the circle.

Brandon and Mom were in view, and I could see them becoming weaker from the tug of war.

The aura came into sight, and it was dark. Darker than mine. Darker than Dad's. It was like a black hole in time and space. I looked at Brandon.

He knew. His face was in a grimace. In a labored movement, he shook his head back and forth.

I looked past him to Sorin.

His concentration was solid on our mission. He hadn't seen what Brandon was about to take inside him, but in my heart, I knew he'd been part of the decision I'd been excluded from in this plan.

Betrayal. They'd made a pact behind my back, and the betrayal threatened to blast my last little wedge of light away.

Vampires tried to cross the fire to get to Alastair. Ash floated in the air at their attempts. The fire kept them at bay, but it didn't keep the witches loyal to Alastair away. They exited the castle and came toward us. We were out of time, and Mom and Brandon grew weaker as Sorin and I grew stronger.

My eyes went to the aura and back to Brandon.

He mouthed, "No."

He'd never be Brandon again if I didn't stop it. The thought of his kindness and warmth eaten away from the abyss Darkness leaves was more than I could sacrifice. He'd just found love, and I wouldn't allow that to be taken from him. He wasn't gifted to withstand Darkness like I was nor could he destroy it as I could. It had to be me.

Energy flew from one of my hands toward the aura and toward the advancing witches. The aura disappeared. The witch guards fell to the ground.

The aura reformed into a dark mass. *What the fuck!*

"Brie, you can't stop it. We need to contain it," Sorin said through gritted teeth.

"Brandon is not a box built to contain evil. He's my brother. Your son. Not happening," I yelled to Sorin over the roar. "And don't give me bullshit about destiny or duty," I said to Brandon.

He didn't move. Didn't say a word. Sweat ran down the side of his face. He concentrated on anchoring us in place. My Darkness barely at bay. His eyes closed. It was harder for him than for us. Darkness didn't live in him like it did Sorin and me.

"No, he's a conduit, and he knows what he is doing."

"A conduit?" I whispered under my breath. My eyes sought out Brandon's.

He opened them this time and met mine. The struggle behind his answered my question.

He knew.

Sorin knew.

Now I knew.

Brandon anchored us in place not to Light but to receive Alastair's dark aura. They knew I wouldn't agree to my brother being the recipient.

My lids flitted closed. Tears pooled in them. I wouldn't watch the Darkness flow into him. I imagined myself in front of the tiny wedge holding the door open in my pink aura, and I kicked it out of place. Darkness curtained my vision, and the burn jolted me when it flowed into me. My body absorbed it. Lavished in it. My pink aura, the good part of me, pushed back. The struggle between light and dark raged inside of me. The black aura caressed the chinks in my armor until it squeezed in to stake its final claim. Even before I opened my eyes, I sensed my pink aura had been extinguished.

Lost again. I wanted to let go, and it was only a time before my feelings and emotions drifted far away until they were winked out. I'd lost myself in the Darkness. To not have to fight to be good anymore. It was easier to not care. It was easier to not love. It was easier to not feel.

Except even in the dark, I cared. Even consumed in Darkness, I loved. I buried it, but it was still there under the numbness.

Brandon collapsed between us.

My eyes flamed and heat built in me. I looked to Sorin. His eyes full ablaze. He must have called Darkness to him too.

My knees gave way. I dropped beside Brandon and steadied my hands over him. No healing energy came. Darkness forbid it and consumed my desperation.

I glanced at Sorin, and he turned and walked away without a word.

Solitude. I understood his choice in a way no one else could. The only time the Darkness allowed peace within its capture. He left to keep from destroying those he loved, and I was the only one who would get it.

Love. It's what both of us chose today more than once.

Mom's voice behind me jumbled in my head. *Closing the circle.*

Steps pounded past me and drew my eyes up. *Mom.*

She chased after him. I'd never seen her run after a man, but he disappeared into the dark of night before she could catch him.

"Mom, Brandon needs you." My voice boomed out toward her.

Tears stained her cheeks. She let out an ear-splitting wail. "Heal him, Brie," she pleaded.

"I can't," I whispered.

I scrambled to my feet against the weakness beckoning me to stay on the ground. Darkness answered and filled me with heat and power.

"We need to get you both home," I said.

Mother gained composure. "You need to make sure Alastair doesn't get away," she said, wiping tears away. "Go now, Brie."

"Send the guards to find me when they get here," I said. "They need to be ready to contain me."

Ella appeared from the shadows. "I couldn't get near with the flames," she said.

"I might still need you," I said. "We need to take care of Alastair first though."

I wanted to lay on the ground and fold in myself. To rest the weariness in me. To sleep the reality into oblivion. I made the way to where Alastair laid on the ground. Ella followed. The pit in my stomach grew with dread of the anger I'd meet when Alastair and I came face to face. Darkness would be ready for it, and I hoped I was strong enough to resist.

His hair turned a stark pure white. After closer examination, I found his skin showed age. Lots of it. He looked every bit his two hundred years.

His labored breaths gasped for air.

I crouched beside him, not wanting to get too close. He couldn't do anything, at least not with magic.

He motioned for me to come closer.

I inched his direction with Ella at my side.

"My essence," he said, his voice hardly audible. "I'm dying."

That wasn't the plan. Not unless it was the only choice. I sucked in air and gagged. *The rot of death.* My powers couldn't heal him. Darkness drove that one away. Darkness whispered to finish him, and I struggled to fight against it.

What would the cost be to the rest of the coven? To the humans? To the vampires? If I let him die like this, would the power die with him? Darkness relented, seeming to agree with saving him.

"Damn it." I positioned my hands over him. My fingers spread wide. *Heal his body, not his powers.* I repeated the mantra in my head. Not sure if Light could discern the difference, but I hoped it would obey my command.

But light didn't appear. A drop of Darkness fell from my index finger to his chest. The age wiped from his skin, but his hair remained bright white like a battle scar.

He sat up. "Thank you." His voice normal.

"The guards will be here to take you into custody," I said. Darkness nagged at me to take him somewhere. I bit down on the inside of my jaw to give it something else to focus on, but the craving it had for Alastair was strong. Hard to ignore.

"I would expect nothing less."

My head tilted to the side, taking him in. His calmness about being arrested unnerved me. "You know you are being arrested for crimes against... well, everyone, right?"

"Yes, I understand. I must pay for the havoc I dealt."

He never agreed or relented. He had a plan. "Not exactly what I expected from you."

"What did you expect, my queen?"

"I expected you to fight until the end."

"I remember every detail, but I don't agree with my actions."

The contradiction confused me. Was this another of his ploys?

Footsteps thudded across the ground, and the guards appeared in the doorway.

I stood and straightened my jacket. "Take him to the cells at the mansion."

"Yes, Your Majesty."

Alastair rose from the ground and extended his hands to them.

The guard cuffed him and bound his magic, or lack thereof, to the cuffs. I studied the creases around his eyes. The corners seemed to turn down. Same with the edge of his mouth. I sensed again for Darkness and found none in him except for the single drop I'd put there.

We'd freed him from his troubles it would seem. *What had been the cost?* We'd used dark magic from the Fire Book. *Had I given myself over to dark?* I still felt some measure of me. *But was I fooling myself?*

"Ella, I do not need you right now, but the day will come when I do. When it does, will you do for me what I couldn't do with Alastair?"

"If that is what you wish and it is necessary, yes," she said, her tone solemn.

I scanned the area for Mom and Brandon. They needed healing. Their hearts more than their bodies. That would take time. A lot of time. I located them and saw Brandon on his feet, leaning against Mom.

"It's good to see you up," I said. I meant the words, but they stirred nothing inside me. Darkness layered anger with a hunger for power over everything else.

He hugged me to him. "Sis, I'm sorry. Dad said we shouldn't tell you."

I hugged him back, but there was no warmth. "Sometimes secrets can help people. Still not a fan of them, but he did it for us."

"Where is he?"

"He's in solitude." Tears fell from the corners of my eyes, but I couldn't reach the sadness in me. Darkness reduced me to mechanical actions. Aware but unable to act. "Let's go check on our people."

"What about Alastair? Is he..." He choked on the words.

"He's alive." I paused. "I couldn't let him die."

"You saved him? Why?"

"For Cal. We know what it's like to think your father is dead. We've experienced it twice. I couldn't do that to someone I care about." I recalled the words from memory unable to connect to the emotion of them.

"Light lives in you, Sis. Grandmother would be proud."

I forced a smile. Light didn't live in me anymore. Only Darkness and a numbness like when bitter cold bites into you. Alastair's evil became part of me. My stomach hurt and nausea waved over me.

Brandon wrapped his arm around my shoulder and side-hugged me.

"Let's go home."

Home. My husband-to-be waited there because the elders and my family thought he'd be a distraction here. We'll never know if they were right, but he meant everything to me. The only reason I agreed was to ensure his safety. I had to face him and tell him I killed some of his people to stop Alastair. He'd be the one that had to deal with that fall-out, and it wouldn't make it easy for him.

I'd killed witches too in my haste to destroy Alastair's evil aura. *Had they been given a choice? Had they intentionally sided with Darkness?* Their deaths would have to be something I lived with regardless of whether they were forced or chose to follow him.

Solitude would be where I would go, and with Cal named as my unofficial successor, the coven would be safe.

"There's our ride." Brandon linked his arm through mine and Mother's. He led us to the SUV the guards brought for us. Nick stepped out of the vehicle and made hasty steps toward me. I couldn't meet his eyes. Brandon hadn't said it, but mine would be as dark as Sorin's had been.

The ground rumbled around us. I looked down. *Not an earthquake.* A force shoved me back hard enough that I flew in the air. Waves of heat passed over me. I lost contact with Mom and Brandon. Everything fell silent when I hit the ground. I gasped for air. My back ached. I rolled to my side.

One of the SUV doors laid at my feet. No glass in it. The metal was charred with burn marks and bent into an almost unrecognizable position. More twisted metal a few yards away. The remains of the SUV, a shell really, flamed like a bonfire doused in gasoline. It set askew from where it was originally parked. Black smoke billowed up to the sky from the scene like a smoke signal. The vampires knew we'd be weak and vulnerable after containing Alastair. Darkness rose in me and brought rage with it.

I struggled to my knees. My ears rang. I shook my head in an attempt to clear it and stop the ringing sound. To my right, Brandon and Mom sat up.

Brandon's hand went to his forehead. A gash across his head bled, causing a red stream down the side of his face.

I tore the edge of my shirt and folded it. Pressed it against his head. I grasped his hand and put it over it. It was the motions from training. "Press down. It's a good size cut. Anything else hurt?"

"Where is Nick?" I asked, my first hint of emotion was fear for him.

He shook his head and looked past me to the car.

I knew what he thought, but Nick and I were blood bound. I'd be crushed from the inside out. *Or would I with Darkness?*

Gifted with vision, and we didn't see it coming. Where the fuck is Nick?

I crawled to Mom. Her eyes were on her hands. "Are you okay?"

She didn't answer.

"Mom, are you okay?" I asked louder, touching her shoulder.

She flinched. *Shock.*

I looked her over and didn't see any injuries despite some scratches, bruises, and blood splatters on her clothes. Pretty remarkable actually. I noticed spots of red on my clothes. Swiveled toward Brandon. The blood could be from his wound, but there was lots of it. My eyes fell closed to avoid acknowledgment of what it meant.

A guard. Maybe more than one.

I stumbled to my feet and the edge of the tree line. My stomach wretched the contents from it. It emptied completely. *Where could he be?*

The sight when I turned around sank like a dagger in my heart. Movement made me aware some needed help, but I only wanted to find Nick. I had to find him and Darkness didn't disagree.

A hand grabbed my ankle, and I stopped. A guard had a metal shard protruding from his leg. The bloody site pushed Darkness back. The guard needed a healer. I didn't want to taint anyone with Darkness, which meant I couldn't heal with magic.

I reached down for his hand and squeezed. "Help will be here."

"Your Majesty, you need to get out of here," he whispered.

"I'm right where I need to be. I'm fine, and you will be too." I squatted down next to him.

Alastair. Or his followers. Or both.

"Did you have contact with the SUV Alastair was in?" I asked the guard.

"It left about ten minutes ago. They weren't due to check in yet," he answered, his voice strained through the pain.

A hand slipped over my shoulder. Bloody fingertips squeezed against my skin. I followed the arm up to its owner. *Nick.*

"Thank the Goddess." Darkness stabbed me in the chest, but I ignored the pain. Seeing him in front of me, jarred some Darkness's hold loose. I wrapped my arms around him.

"Are you ok?" He patted me down.

If I'd had any wounds, Darkness had long since healed them. "I'm fine, but many are not. We need help, Nick."

Ella came into view. "You need to go and go now," she said, her voice frantic. "They plan to liberate Alastair."

"What do you mean liberate?"

She met my eyes and didn't shy away from the Darkness there. I saw fear in her, but it wasn't for what she saw in my eyes. "They will intercept him and take him to the old chapel near the first battle."

The memories of that battle flooded in. I chose love that day and set this prophecy in motion. I condemned Sorin back to Darkness that day unknowingly. *It's only fitting that we end this there.*

"My mother and brother are here. I can't leave them." The guards all seemed to be accounted for. Injured but alive. Except one. One was missing. Alastair wasn't a warlock any more. His magic was gone or at least I hoped it was. But he was a master manipulator.

My heart ached that anyone was lost. Darkness was behind a dam for the moment, likely temporary, but I need to move forward while my thoughts were clear.

"I'll make sure they return to your coven safely. I give you my word," Ella said.

"If you cross me, I'll bring the full wrath of Darkness down on you, and that is my word." Darkness delighted in the threat and made my words bitter.

"Which is why you know you can trust me. Now go," she said. "Before it's too late."

I took Nick's hand a teleported us to an old meeting spot near the field and across from the dilapidated church.

TWENTY-ONE

N ick crouched next to me. I looked him over and didn't see any open injuries. I should have asked. There was no movement and no lights at the decayed chapel.

"Are you sensing them?"

"Nothing yet. Someone is blocking me," I whispered. "I knew it was too easy. He's a master of distraction. He won again." I sucked down my anger, afraid Darkness would use it to destroy the block in place.

"No, he didn't. You're still alive, and I can't believe I have to say that," he said.

"Ella told you."

"She's my subject, Brie. She would face her death if she lied to me."

I understood. Cal or Brandon would have done the same. "I need to tell you something, Nick," I paused. "About the ceremony tonight. It didn't go as planned."

"Your eyes already told me, and I'm still here by your

side. I told you Light or Dark doesn't matter. You are my everything," he said, his voice quiet and reassuring.

I nodded, but Darkness found a break in the barrier and pushed through and dulled the moment. His words should have put me at ease. They should have warmed me. But there was nothing. My solitude would come, and I hoped he would move on when the time came. "Alastair doesn't want me dead. He wants me weak. He wanted to break me. What I don't understand is why he'd give up the Darkness. He had to have known I would intervene."

"He was counting on it, my love. He gambled with your life and his. You could have died today. You do realize that, right?" Nick's voice broke.

"We can die any day. The gift of visions doesn't prevent that. I can't figure out how neither Cal nor I saw this though."

"You've said it many times. It's a gift. You don't control it."

"No, I don't. You're right." If I didn't see it, then maybe Cal hadn't either. "You do think we can trust Cal, right?"

"You're his biggest advocate. Why are you questioning him now?"

"It just bothers me we had no clue."

"Alastair is resourceful. I think that's what we are witnessing."

"Maybe so."

Light flashed in front of the church, and my other SUV came into view. *Mother fucker.* All the rage in me directed at him.

"Brie, it's getting warm over here. Maybe take a couple of

breaths." I glanced at Nick. His brows furrowed together. The grass around us wilted.

"Sorry," I said. "I'm going down there. You should stay here."

"Not a chance, my love."

I gave him a sad smile. I planned to unleash all the dark power at my disposal on Alastair. Nick would be done with me once he saw the callousness of it, and I'd be free to move on to a life of solitude.

Lights flickered on in the old chapel. I snaked my way down and Nick followed. We sidled up next to the SUV. There was no cover to be had between here and the door. I took Nick's hand in mine. He laced our fingers together. *Cloak.*

Pain seared over me as Darkness, not Light, answered my request. Singed flesh hit my nostril, and I dropped Nick's hand as well as the cloak. "Are you ok?" I whispered.

Nick stared over my shoulder. The hair on the back of my neck stood up.

"There's my Dark Queen. I was so hoping you would come, Brie," Alastair said.

I turned to face him and put myself between him and Nick.

"Won't you come inside? I'd love to give you both a history lesson." He gestured to the door. Two vampires and two witches moved in around us. Hell's Fire could burn them all down, but it would take Nick too. *Inside it is.*

"I should have killed you." I walked past him and shoved my shoulder into his.

"But where would be the fun in that?" he asked.

Darkness coursed through me, but the difference between Alastair and I is he didn't need it to be evil.

Stockades were set up inside. *Two.* It was like he knew both Nick and I would come.

"If she struggles take it out on the former Vampire King," Alastair said, waving his hand in Nick's direction.

They maneuvered us towards the stockades. Darkness and I agreed on the desire to fight, but I wouldn't risk Nick even as Darkness prodded me with pain.

Alastair's men placed Nick and me in stockades and locked them down. He meant it as an ultimate insult to our history of persecution. Witches, especially during the Salem Witch Hunts, were placed in stockades before being hanged. It was a threat and a humiliation. Stefan had used the same device on me, and I wondered if Alastair had given him the idea.

He went through the history, which I already knew. Sorin had told us before the battle with Stefan about how witches once used a spell to create witches that required a decapitated vampire's blood. It allowed the creator to control the new type of witch.

Nick knew the history as well, but he stilled as Alastair spoke.

"What many don't know is that the dark witches created vampires for this specific purpose. The dark witches thought the vampires could be controlled, but that turned out to be only partially true. The older a vampire became; the harder they were to control. And never turn a pure-blood witch into a vampire, because there is almost no control," he said, pleased with himself.

I'd deciphered it from the old scrolls and kept it to myself, but Mom and Dad knew. The Elders knew. And soon the entire vampire and witch populations would know that the dark witches created vampires. Our ancestors, at least the portion that turned dark, were responsible for the birth of the vampire population.

"But how does one become a dark witch without allowing Darkness to claim them?" Alastair said, amusement in his voice. He ran his hand over my cheek. "With a Dark Queen of course."

"I'll never be your Dark Queen," I said, straining against the stockade.

"You already are, Brielle."

He whispered an incantation in Nick's ear. When he was done, he touched Nick's temple. "Forget until I call on you."

He repeated with me, and the words uttered so fast I couldn't make them all out. I understood enough to determine his plan. He planned to make me a bomb and make me forget until he was ready to use me. His incantation suppressed my Darkness, and that might be the only salvation. Darkness doesn't like to be suppressed.

His fingers pressed into my temple. "Forget until I wake you."

)) ● ((

"WE'RE HERE, BRIE." Nick's soothing voice roused me from my sleep.

I blinked away the disorientation. The smell of leather

around me. I was in the backseat of an SUV. I turned to Nick. Our eyes connected, and the full force of our love stole my breath. Darkness didn't try to eat away at it. I didn't feel Darkness at all. I sighed, the relief of its missing chaos welcome.

Nick held out his hand to help me from the car.

"Do you want to clean up first or go straight to the hospital area?" Nick asked.

I looked down at my tattered and red-spotted attire. "If I go to my room, I might not come out the rest of the day." The sun peaked over the horizon, emphasizing my point.

"Let's go see your guards then." He extended his arm to me as Brandon had to Mom and me right before the SUV blew up.

My hands shook, but I slid an arm through his for support.

His eyes narrowed. "Are you sure you are up to this?"

"Yes, I need to see them." I owed them my gratitude, and they would hear it from me today.

He escorted me down the empty hall to the hospital wing. Metal clinks and bangs echoed through the space beyond the door.

I inhaled a deep breath and let it out slowly.

"Ready?"

"Yes," I said. "What about you? The blood?"

"Brie, I need blood to live, but I can control the craving. I'll be fine."

He pushed the door open.

Everything stopped. Everyone stared at me.

"Your Majesty," the head of the hospital, a gifted healer and medical doctor, greeted me. "Do you need assistance?"

"Please continue," I said, my voice gravelly. "I just came to check on the injured guards."

"No life-threatening injuries, Your Majesty."

"Please call me, Brie. That is wonderful news. Do you need any help? I am gifted with a powerful healing aura as well."

"Yes, your ... Brie." He shifted awkwardly. "I'm aware of your many gifts."

"I'm aware my Aunt Cecily often visited the ward and used her healing powers to help the sick." I reminded them of the precedent the former queen set.

"Very well. We haven't made it to the ones in the back yet. Our technique is to only heal them to about eighty percent, so their bodies do not forget how to heal themselves."

"I see. I will honor that technique as well," I said. "Since there are no life-threatening injuries."

His eyes shifted to Nick.

It annoyed me that after Nick's sacrifices he was still looked at this way. "I can vouch for my future husband. It will not be a problem."

"Of course, Your Majesty." He shifted to the other foot. "Brie."

Nick and I walked to the back of the room. The first guard I spoke to after the accident was there. His leg propped up on the bed. The metal shard still sticking out of it. The healers were in triage mode and hadn't made it to him yet.

"Your Majesty," he said.

I took his hand in mine and squeezed. "Brie, please. I'd like to help heal you if you're ready."

"It would be an honor, Queen Brie,"

I coughed over the laugh at how he addressed me. Nick pressed a hand to my back.

"I'd really like this piece of metal out of my leg," he said, his voice tinted with discomfort.

"Let's have a look at it then." I studied it for a moment. It was deep, but it wouldn't leave permanent damage if healed correctly.

Nick handed me the scissors from the tray next to us.

"Reading my mind, I see." I smiled at him. The scissors cut through the material of his pant leg in short work to expose the wound. "Sorry about the pants," I said to the guard.

"I have others," He smiled.

"What's your name? I don't recall seeing you before today."

"Drake. Alan Drake. I was on Queen Cecily's detail as well. I usually do the prep work, but I moved up when several of the others retired."

"Ahh. That makes sense. It's going to hurt when we pull this out, and I'm sure you are aware pain medication doesn't work so well for us. Do you want something to bite down on?"

"No, Queen Brie. Give me a moment to center first."

I smiled at him and nodded. I'd heard of the guards' techniques for controlling pain, but I'd never seen it in action. I sensed his peace.

"Are you able to help?" I asked Nick.

"Of course." He handed me the forceps.

"It's going to bleed a lot, so we have to be quick. Can you pull it out while I clamp it down?" I worried about him being around the blood, but this wound would produce less than we saw after the explosion. My memories blurred around it. I focused on Alan.

Nick grasped the edge of the obstruction. "Brie, I've seen worse wounds. I'm ready when you are."

"Here we go. On the count of three pull it out. 1... 2... 3..."

In a swift jerk, Nick yanked the piece of metal free.

I clamped down the worst bleeds. "The worst is over, Alan. We are ready to heal."

He squinted his eyes and nodded his head. Beads of sweat formed above his lip.

Nick took over the forceps to hold the bleeders closed.

"When my aura starts to heal, remove the forceps. We don't want Alan to have them sticking out of his leg. That might be worse than the chunk of metal."

Alan made a weak chuckle.

My hands found their place over the wound, and I closed my eyes. Quiet focus took hold. *Heal.*

I opened my eyes to see the wound pink and scabbed. *Maybe a little more than 80%.*

"Feel better." I placed my hand on his shoulder and gave him a quick squeeze.

"Yes, Queen Brie."

Nick dropped the tool on the bedside tray.

"Brie. I'm fine with you saying just Brie..." I grabbed my forehead against the dizziness and swaying room. My field of vision narrowed. The sensation of falling.

"Brie?"

I heard Nick's voice, and my body lifted.

"I'm taking her to her room. You can check on her there."

Clicks quick together. Quick snaps of lights. A buzz in my ear. Nausea.

)) ● ((

I PUSHED up in the bed and grabbed my pounding head. "What happened?"

"You passed out." Nick's eyes focused on me.

"That's weird."

"And you have this now." He flipped the sheet back.

A well-placed bandage was on my leg. I lifted my leg, but the pain forced it back down. "What happened to my leg?"

"It would appear you took on the wound of the guard you healed."

"What?" *What the actual fuck.*

"It's baffled the healers as well. They said they've never seen it happen."

"So, I can't heal anyone until we figure it out?" Something was off in my magic for this to happen, and it worried me. *Could some of my magic have been siphoned off during the ceremony?*

"Exactly."

I studied the nasty wound. It was red and fresh looking. "And they couldn't heal this thing?"

"They did."

"Let me guess. Eighty percent?" I rolled my eyes.

"You got it."

"That's a shit rule." I moved the leg and winced. "Hmmm. Guess I shouldn't try to heal myself either."

He shook his head. "They did not recommend it."

I nodded. "How long to heal then?"

Nick's brows furrowed together. "The doctor said maybe a week if you heal like a regular witch."

I swung my legs over the side of the bed.

"It's going to hurt," Nick warned.

"I figured. Everything always does." *Get it over with, Brie.*

Nick stood beside the bed and held his arm out for me.

"I've been leaning on you a lot lately," I said, placing my hands on his forearms.

"I'm not complaining."

I placed my feet on the ground. The pain intensified tenfold when I put pressure on the leg. My fingers dug into Nick's arm, but he didn't budge.

"You're my rock, Nick." I gritted through the pain.

"I will always be your rock." He met my eyes with so much encouragement in his. "We need to get you better for the wedding."

I stepped forward on the injured leg. "Fuck me."

"That can be arranged." He wagged his eyebrows at me.

I erupted in laughter and fell forward. My rock caught me and leaned me back upright.

"We need to find Alastair," I said. "And you need to find out why Ella sent us to that empty chapel."

"Cal is on the Alastair hunt. He thinks he has the best chance of finding him. Ella swears by her intel that Alastair was meeting someone there."

"How did we miss him then? Could they have moved that fast?"

Nick shrugged. "I don't know. The explosion is affecting my memory."

"Same. It's all fuzzy for me after the SUV blew up," I agreed. "I want to talk to Cal."

"Tomorrow. Doctor's orders."

"My real doctor or you?" I looked up at him under my lashes.

"Both. Ready to take a couple of steps?"

I sucked in a breath and stepped forward with gritted teeth. "Gahh! Damn it that hurts!"

"It will get easier. The wound was deep. There was nerve damage." His face creased with worry lines.

"But it will heal right?"

"Eventually."

I eyed him. "You can embellish a little. It wouldn't hurt my feelings."

"Step."

My teeth clenched together, and I pushed the leg forward. Sweat beaded on my forehead and palms. "This fucking sucks." I gasped for air. "Sorry. I usually keep all that in my head."

"At least I know what you're normally thinking in that profanity-laden brain."

I laughed hard and took another step. It was easier. Pain more manageable.

"If I make you laugh, you don't complain. Noted."

"Aren't you smart?" I paused "Ass."

"And sarcasm. Yes, you'll be just fine. I'll be able to take you back to bed sooner than I thought." He winked at me and kissed the tip of my nose

"You didn't think you'd get rid of me so easy, did you?"

His smile faded and he wrapped his arms around me. "I hope to never be rid of you." He pressed his lips to mine.

My body tingled awake wanting something it had missed. Apparently, a lot by the reaction below the waist.

Nick pulled back and looked into my eyes. The desire in his stirred my body to life.

"You need to not give so much of yourself," he said in a stern tone.

"I can't not be me."

"You're right. I guess I'll have to buy a gilded cage." He lifted me and placed me on the bed.

"I'm a witch. That's not going to work."

"I guess a gold ring will have to do."

"Are you talking about our wedding?"

"Yes, vampires don't have any kind of joining ceremony other than being blood bound, and we've done that."

"But you're traditional and want a traditional human wedding? Like in addition to the handfasting ceremony we have planned/"

He knelt beside the bed and brushed loose hair from my face. "Yes, I'd like that."

"I think we could combine them without a fuss," I said, smiling up at him.

He took my hand in his and brought my knuckles to his lips. "You can have whatever you want. Haven't you learned that by now?"

"So can you. Haven't you learned that by now?" I winked at him.

A challenging brow shot up. "I know exactly what I want."

"Then take it." My voice was raspy.

"Yes, Queen Brie."

I laughed and wrapped my arms around his neck.

He slid into the bed next to me.

A knock at the door made us both jerk.

"Are you kidding me?" I looked up at the ceiling like the response would be there.

Nick rested his head on my forehead.

Another urgent knock tapped against my door. "They're not going away. It might be news of Alastair."

Nick stood and took my hand in his. He pulled me to my feet and swept me into his arm. His unnatural speed carried us to the door. He set me on my feet and stood behind me to steady me.

I eyed him over my shoulder and smirked, sure the placement was to prevent view of his crotch.

The wicked grin on his face said I was right.

My hand grasped the doorknob and with a deep breath, I opened it.

The guard I healed stood there. I was both happy and surprised to see him. "Alan? You're out of the infirmary?"

"I am thanks to you, Queen Brie."

Nick snickered behind me, and I casually pressed my elbow into his ribs.

I tucked my robe tightly around me. "What can I help you with?"

His expression turned serious. "Cal has news of Alastair and asked if you'd join him in the library."

"Of course. Will you let him know I'll be there shortly?" I asked.

"Yes, Queen Brie."

I touched his arm. "Alan, I'm glad you are feeling better."

He nodded. "Thank you, Ma'am."

I shut the door. Nick and I both giggled.

"Queen Brie, we need to get you dressed for a meeting unless you plan on going in your robe."

I put my hands on my hips. "Don't make fun of him. He's a nice young man."

"I'm not. It's funny because it bugs you."

"Are you jealous?" I teased.

"No, I know you like older men." He wrapped his arms around me.

I pushed him away.

"Time to get you dressed." He made a motion to pick me up.

"I'll walk. I need to get used to it."

I hobbled, ignoring the pain, to the closet with my hand on his arm. I picked out pants and a blouse I thought would be easy to slip on, but I couldn't bend the injured leg very well. "I think I need help with the pants."

Nick's wicked grin returned. "I'm always glad to help you with your pants."

I shook my head and laughed. "What has gotten into you? You're impossible."

"I'm just happy. I will be marrying the woman I love in less than a month. That's as far as they are going to go while you're sitting." When the ancestors chose the third Blood Moon in the tetrad for the wedding I thought it a blessing, but I wasn't as sure now.

I looked down at the pants around my knees. "Oh." I pushed off the bench into a standing position, steadying myself with my hands on his shoulders.

He eased them up. His lips brushed my belly as he got them to my waist. "I assume you can finish. I much prefer unfastening them."

I swallowed hard. "We can have dinner in here tonight."

"I like the Queen's choice." His nose skimmed my cheek. He crushed my lips with his.

My breaths came in a ragged burst when he broke away. "I hate meetings."

"Still complaining? I'll fix that tonight."

"God, I hope so." I smiled.

"Make the meeting fast," he said.

"You're coming with me, right? I'm not sure I could stick the landing if I teleported." I tested the weight on my injured leg, and pain radiated through it.

"Of course." He picked me up again. "I'm your ride there." His swiftness carried us to the library.

"You're going to make me lazy," I said.

He sat me on the ground in front of the door. "I assume you want to walk through the door."

"Yes, you assume correctly." I took his hand in mine. "You don't mind if I squeeze a little? Do you?"

I opened the door.

Cal looked up from the books spread across the table in

front of him. Brandon seated on the opposite side. His head wound completely healed.

I limped across the room to hug my brother. "You recovered quicker than me."

"You look like you're going in the opposite direction."

"Ehh. I'll survive."

Cal met me halfway for a hug. "You don't look so bad."

"You can tell a lie." I smiled at him. A bit of awkwardness hung in the air.

"Did you find your father?"

"Yes," he said. "He's still on the move."

Nick helped me onto one of the barstool like chairs around the table. "What's his destination?"

"London."

"It's a smart move. I'll give him that. London will always be loyal to him. They'll protect him there." I'd have retreated in the same manner given the situation.

"He has a fortress there too, and I do mean fortress," Cal said, sounding frustrated.

Brandon took the seat beside him and scooted close. His arm moved under the table. Cal glanced at him. He must have put his hand on his leg. I liked seeing them as a couple and both having joy in their lives.

"When can we fly out?" I glanced between them.

"You can't go anywhere until we figure out if and when you can heal again," Brandon said.

"A hurt leg doesn't mean I can't wield my powers." My hand instinctively went for my necklace and caressed it.

"It's not the leg. Something is off with your powers, and

it puts you at risk," Brandon said. "I can sense it. I can smell it on you."

I sat up straight. "What do you mean you can smell it on me?"

Brandon wrinkled his nose. "It smells sour."

"Like rot? Like death?" My stomach knotted. I'd named Cal as my successor in private, but we hadn't done the formal ceremony. There should not be a bond to start the process without the ritual.

"No, like sour milk." The side of his mouth drew up in a grimace.

I let out a breath in relief and wiped my hand over my face. "I wonder what that means. What does Nick smell like to you?"

Brandon sniffed in Nick's direction. "Kind of like whiskey."

I laughed. "That's what he smells like to me too. Vanilla and whiskey."

Nick looked at me and cocked his head to the side. "You never told me."

I shrugged. "I thought you liked a sip of a little finely aged whiskey."

His brows bunched together. "Interesting."

I turned back to Cal and Brandon. "Back to Alastair. What do we know? Does he have any powers?"

"I don't think he does. He's called some powerful witches to him though," Cal said, his voice deflated.

"He's still a warlock. We only pulled his dark aura. That's not the root of the power," Brandon said.

"I always thought they were linked. He said he was

dying, and I healed him," I said. "I gave him a drop..." I grabbed my head. The memory hurt. I swallowed against it. "A drop of my aura." *Why can't I remember it? I know I did it, but I can't see it in my mind's eye.*

Nick's eyes burned into me. *He said his memory was distorted too.*

"Hmmm. The aura would have weakened him, but he'd still have power. He shouldn't have needed you to heal him," Cal said.

"So, he lied to me. Why? Why would he want me to heal him if he'd heal on his own?" I played the ceremony events in my head, and I saw it clearly up until the point I walked up to him. Then it was fragments until we returned to the Great House.

"I don't think it's a coincidence he asked you to heal him, and then your healing powers went wonky," Brandon said, his face twisted in disgust.

"I agree with Brandon. He did something," Nick said, anger threaded in his words.

"Dad is a skilled manipulator. I wouldn't put it past him," Cal said.

"Great. Just great. He's hexed me in some way, and we have no idea how or why." Danger stirred in me. *Darkness? I hadn't felt it since we returned. Or was this it? Why can't I remember what Darkness felt like?*

Nick slid his arm around my waist. "Maybe we do, Brie. You said yourself at the castle that he wanted you weakened."

"I meant emotionally."

"Maybe he's trying to hit you physically and emotionally at the same time," Brandon said.

"We have to know what he's done first before we can reverse it," Cal said.

"Can you see a solution for this?" I asked my twin.

"No," he said. "I can't."

"I'm tired," I said. Exhaustion made me weary. "Would you two mind working on it together? I can join you after I rest?"

"On it, Sis," Brandon said.

"We'll touch base in the morning." I limped to the door.

Nick opened it for me. "You're getting around better." He closed it softly behind us.

"It's feeling a little better, but I think I need help back to our room."

"Lazy already." He nuzzled the side of my neck.

I laughed. "Preserving my strength for other things."

He gathered me up in his arms and sauntered down the hall. "I like the sound of that." He pressed his lips to the sensitive place behind my ear.

Shivers ran down my arms. "You don't seem to be in much of a hurry."

"Savoring the moment. It won't last forever."

"There will be lots of moments to savor."

He didn't set me down at the door this time. His hand was able to maneuver and open it. "I plan on doing a lot of savoring tonight." He walked through and kicked the door shut.

"It's been a while since I've seen you do that." My insides clenched.

"Does it make you weak in the knees?"

"Oh, it does more than that," I said.

He slid me down his body into a standing position. His strength positioned me so there was no weight on my bad leg. "Does it now?"

"It stirs desire deep in my belly and further." I took his hand and placed it between my legs.

"I like it when you talk like that. Marry me." His hand moved.

The heat grew in me. I tugged his shirt up over his head. "I am, and I'm already Blood Bound to you," I said, my voice breathless.

"I want you tied to me in every possible way," Nick whispered against my ear. His breath tickled.

"You can have me any way you want me. Tied to you in every way possible." Hearing him saying it and repeating it myself made my core clench.

"I'm going to hold you to that." He undid my blouse and slipped my pants off. His lips covered mine and he tugged my underwear off.

He sat me on the edge of the bed and urged my legs apart. He trailed kisses down my neck to my breasts. He lavished them before moving down my belly. His tongue stroked between my folds, and his finger found the spot.

The pressure built in me. I moaned and lifted my hips.

Nick growled against me and increased his pace.

My fingers gripped his hair. I arched my back and let the magic happen. His tongue circled while he sucked, and it drove me over the edge. "Nick." His name was nothing more than a moan on my lips.

He kissed the inner part of my thigh and stood up to undo his pants. They fell to the ground and exposed his length.

I scooted back on the bed. He crawled on top of me and caged me under him.

"Tell me I'm yours forever and you'll marry me," he said.

I loved him in every way possible.

"You know you are." I placed my hands on either side of his face and kissed him.

He hovered over me. "I love you, Brie."

"I love you forever, Nick," I said. He plunged into me. I moaned against his mouth. He pulled back slowly and drove in again. "Nick, please."

He increased his pace until I tightened around him, and we found our release together.

His forehead rested on mine. "Forever, Brie."

I smiled and kissed him. "Forever."

He rolled off of me and pulled me against his side. His lips pressed against my forehead. *I'd take this and everything else he wanted to give. Forever.*

TWENTY-TWO

The month went by in a blur of wedding preparations, and my nerves were high. Everything had to be perfect.

Mom entered the room. Her smile big, and her eyes shiny. "Today is your wedding day, Brie."

I spun around for her in my blue gown. *It's really happening. I was going to marry my love today.* Happiness I'd never known before welled in my chest.

She kissed my cheek. "I was wrong to be against the strapless gown. You look stunning."

"I never thought I'd get married, and here I am. In love. Happy." My insides threatened to explode with excitement, but I'd never tell anyone that.

"I think that's the reason your dad made it back. He wanted to see his daughter get married for love."

I'd smiled so much the last few weeks. We still had to finish our business with Alastair, and I worried he would interfere with today. All the measures within our means had been taken to ensure he wouldn't. *But this is Alastair.*

"Dad always planned to come back. He fought to come back. Love and Light guided him home." It meant so much to have him here. I might need solitude one day, but it wouldn't be my wedding day.

"He's given up magic again. I'm not sure that is the same as choosing Light," she said, her eyes looked distant.

I held her hands in mine. "I know, and I understand. We're two different people, Mom. He has to do what works for him."

"You are unique. Your Grandmother knew it from the beginning. I just wanted you to be healthy and safe. You have overcome so much in your life, and I'm so very proud of you."

It wasn't the first time she'd said it to me since Grandmother passed on, and I believed it a little more each time.

"And I'm thankful I have you here with me." I hugged her.

She smiled. "You have your something new and something blue. I hope you will accept this as your something old," Mom said. She reached into her pocket and pulled out a bracelet with diamonds and a gemstone the same color blue as my dress.

"It's beautiful, Mom."

"They're star sapphires. My birthstone. Your Grandmother gave it to me for my eighteenth birthday."

The narrow cuff fit my wrist perfectly. Nine blue star sapphires graduated in size to the middle and back down again on the other side. A row of diamonds flanked them on either side. Truly beautiful.

"It was your great great grandmother's. Handed down to your great-grandmother who died before she could pass it to your grandmother. Your grandmother received keys to a safety deposit box when she turned eighteen. I should have given it to you when you came of age, but we were not in a good place. I think maybe it was meant to be today for you."

"Me too, Mom. I love you."

"I love you too." She hugged me tight to her.

My heart was full today.

"Do you know the significance of the star sapphire?"

"Communication, right?"

"Yes, a blue sapphire is for communication and good judgment. A star sapphire enhances those abilities. It aids in organizing disordered thoughts."

"I need that for sure." My memories had been disjointed since the ritual. The healers thought it was trauma-induced, but Nick had a similar problem recalling the time around it.

"Keep it close to you when you meditate. It should help discern the messages." She'd thought about this gift. I told her how much I missed Grandmother's guidance after meditating, and she mentioned she wished she could fill that space for me. In her way, she did it.

"This means so much to me. It's like I'll always have a piece of the family with me." Tears pooled and spilled over.

"Don't mess up your makeup," Mom said. Her thumbs brushed under my eyes, wiping the tears away.

The bracelet and love behind its journey filled a little piece of the vacant spot in my chest for Grandmother. She would have been a big part of this day, but I know she is watching me from her position on high.

"And here is your something new." She handed me a small blue velvet box.

I flipped open the top to find earrings that matched the bracelet. "Mom, they are beautiful." My eyes teared up again.

"Stop crying. Besides messing your makeup up, mine is going to get messed up crying with you."

I giggled and hugged her. "We better get out there then."

She nodded. Her fingers patted under her eyes.

The earrings slipped into my ears easily. I stared at my reflection in the mirror for a moment. My strapless gown was fitted at the bodice with a sweetheart neckline and then flared out in a ball gown style. It shimmered like the ocean, and the only beading was reserved for the stones at my waist. I'd opted for a traditional updo, and I felt like a princess. *Like a queen.*

"You look perfect." Mom squeezed my shoulders.

We made our way down the hall to meet Sorin in front of the chapel. He had dark circles under his eyes, but he looked well otherwise. Darkness would do that to a witch. Make the witch look healthy unless the observer knew what to look for as a sign.

"My beautiful daughter. You look exquisite. Every bit the queen." He kissed my cheek. "How's my tie?"

"Your tie is perfect, Dad." I gave him a peck on the cheek and straightened his blue tie perfectly matched to my dress. "Nick?"

"He's in the chapel. Brandon has him covered."

He meant it lighthearted, but it was true. One of the gifts Grandmother sent Brandon was the ability to share his aura as I did. It's a special gift that only exists in our bloodline, and Brandon was the first male to have received the gift.

Mom and I exchanged cheek kisses. "See you inside," she said.

"I'll be the one up front." My voice squeaked.

She and Dad laughed.

Christopher took her arm and escorted her through the doors. He'd taken up permanent residence at the coven at my request. Ella saw to his schooling and training, so we would be able to take a few days for ourselves.

"Are you sure you want to marry a vampire?" Dad teased.

"I'm sure."

"Are you sure you want to get married? We can turn around and go the other way."

"I'm sure, Dad." I laughed.

He chuckled. "Okay, let's get you married then." He nodded to Alan, my guard who attended the door.

Alan peeked inside to make sure Mom had been seated as planned. Once she had been, he nodded to the attendant posted at the other door. They pulled them open simultaneously. Horns blew from just inside.

"All stand for Queen Brielle," Alan announced.

The guests rose to their feet in a shuffling noise.

The music started. I declined to have the wedding march played. Instead, I requested a song Nick and I had danced to. Dad and I stepped through the doorway.

My eyes raced to the front to find Nick. My heart beat out of my chest and nowhere to wipe my sweaty palms.

Nick stood at the front with my brother by his side. He wore a well-fitted tuxedo and looked as steady as a rock. His eyes left the floor to capture mine. Even though his were a blur to me from there, I could still feel the connection when he locked onto me.

My breath caught in my chest, and I sucked in a deep breath.

"Ready?" Dad whispered to me.

I squeezed his arm where my hand rested. "Ready."

We stepped forward together. My dress rustled with each movement. When we reached the end of the aisle, Dad extended his hand with mine over it.

Cal greeted me and my father with a smile. "The Queen of all Covens has chosen to enter into marriage. Who gives her to this union?"

"Her mother and I do," Sorin said. His voice cracked in the middle. No one had to stand up for the Queen at her wedding. It was my special request, and a nod to the place of honor my father held for me as well as the traditional human wedding Nick wanted.

I glanced up to see a smattering of tears at the corners of Dad's eyes.

He placed my hand in Nick's, kissed my forehead, and stepped back to take his place by Mother's side.

My eyes came back to Nick. A huge smile spread broad across his face. He was so handsome. I blushed at the intense gaze he pinned on me.

He mouthed, "I love you."

I mouthed it back.

Cal cleared his throat and drew our attention.

"The Queen of all Covens and the King of the Vampires wish to take a moment to acknowledge the Queen's Grandmother. Had she lived, she would be performing the ceremony today. As the Queen's closest advisor, I am, but a poor stand-in for such a large presence. Please give a moment of silence for Her Majesty's Grandmother."

The room grew silent in respect for her. I warmed on the inside, and tears threatened the edges of my eyes again. Nick squeezed my hand tightly.

Grandmother, if you can hear our prayers, you are remembered, and all this is because of you.

"Thank you," Cal said after several moments. "The ceremony will begin. Please stand and join us by facing the corners as they are called."

"May the East bring openness to your marriage. May the South bring warmth to your home. May the West bring trust to your union. May the North bring security to your marriage."

We held our hands, fingers laced together, out to him. He laid the red ribbon across our wrists. *We made it.* Love won the day, and every look, every touch, every word with Nick reminded me how much we had.

"Do you promise to honor and respect each other?" Cal asked.

"We will." Nick and I said in unison.

Cal wrapped the ribbon around once.

"Do you promise to ease each other's burdens and pains?"

"We will."

The ribbon wrapped a second time. My heart fluttered in my chest.

"Do you promise to live in the Light and love of each other till the end of days?"

"We will." A twinge caught in my belly, and I tamped it down.

Cal wrapped the ribbon a third time.

"Blessed be the binding that is made."

He wound it around one more time and tied it in a knot.

"Brie and Nick, like your hands now bound so are your lives and spirits intertwined together in your blessed union of love. May you always seek each other in the stars you love and remain steady with the earth under your feet."

"Blessed Be," the crowd said together.

I let out a breath afraid I would cry from happiness.

Cal snipped the ribbon to end the ceremony.

My tattoo tingled and glowed. My eyes fell to my arm to see the second Blood Moon turn white. I looked at Nick's chest.

His palm was over where his mark was.

My eyes found his.

He nodded.

Two down and two left. We were halfway through the prophecy with a mountain ahead of us still to climb.

"Together," I whispered to him.

"Together," he whispered back.

"The bride and groom wish to have a traditional ring ceremony to conclude their vows. They provided the rings before the ceremony, and they have been blessed." He removed the rings from his pocket and placed them on the Book of Light and Love.

"Nick, you may recite your vows and place your ring on Brie's finger."

My heart fluttered like it would fly right out of my hair. I couldn't envision a more perfect or happy day.

Nick picked up the ring. His hand shook as he positioned it near my finger.

"Brie, my life changed when I first met you. You showed me how to live again. I live, because of your passion for life. I love because love lives in you. I found my light in you. My love is devoted to you and you alone for eternity." He slid the gold band on my finger.

A tear escaped and ran down my cheek.

"Your Majesty, you may recite your vows and place your ring on Nick's finger."

My sweaty shaky hands grasped the ring from the book in a tight hold, afraid I'd drop it. I positioned the ring near his finger. His hand steadied, but mine was not.

"Nick, you saved me. More than once, and the world should know I wouldn't be who I am without you. Thank you for putting me first. Thank you for choosing me. Without you, Light would not live in me. Without you, I would not know true love. My love is devoted to you and you alone until the days come to an end and then some."

I glanced at Cal ready for his next instruction. He brushed his tear away.

"Nick, you may now kiss your wife."

Nick's eyes focused on mine until our connection consumed me from my toes to the tip of my head. He leaned forward touching our lips together in a soft dance. His lips released and pressed against mine in two shorter motions.

I wanted more, but I always did with him.

"May I present to you, Queen Brielle and King Nicholas," Cal said. "Long may they reign in peace."

The room erupted in a startling round of applause. The guests were on their feet. It overwhelmed me for a moment, and I squeezed Nick's hand in a death grip.

"On behalf of the newlyweds, we invite you to join us for a reception. Our team will have the banquet hall ready for us," Call said.

"Thank you, Cal," I said over my shoulder.

"You did a great job, my friend," Nick said.

"Brandon, you look a little pale. I can take over now," I said.

I willed my pink aura over Nick. It hadn't looked as bright as before since we faced Alastair, but I guess that was to be expected. Battles changed all participants in some way.

"Thanks, Sis. It's harder than it looks. Congratulations." He kissed my cheek.

"Thank you for keeping him safe for me until I got here."

He winked at me and shook Nick's hand.

"I'll go make sure the banquet hall is ready," Brandon said and went ahead.

"I like being in here," Nick whispered in my ear. "With you."

I smiled up at him. "We can make it a regular thing."

"I have much to be thankful for." He pulled me against his side.

"That's the last of the guests. We can make our way. Your parents will enter the hall ahead of you and take their seats.

Then the royal announcement will be made, and you will make your entrance," Cal said.

"For the announcement at the reception, please just say Queen Brie and King Nick. The less formal the better for us," I said.

"Of course," Cal said. "I'll make sure of it."

He went ahead.

Nick held out his arm for me. "Mrs. Domenico."

I slid mine through the crook of his elbow. "I never said I was taking that name." I winked at him. A little cringe formed inside me at the name.

"We both have two last names by circumstance. We could put them all in a hat a draw for the name we shall use."

My laughter echoed down the hallway followed by Nick's.

"That is definitely an option. As Queen and King, we technically do not have to choose a last name. Let's table it for today."

"Agreed."

A shiver ran down my spine. I turned to look behind us sure someone was there. Sure it was Alastair even though the contacts in London said he hadn't left his sanctuary there.

D ad escorted Mom into the room. They were met with cheers and accolades.

The room quieted, and Nick and I stepped to the threshold. Adulation bombarded us with a thundering sound.

Cal stood next to us and waited for the room to quiet once more. "Queen Brie and King Nick welcome you to their home to celebrate their nuptials. This is a historic time as never before have the Coven and the Vampires had such a close tie. They have chosen to rule as one body, and their reign will be known as The Blood Moon Conservatorship dedicated to keeping the peace for all."

A server came by with a tray of champagne, and we each took a glass.

"To Queen Brie and King Nick. Long may they live. Long may they lead. Long may they love," Cal said. Brandon slipped his arm around Cal's waist. They looked so happy together, and I couldn't help but hope they might be next down the aisle.

Glasses clinked, and champagne was sipped. Our guests formed a procession line to greet us and bless our marriage. The long line lasted for an hour as noted by the clock in my direct line of sight. The blessings were welcome, but they exhausted me.

"Please take your seat. Dinner will be served shortly," Cal said.

Nick and I took our seats at the table of honor. I was relieved to have some space.

"I hate these formal dinners," I whispered in his ear. "Even when it is for us."

"This is for the people. We will have our own private celebration later." He smiled, and his eyes twinkled.

"We need a honeymoon with just the two of us." I wagged my eyebrows at him like he so often did me.

He chuckled. "I think that has been arranged."

"Really? How would we ever travel without the guards?" I rested my chin on my palm and smiled at him.

"We're going to an island. They are securing it as we speak and will keep it secure until we arrive. Then they will monitor the perimeter."

"So not alone." I sighed. *But better than it had been since the battle and Alastair's escape.*

"As alone as it gets for us, my love."

"I'll take it." I rested my hand on his knee and squeezed it.

He leaned his forehead against mine. "I love you for eternity, Brie."

"I love you for eternity, my husband."

"My wife." He brought our lips together for a brief affirmation.

The first course arrived, and I didn't want to eat. I wanted to be alone with my husband. *My husband.* The word danced in my head and sparkled inside my soul. I had my own personal glitter fest going on inside me. Another first.

I looked at the ring on my finger. *I'm Nick's wife. Holy shit! It's real.*

"This is our normal," I said.

"This is our normal." He picked my hand up and kissed the knuckles.

I stared into his eyes. The connection took over and wound us together from our innermost secrets to our outer-most extremities.

The second course arrived, and I glanced over it.

"How many courses are there? I'm ready to get my wife in my arms for a dance," Nick said, our eyes locked on each other.

"I think I talked Mother down to three. If you count the cake, we have four."

Nick leaned back and settled in. His arm draped over the back of my chair. "Your mother certainly likes her parties."

"She has her reasons."

Nick wrinkled his nose at the salad in front of him.

"Salad not appetizing?" I smiled. "You might find the red wine a bit more appealing." The vampires had a special mixture in their wine thus the different glasses so a witch didn't end up with a swig of blood.

"That's not what I want either." His fingertips brushed over my bare shoulder and down my arm.

Goosebumps sprung up in the aftermath. My insides quivered.

"There's still another course. Plus cake. Plus our first dance."

His fingers reversed course going back up from where they came. He traced a few circles at the top of my shoulder. His hand drifted down my side and over my hip.

I sucked in a sharp breath. My heart pounded against my chest like the first time we kissed. Anticipation grew in me. I swallowed hard against it.

"You might want to take it easy. We have a couple more hours."

"I assure you I am in complete control." He pressed his lips to my shoulder and his breath skated across my skin.

I chanced a look into his eyes.

He leaned into my ear. "You are the queen. You can leave the party whenever you want. And we could—" His breath tickled my ear.

He tempted me. I wanted to go. "That would make me a poor hostess."

He took my hand and placed it on his knee and pressed down. "Since when do you care about the rules?"

"I don't, but I do care about making my family proud," I said. "Including you."

He kissed the tip of my nose and sat back in his chair. "Damn your sense of duty."

"Don't tempt me. You know I want to get out of here."

"As you wish." He shifted in the chair.

The third course arrived. A choice of steak or fish chosen on the little RSVP cards mom sent with the invitations. Nick and I both chose steak prepared medium. Mom quizzed him before to make sure he didn't want it rare. I'd rolled my eyes, but Nick's patience allowed him to explain to her how he still enjoyed food. She'd been genuinely surprised.

"Eat something. You'll need your strength later."

"Will I now?" My brows went up in mock surprise.

"I think you know the answer." He laughed.

"I hope you can live up to my expectations."

"Careful or I will throw you over my shoulder and carry you to the room now."

Laughter rumbled from my belly and out my mouth. Loud enough to turn a few heads. I nodded and earned smiles in return.

Nick kissed my temple. "If they only knew what we were talking about."

Heat rose in my cheeks. "Oh, most of them are married or bound so I think they understand full well."

"That's a bright shade of pink on you."

"Shut up," I said through giggles. "Finish your steak. You're going to need your strength."

Nick coughed and smiled. He down the wine laced with blood.

"Who's ready for cake?" He stood up, extending his hand toward mine.

"Do not smash it in my face," I said when he pulled me to my feet.

"No promises."

I formed a tiny energy ball in my free hand.

"You wouldn't."

"Smash cake in my face and see."

We stood behind the table where mother directed us.

Nick's hand covered mine in warmth. Still amazed a vampire could generate warmth. Together we slid the knife down through the cake.

Red velvet. She'd refused it when we discussed it, but she gave in to me after all.

I looked up and gave Mom a small smile. She smiled and nodded.

Nick held up the plate with the slice on it. His fingers picked off a small piece. He placed the small bite in my mouth.

"Mmm. It's good."

I got a larger piece. "Your mouth is bigger."

"Not really," Nick said.

I shoved it in and wiped icing on his cheek.

"Really, Brie?"

He stuck his finger in the icing and smeared it down my nose. His laughter was contagious to the crowd.

I grabbed a napkin and cleaned it off my face. "Very funny."

His finger wiped through the icing on his cheek. He licked it from his finger.

A tingle in my belly stirred.

"Can we dance now?" His patience started to wear. I didn't blame him. I was ready to bed my husband.

"The first dance is with Dad. Halfway through you cut in."

Nick escorted me to him. "Sorin, my wife would like to dance with her father."

Sorin smiled. It was tight like he struggled. "She is the queen, so who can refuse her."

Dad led me to the dance floor.

I winked at Nick from across the way.

The music started. *A slow song thank the Goddess.*

"I'm so proud of you. Your grandmother would be beyond proud. I've never seen the strength in someone that I see in you."

"Dad..."

"You are the queen your people need you to be. You are the queen who will bring peace. You are the queen who overcame Darkness through Light. But most of all, you are the daughter who inspires me."

Tears burned my eyes, but I held them back. *If I overcame Darkness with Light, why can't I remember it?*

"You are the one who inspires me, Dad. Without your guidance, I would not have found my path. Without your love, I would not have had the strength to make the choices I did."

"You give me credit when you should be giving yourself the credit." He kissed my cheek. "I think your husband wants to dance with you." Dad spun me around into Nick's arms.

"Hello, wife. I missed you."

"Hello, husband. My face hurts from smiling so much today."

"I hope it wasn't forced." His forehead wrinkled.

"Not at all. It's because I am so happy," I said. "Happier than I ever remember being in my life."

"I should have known you wouldn't choose traditional." Nick eyed my gown.

"There have been a few other royals who have worn blue, so it's not unheard of," I said. "But it has been a while. I guess even someone as old as you may have forgotten." I leaned into him.

His arm tightened around my waist. "I bet I can outlast any other old man you know." He winked at me.

"You'll have to show me later."

"How about now?" His arm swept under my knees, and he scooped me into his arms.

"Are we leaving our party?" I asked in mock surprise with a smile.

"We are." He planted a firm kiss on my lips and carried me out of the ballroom.

Man and woman. Witch and vampire. Queen and King. Husband and wife.

No matter what label was put on us, our lives were only complete when we were together. Each the half that makes the other whole.

TWENTY-FOUR

$$\text{))) ● (((}$$

The guards carried our luggage out to the black SUV. The private jet was on the ready for us at the Coven-owned airport a few miles away.

Brandon pressed his shoulder against mine. He came to see us off. Neither of us wanted a huge send off. "Does Nick know what kind of crazy he is marrying into with this family?"

I laughed. "I think he does. He's seen and heard a lot already, and he hasn't gone anywhere."

"Family is important to him."

I nodded. "It is. He wants a family. Kids of our own." I thought back to my vision of us with children.

"Vampires can't ..."

"I brought that up, and he said we'd figure it out, so maybe adoption one of these days."

"Do you want kids?" Brandon asked, a brow raised.

"I never gave it any thought before, because I didn't think I'd get married. I do want them, but only if it is with Nick."

"The prophecy throws a wrinkle in that doesn't it?"

"Don't make me hit you with an energy ball today. I'm off Queen duty for two weeks."

"You wouldn't."

"Try me." I shoved my shoulder back against his. "You and Cal could be next. How do you feel about that?"

Brandon shifted his gaze to the ground and pushed around a pebble.

"I've never seen you so interested in a rock before," I said. I could avoid the tough question, but that wasn't how it worked with my twin. "Does Cal not want to get serious?"

"We're just taking it slow and seeing where it goes," Brandon lowered his voice. "But I really like him, Sis. A lot."

I smiled. "Brandon, you deserve happiness. It's okay to go after it. If you want to be committed to him, talk to him about it."

"He's got legitimate concerns about succeeding you to the throne." Brandon's eyes skittered around us.

I knew where he was going. It was a different set of expectations for royals, but rules were made to be broken. "Just because there has never been a warlock with a warlock mate on the throne, doesn't mean there can't be. Besides, I'm not planning on going anywhere for a long while. We'll have plenty of time to make the haters see the truth, and the ones that don't might find themselves without a coven."

He gave me a side hug. "Thanks for your support, Sis. Mom's been all on this tangent about me having to give her grandchildren since you and Nick can't."

"Just tell her she's going to have to wait at least a decade for any grandchildren if she keeps pushing," I said. "That will give her something to chew on for a while."

Nick and Cal walked up.

"All the arrangements are in place. Have a glorious honeymoon, and I promise to handle Coven business to your standards. I will not bother you unless it's an emergency," Cal said.

Brandon planted a kiss on Cal's cheek and slid his arm around his waist. *Looks like someone is ready to be official.*

I winked at them. "I trust you to have the greater good's interest in everything you do while I'm away."

I hugged them both.

Mom and Dad walked up with their hands entwined. "It seems love is in the Coven."

Mom blushed and Dad chuckled. We exchanged hugs.

"The car is ready whenever you are," Cal said.

☽ ☽ ● ☾ ☾

WE LANDED at the private airport on the island. Alan accompanied us on the plane, and we were met by a warlock and a vampire guard in charge jointly of our security while we were on the island. Jeeps sat on the tarmac to take us to our home for the next two weeks. Excitement for the time alone with my husband danced inside me. *My husband.*

The warlock, Kace, ran through the security system and monitoring. He pointed to a white button on the wall. "There is one of these panic buttons in every room. Should something happen, press it, and the team will arrive within sixty seconds. There are two panic rooms. One in the master bedroom and a bunker under the house. The entrance is here to it." He pressed another button on the panel, and the floor slid back to reveal a hidden entrance.

"The kitchen is fully stocked, and a chef is on call twenty-four hours seven days a week while you are here. If there is something you need that is not here, just dial zero on the intercom. We'll have someone retrieve it for you. Any questions, Your Majesties?

"None from me," I said. "Thank you."

"There is something I want to ask," Nick said. "Can I walk you out while we talk?"

"Of course, Your Majesty," Kace said.

Nick winced at the moniker. I smirked. He was going to see why I asked people to call me Brie.

I watched them walk out the front and head over to the sliding glass door. The beach looked beautiful with the white sand contrasting the water the color of Sleeping Beauty turquoise. I stepped out for a closer look.

The sand was warm under my feet, and sweat gathered on the back of my neck. Despite the cool breeze blowing off the water, sweat beaded on my forehead and in the crook of my arms. Nausea hit me in waves. My head swam. I dropped down on one of the lounge chairs.

Darkness slammed down around me like a cage, and I remembered. I remembered everything from the day we took Alastair's aura. The day I surrendered completely to Darkness. It'd been dormant and patient as it waited for this moment. I closed my eyes. The flames there roared like a forest fire.

Nick's footsteps thudded across the sand. I looked over my shoulder and met his gaze. Fear looked back at me. His forehead bunched up. He remembered too.

To be continued...

☽ ☽ ● ☾ ☾

Brie will come face-to-face with Darkness one last time, but will Nick and her friends stand with her?

SUSAN PERSON
Queen of Sacrifice
The Blood Moon Prophecy Book 1
QUEEN OF SACRIFICE
1
QUEEN OF DARKNESS
2
QUEEN OF MOONS
3

ACKNOWLEDGMENTS

Thank you to all those who helped me through my grief while finishing this book. I lost my mother before this one was finished, and I don't think I could have written the words for such emotional scenes as planned for this book if it weren't for those who were there to support me. I wrote book 3 immediately after it and carried the momentum into it.

To my family, thank you for the support and cheering me on, many times when you didn't even know how hard I was struggling.

To the fans, it is your reviews, emails, social media messages, and random greetings that keep me writing. Thank you!

Last but far from least, thank you to my editor, Dawn Alexander, who challenges me with every book to improve and grow as a writer. When I think there is no more emotion to squeeze out of a scene, she is there asking for more and is always right. Even when a scene has gutted me to write, she finds places where there is more to give. She reminds me of what is good in the book when I start to second guess something and works through the difficult scenes with me, even when I give her nightmares (literally). I couldn't ask for a better editor. Thanks for keeping me on track, Dawn!

ABOUT THE AUTHOR

Susan Person is a multi-contest finalist in the paranormal and dark paranormal categories. Recently, she returned to college to pursue a degree in anthropology and graduated in May. Susan enjoys meeting writers and readers alike at conferences. She knew at an early age she wanted to write powerful heroines and fulfilled that dream by writing badass empowered heroines who take charge in their paranormal worlds.

Susan grew up on a thoroughbred horse farm before moving to the big city of Dallas. She considers herself a Texan but is loyal to her home state of Arkansas. A lover of travel, she has visited several countries with many more to go on her list. She particularly loved dowsing at Stonehenge. The outdoors are a place Susan finds inspiration and can often be found in a park, at the lake, or on a road trip. She especially loves the mountains. Furry animals hold a special place in her heart, and dogs tend to seek her out as a friend. A friendship she happily returns.

Connect with her at susanperson.com

Also by Susan Person

The Blood Moon Prophecy

Queen of Sacrifice, Book 1

Queen of Darkness, Book 2

Queen of Moons - Book 3: Coming in February 2023

A Vampire Ice Age Series

In Blood & Ice, A Vampire Ice Age Series - Book 1

Reclamation In Ice, A Vampire Ice Age Series - Book 2

Book 3: TBA in 2023

Enchanted Rock Immortals World

Fae Undone, The Enchanted Rock Immortals Clan Fae 1

Fae Redone, The Enchanted Rock Immortals Clan Fae 2

BOOK 1 QUEEN OF SACRIFICE

Sacrifice was something she was used to. But will surrendering to her coven's demands mean giving up on love?

Brie Danforth had lost much in her youth. As a vampire-hunting witch, her destiny was to be the best of her kind. Love wasn't part of the plan and definitely not with a high-ranking vampire.

And when Nick shows up during one of her hunts, she can't bring herself to end the handsome blood-sucker.

But when a surge of power knocks her unconscious, Nick is there to catch her instead of draining her. When fate puts the beautiful witch he helped escape from his brother's torture years before in his arms, Nick refuses to let her disappear from his undead existence a second time... even if it means betraying his vampire life.

Will they have to forfeit their love to survive The Blood Moon Prophecy?

Queen of Sacrifice is the first book in The Blood Moon Prophecy paranormal romance series by Susan Person. If you like vampire and witch romance, magic, and a headstrong heroine leading the journey, this book is for you.

Pick up *Queen of Sacrifice* to start this magical series by Susan Person today.